The Devil

of

Charleston

PRESS
A Superior Publishing Company

P.O. Box 115 • Superior, WI 54880
(218) 391-3070 • www.savpress.com

First Edition

Copyright 2005, Rebel Sinclair

First Printing
Second Printing
Third Printing
Fourth Printing
10 09 07 05 9 8 7 6 5 4

Cover design: Debbie Zime

Cover art: Judy A. Beschta

ISBN Number 1-886028-69-9

Library of Congress Catalog Card Number: 2005900940

Published by:

> Savage Press
> P.O. Box 115
> Superior, WI 54880

Phone: 218-391-3070

E-mail: mail@savpress.com

Web Site: www.savpress.com

Printed in the USA

The Devil
of
Charleston

Rebel Sinclair

For D.C., with the deepest of affections
and also for Glenn

Preface

Charleston, South Carolina, was originally founded in 1670 as "Charles Towne," named for King Charles II of England by the Lords Proprietors. For their service in aiding Charles II to the throne during a time of upheaval in England, eight Lords Proprietors were granted territory in the New World from the present-day North Carolina/Virginia line southward to approximately New Smyrna Beach, Florida. The word "Carolina" is also derived from the Latin version of Charles, *Carolus.*

The name "Charleston" was not official in South Carolina until 1783, when the city became incorporated. The modern spelling has been used for easier reading, and also to better reflect the local pronunciation, "CHAL-ston."

Therefore, on every morrow, we are wreathing

A flowery band to bind us to the earth,

Spite of despondence, of the inhuman dearth

Of noble natures, of the gloomy days,

Of all the unhealthy and o'er-darkened ways

Made for our searching; yes, in spite of all,

Some shape of beauty moves away the pall

From our dark spirits.

—John Keats, Endymion, Book I

Prologue

<u>Charleston Harbor, July 1692</u>

Scents of the sea and rotting wood floated through Bridge's Wharf, the last dock in line down the eastern side of the nestled peninsular city. The dock was full of varied wonders; sights of tall-masted ships and schooners that plied the greenish-gray waters of the harbor, barges that awaited the turn of the tide to take them up the Ashley River to the west, and the pouring of man and beast over the hard packed ground in between. Outgoing ships sat low in the water, their holds stuffed with rich deerskins from the Indian trade, grudgingly inching their way out of port into the vast seas beyond, their courses set for Europe, India, and Barbados.

A dark-haired boy, naught but eight years of age, dashed as fast as his legs would carry him down Meeting Street, his bright blue-green eyes darting through the throng as erratically as his body movements. He made a sharp left and delved into the crowd along Bailey's Creek and past the unorganized market, the odor of hay, barnyard animals, and unwashed human bodies thick in his nostrils. The booming tones of an auctioneer rang in his young ears. It took a bit of artful dodging to make it to the end of the market without incident, the press of the crowd jostling him this way and that.

He turned right down Bay Street that lined the easterly side of the waterfront, coming at long last to the wharfs he loved so much. Scanning the heads of the passersby, the boy found the prominent, steadfast shape of his father walking down the planks of the dock to his fleet's flagship, the merchant vessel *Seascape*. It was his pride and joy. Though not as fast as the sloops and schooners that made up the rest of his regime, Benjamin Ashhurst's 110-foot, three-masted square-rigger *Seascape* boasted thirty cannons and a hold that seemed bottomless. A by-blow cousin to the lord proprietor Lord Anthony Ashley Cooper, Earl of Shaftsbury, for which the rivers on either side of Charleston were named, Benjamin shared a diluted blood tie, but his wealth and riches were his own. He had grown fabulously rich in the shipping business, and the customary Chinese rope that curled around the front door archway of his townhouse rivaled most every shipper in town. Respectable and proud, Benjamin Ashhurst was a high-standing member of society in the fledgling community.

Naturally, this sort of vast monetary income did not come without its related tribulations. Beating out several other merchants in the colony for an extremely good contract with Atlantic Import & Export, Inc. had brought bitter resentment from Ashhurst's rivals. Talk had begun to circulate about how Benjamin was no more than a bastard castaway that had made his wealth by lucky and unscrupulous means. It was also a strange coincidence of luck and fortune that Ashhurst's ships never seemed to be assaulted by the French or Spanish who were forever lurking about the harbor; but *Seascape* was definitely a sight with her cannons, and the critics had to be content with that, as well as the fact that Benjamin was certainly rich enough to pay off any number of pirates and ensure their black-hearted loyalty.

Pirates were no menace to the Charlestonians at the time. Settlers were grateful for the money and merchandise they brought, as well as their heavily armed frigates and sloops. The French and Spanish usually thought twice about assaulting the harbor when any number of pirate vessels were docked at the wharfs, an occurrence that had become more of a regularity with each passing month. Rough and crude the men were, drunk and shameless in front of a lady most of the time, thinking it a bawdy sport to see how quickly they could make her blush; but pillaging of the town itself was so slight it was nearly non-existent, and that was enough for the colonists. They were starved for cash and protection, and they would take it where they could get it.

As the boy watched his father ascend the ropes to the upper deck of the *Seascape*, he wished more than anything that he could be there with his sire, standing straight with his head tilted as Benjamin did. But he had been forbidden from the docks unless his father brought him, unaware as he was in his youth of the dangers. He hated having to stay home with his mother and Mammy. He was entirely too old to have a mammy, and when he had informed his father of this, Benjamin took one look at his frazzled wife's huge eyes and only laughed, saying, "I'm proud of you, Royal. You'll be a real man someday."

So, it was with great disheartenment that Royal dug his toe into the dirt, knowing he could only watch and advance no farther. He shouldn't even be this close to the docks, either. Mammy had told him his limit was the end of the market. If he passed that, she'd told him he could be caught by a ruffian and taken to the slave market on White Point and sold to a man who would beat him, and he would never see anyone who loved him again.

Even as he thought that his frustrated heart over this limitation was the worst thing in his small world, his eyes fell on his father, deep in discussion with one of the crewmen on deck. The sun was shining brightly, with nary a wisp of cloud. The soft ocean wind caressed his dark hair, teasing it into a misshapen mop, belying the high temperature. The day was so perfect it could have been a painting.

Yet even the clang and clatter of the docks themselves could not conceal the explosion of the musket that came from nowhere, piercing the tidy hum-drum into silence and then uproar. Royal watched his father crumple from the ankles up. Blood pooled onto the deck beneath his limp form, its ghastly crimson glistening in the unblinking sun. Royal couldn't do anything, couldn't will his eyes to move from that image. He was frozen in place, unaware that his toe had dug a sizeable hole in the ground. He was just a boy with no thoughts of recourse or revenge as the tears burned his eyes, blurring the scene before him.

1

"I've had it with these damn pirates!"

Every now and again, something else would emit out of the governor's mouth, but that had seemed to be his favorite speech for over an hour now as he looked with disgust at the ever-mounting stack of complaints from local and overseas merchants that were threatening to bury his desk. His secretary, Jonathan Rembert, was at a loss. He had learned in previous service that not saying anything at all was the best policy at this point, but he himself was getting tired of silence, and there were things he needed from the governor in order to complete his duties for the day.

"Motley lot, all of them…"

"Ahem…Governor Johnson?" Rembert gently interjected, earning himself a scowl over the mass of parchment. "I was hoping I could get your attention on this tax proposal…"

"Taxes! No one is going to be able to pay their taxes if these brigands keep at it," Johnson snarled, rubbing at his sore neck. "And I have a terrible feeling that things are going to get worse before they get better. Charleston has become a marauder's haven and it seems there is little I can do about it. North Carolina's Governor Eden isn't helping matters either. I swear he's as bad as they are and making it harder on the rest of us with his pardons…"

"Not to alarm you, sir, but I've received word that a few months ago Hornigold and his protege Edward Teach, now known as Blackbeard, captured the French slave ship Concorde of Nantes just off the island of St. Vincent. The lot made out with a treasure trove of gold dust, slaves, and jewels that were en route to Martinique. It's one of the biggest conquests since Henry Jennings took his galleon prize off the Florida coast three years ago. Apparently Blackbeard has taken the Concorde for his own."

"When was this?" Johnson demanded.

"Um, last November, sir…"

"And we're just hearing about it now?" Johnson roared, scooting his chair back from his desk and holding his hands over his face. "By all that's holy, what do we pay our scouts for, Rembert? Who hired them?"

Jonathan Rembert flushed. "I hired them, sir. And if you want me to find others, I can start on it tomorrow."

The governor's face relaxed as his focused his keen eyes on his assistant. "I apologize for my outburst, John. I know it's not your fault. I hope you understand that this feeling of powerlessness is grating on my nerves and I am at a loss on to how to proceed."

"A lot of the colonies are trying to raise funds for ships from the Royal Navy, Governor. While I don't think it's quite right that Mother England leaves us to fend for ourselves like she has, one sight of a Navy frigate would have those rat bastards scattering for cover."

"There just isn't enough money in the treasury, nor much surplus to be had from London," Johnson sighed. He sat deep in thought for an extended length of time, the creases on his forehead growing deeper with each passing minute. "And as for hiring locally, shipbuilding may be advancing, but so are the fees and, consequently, the builder's wallets. Right now, all we can do is cross our fingers and hope for the best. At least Colonel George Chicken and the Goose Creek Militia have the Yemassee Indians under control with their latest victory at Monck's Corner. That's one less worry on the table."

* * * * *

Royal Ashhurst sat in his small, simple office on Tradd, just off Bay Street, thumbing through his own mass of parchment that was stamped with overdue markings and threats of foreclosure. Other than his desk and the spare wooden chair across from it, the room was empty but for an odd crate and a small oil painting of a merchant ship at sea, hanging crookedly from a rusted nail. Hazy sunlight filtered in through dust-clouded window panes, casting the room in a tired glow. Mildew was doing its best to creep up the walls despite efforts otherwise, inching ever closer to the cobweb suspended in the corner that had been keeping residence there as long as he had.

Seven months ago Royal had taken the paltry funds he called his own and dumped them into a new 70-foot, 280-ton Dutch flute. The endeavor was risky, but it was the only choice he had; he needed to add a third ship to his tiny regime, and the flute was the best all-around pick. It was a bit more expensive than he had wanted to front, though comparatively reasonable in price to the rest of the vessels he had looked at, with an increased cargo capacity over similarly-sized ships. Another added benefit was that it only required twelve crewmen to sail.

Stormchaser was gorgeous. The only problem was that it had yet to pay for itself, and with his dilapidated brigantine *Courtesan* careened for the fourth time in two months, the workload had fallen to the swift but small sloop *Navigator*. The unfortunate careening of *Courtesan* in Barbados when *Stormchaser* was already on her way back to Charleston from her maiden voyage to London left no avenue of contact, and the goods the brigantine were holding were pretty well dead in the water until she could be patched together yet again and set to course. The only thing Royal could even anticipate was that *Stormchaser* brought back a decent amount of income with her when she came. Projections when she had set sail a month ago had set the market price of indigo higher than he could have hoped, but even then his creditors would be kept silent only long enough for *Courtesan* to make it back, trusting that by some miracle she did so on time. He didn't even want to entertain the passing news of tropical disturbances in the atmosphere that had floated through the taverns. Royal knew hope was being held together by a weak thread, but he couldn't cut it loose until he was forced to.

He sat back and closed his eyes against the bills and the sad, drooping walls of the infinitesimal room, unable to stop an odd flood of memories from washing through his brain. The brutal recollection of his father's murder, as clear as the moment it had transpired, gave way to the years after, when his mother, over-burdened and underfed, sought refuge but instead found a similar fate. The familiar face of Mammy had long gone; she had stayed as long as she could until hunger, too, had driven her to find other employment. The riches of his youth had begun to slip away at the point of his father's death. Barely twelve and on his own, Royal had made his bed in the stables of various townhouses before he had been run off with rapier or pistol.

Queen Anne's War had given him a bit of a sporting chance. After years of drifting from vessel to vessel, he had found refuge aboard the *Great Lady*, a privateer ship captained by Johannes Wylie. He had worked long and hard, the sun burning and then bronzing his skin, fighting his way through numerous encounters with enemies and earning respect for his unabashed loyalty and strength in battle. Wylie had captured *Forever Decent*, a schooner loaded with gold dust, and Royal had been voted to captain it successively for three years, as was standard by most privateer articles. It was through careful savings of his often meager share of the spoils over time that he had been able to collect enough money to purchase the leaky *Courtesan*. Through all the moldy, worm-infested meals and sickening smells of the bilges in calm seas, during the weeks he lay in his bunk recovering from shrapnel cuts and sword thrusts, passion for the day he would avenge his parents and rebuild the empire that had been stolen fueled him.

Enough time had passed where he could've been forgotten by Carter Seymour, proprietor of Seymour Transport Incorporated, the man whom Royal knew without a doubt had been the one responsible for destroying everything and everyone he had ever loved. In his growing years, he had even witnessed Seymour strolling the deck of the *Seascape*, outrageously renamed *The Prize*, standing on the very same boards his father had. It was almost too much for Royal to watch without killing him on the spot. But revenge would be sweet and slow when he took it, not quick and merciful. And, Royal vowed, he would be in a position to relish Seymour's demise.

Royal could've been forgotten, but wasn't, and all because of one hotheaded mistake.

Royal toyed with his father's ring that still adorned his finger despite all these years and all the attempts to capture it from him while in a drunken haze. He thought of Seymour and the great pains he had undergone in order to smear Royal's reputation through the gutters of Charleston when he realized the unexpected thorn in his side had returned and the threat it presented him. There had been "accidents"—close calls to himself and certain sabotage to his ships. Masts had been cut to break beneath a sturdy gale. Crewmen were hard to find because of fears they would be cursed for working for the devil, now a favorite belief of Charlestonians. The attempts on his life had all but stopped in the last year, however. Royal knew that somewhere Seymour was enjoying this slow, destructive cat-and-mouse game, preferring that to finishing the job quickly as he had with Benjamin Ashhurst.

Why Seymour had turned on his family when he had more than enough riches in his own right Royal couldn't fathom, but the question gnawed at him endlessly. From what he had been able to gather, Seymour had been a trusted friend and investor. After Benjamin's death, Carter had taken the business for his own. Royal's share—the full three-quarters of it—should have been held in trust for him until the age of twenty-one. Yet with Royal's disappearance and being believed dead, it had all gone to Seymour under binding law. When he returned to Charleston in 1714, suspended in the midst of shady exploits, he found any attempt to access his father's records stymied. His own enterprise had then begun from scratch.

The few shipping contracts Royal had been able to procure came either from sullied landowners selling a substandard product or old friends of his father who gave him odd jobs out of pity, and if he hadn't needed the work so badly Royal would have told them all to go to hell. None would admit openly to working with him. Seymour, he was certain, was beyond question the instigator behind the sabotage of everything that bore the Ashhurst name. He had intended for Royal to be seen as an advocate of the devil, having been assumed dead for years and suddenly resurrecting himself before their very eyes. It stirred up no end of superstitions, Gullah or otherwise; to most it was just plain strange and they did not need much convincing.

He knew his clients would outright lie about his services if asked.

Every time he met with one the hour was late and he was ushered in through the back door, mistrust and something akin to fear gleaming in the depths of their eyes.

He had turned thoughts of piracy over more than a few times, and though the money wasn't great it was probably better, and no doubt easier to garner, than the few doubloons he made now. But Royal's will would not allow him to stoop so low, to become something he hated because it took less drive and hard work. Privateering was an option, but though he had been good at it, Royal held little taste for it. He was well aware of the repercussions of theft. Once pirates had protected Charleston; now they were a menace, especially to him and the other merchants of the colonies. He couldn't afford to lose a scrap to them, and that was another worry that had left its line in his forehead. The piratical numbers had been increasing exponentially over the last six months and there was no telling what might happen were the trend to continue uncurbed.

The creak of his office door startled him. Though the portal held a meek sign stating his occupancy, it never received visitors unless they were expected creditors who were always early if not punctual. Since none were scheduled this day, Royal surveyed this alien to his abode with disguised curiosity, his unmistakable aquamarine eyes noting everything about the stranger through heavy lids. He was affluent of dress and poise, had hands that worked with quill and paper rather than ropes and crates. He was of medium height and build, yet there was a determined air about him. He held intelligent, dark amber eyes that gave away nothing.

"Can I help you?" Royal queried softly.

"Captain Royal Ashhurst, I presume?" At the slow nod of agreement, Royal's guest continued. "I am Jonathan Rembert, aide to Governor Johnson. Pleased to make your acquaintance."

"Charmed, certainly." Royal's tone may have been drab and void of emotion, but the wash of nervousness that pooled in his stomach at the announcement for whom the esteemed Mr. Rembert worked was completely the opposite. "Though rumor states I haven't gone by 'captain' for some time now." His curiosity piqued, he leaned back in his chair with his long, tanned fingers laced together, awaiting a further narrative by Mr. Jonathan Rembert.

Rembert didn't know why Ashhurst didn't say anything more; he was simply watching him with an intense look in the depths of his strange, mysterious eyes, the likes of which Rembert had never seen before, so unnatural they were in color. He could see why people gossiped about this man, said that he held the light of hellfire in his gaze. But Rembert also considered himself an educated man, and by any account, he had a job to do that wasn't going to be put off by silly talk stirred by the rich upper crust and their bored wives.

"Have a seat, sir. I would offer you a drink, if I had one," Royal stated casually.

"Not to worry, I don't think my business will take that long," Rembert replied, clasping his hands behind his back. "I'll come directly to the point, Captain Ashhurst. I have a feeling that flowery conversation and beating about the bush appeals to you about as much as it does to me."

Royal's dark brow inched up ever so slightly. He liked Rembert already.

"It is my understanding, Captain Ashhurst, that you are not in the best sort of way," Jonathan continued, unabashed. "I'm also certain you are as aware, if not more so than I, of your reputation here in Charleston. Work has been hard to come by, has it not? Contracts that are few and far between make for lean times."

"I thought you were going to get directly to the point," Royal said, smiling.

"Well, yes…pirates, Captain Ashhurst, are ruining this colony, and the governor has instructed me to find someone who would be interested in stopping their shenanigans for a price."

"What about the Royal Navy?" Ashhurst directed, simply glad that Rembert's visit was obviously not leading to an arrest for some trumped-up charge. "A bit out of the price range, Rembert?"

John flushed. "The Crown, shall we say, seems to have chosen other uses for her ships at the present time."

"And what, may I ask, does this boon entail? Pillaging the pillagers? Sailing about, hither and thither, ensnaring all the evildoers? Ransacking the town, single-handedly taking to task fifty crews of as many men per ship or more? Come now, Rembert, even if you get the lot of merchants in Charleston to put up even a small part of their fleet, which you won't, there wouldn't be enough willing manpower to do it."

"Perhaps you would be more interested in listening to what I have to say if I told you what would be in it for you."

Rembert told him.

Royal nearly choked.

* * * * *

Carter Seymour adjusted his cuffs between thumb and forefinger, one at a time, as he prepared to go out for the evening. He appraised himself before the gilded mirror as he barked for his hat and coat, turning this way and that, altogether pleased with himself and the impression he made. His glossy gray hair was neatly combed, and though his temples were spiked with white, he liked the distinguished sign of his age and the roundness of chin and midriff. Social comfort attributed to the size of his girth, holding countless lavish meals beneath the belt, such as the one he was expected at presently.

With a scowl, Seymour took the called-for items from the wide-eyed slave who brought them, flicking off a bit of lint from the coat with distaste. He didn't like darkies, thought them stupid, and they only proved it over and over again. If it weren't for the fact that he didn't have to pay them a wage, he would have been done with them years ago. In Seymour's estimation, the only real good they did him were the cash sales he generated from the shores of West Africa when he brought them over and sold them. Nasty beasts they were.

But these ideals weren't in Seymour's head at the present. He was thinking rather about the delectable Josephine Beckham, daughter of Michael Beckham, insurance broker, whose presence would grace the table across from him this night. While her father was little more than a sniveling, groveling servant of the hierarchy at his underwriting firm, the man had managed to sire a daughter that was the secret erotic dream of every man in Charleston with clear eyesight. Barely twenty years old, she was young enough to be Seymour's granddaughter, but she had the beauty of a seraph…slim legs, tiny waist, and curves that begged for the touch of a man. Her proud head was blessed with lush mulberry lips, sparkling, almond-shaped emerald eyes, and a wild mass of hair the color of burnished fire. One sight of her drove him mad with desire, and he had thought of little else since he had first seen her on her way to visit her father during the noontime meal two weeks before.

She had been strolling down Broad Street, her hair gleaming gold and copper, held in a prim bun that belied her calling. She wore a day dress of pale blue, the hem growing dusty as it kissed the ground in her wake. Seymour had just finished his rounds at the docks and was on his way back to his townhouse for his own luncheon when he had witnessed her. He had skipped his meal that day to follow her, thinking up some excuse to see the insurers in order to get a little closer. She had barely given him a nod, her glorious attention falling on him for the briefest of interludes before she continued on her errands for the day.

Seymour was not a patient man. An endless procession of sleepless nights had followed that afternoon. Countless mistresses failed to relieve the ache she had stirred in him, no matter their price. The combined air of innocence and seductive kitten that exuded from her made him crave her like no other woman, and he was determined to have her. Seymour cared not a whit about the cost. Whatever it was, he was certain he could afford it.

The dinner affair was fulsome, held in the arched dining room at the Oakley mansion on Church Street. Dennis Oakley was the owner of Seymour's insurance company and came from old money out of Bristol, England. Though it was beneath him to invite one of his underlings to a private dinner with the top of Charleston society, he lowered his standards as a personal favor to include the fidgety Michael Beckham. Beckham pored over policies all day to ensure that the clients had paid their dues on time, and his usefulness ended there. Seymour knew the invite held strings, but he didn't care what they might be at the present; Beckham had brought his daughter as instructed, and that was the bottom line.

Most every eye was trained on Josephine at one point or another. She was radiant in her evening gown of plum and persimmon, her hair coiled atop her head with dreamy wisps curling down around her oval face. Seymour could sense she felt out of place, though she didn't look it. The rich wives couldn't buy her sense of poise and allure, and because they knew it, they hated her for it.

Several of the men had been gawking at her throughout the varying courses of rice soup, shrimp, calamari, and fowl. Seymour felt like strangling each and every one of them despite the mingled feeling of selfish pride, knowing with certainty that Josephine Adelaide Beckham was going to be his, and the rest of them could rot in their lust. They would learn to keep their thoughts to themselves, too, rather than plastered all over their silly faces.

"So what interests take up your sweet time, Miss Beckham?" Seymour asked, catching her eyes across the table. "Painting? The pianoforte?"

"Investments," she replied coolly, ignoring her father's scowl to the left and the audible gasp of disdain from Madame Greenville to her right. "I don't believe in wasting my allowance on frivolous things."

Seymour chuckled. "Ah, Miss Beckham, how refreshingly silly! I must say I am surprised at you, a female playing at broker is a bit like aping a man."

Josephine remained calm, though she wanted to throw her glass of wine in his flabby face. He had been making syrupy attempts to engage her in conversation all evening and her patience for civility was wearing thin. Perhaps now he would leave her alone. Madame Greenville's smug look alongside her did nothing to soothe her temperament either. She didn't care what people thought of her—she wasn't an impractical, empty-headed female and she wasn't going to act that way. "You would be surprised at the things I am capable of, Mr. Seymour."

"I bet I would," he growled, his eyes hot as they traveled over her. Josephine looked away, trying not to gag. He had not disguised his attraction to her in the least, and she wasn't in the mood for it. She didn't care how rich and powerful he was. He was a fat, aging merchant with an egotistical attitude and was quite symbolic of everything she detested. She stared at the clock on the wall, willing it to chime a later hour so she could leave.

Josephine didn't understand why she had been summoned in the first place. Her father made a decent living but he wasn't exactly a social climber. In the invitation there had been a thread of pressure that if they weren't there, on time and ready, repercussions would ensue; and her father, weak as milquetoast that he was, had nearly gone into fits over that. It was beyond mysterious. *"Please be advised that your daughter, Josephine, should accompany you to the gala...her presence has been requested and the request should not be taken lightly."*

Josephine knew she would be lying to herself if she didn't admit that she was ill at ease. She had very few friends because of her odd ways and though she didn't feel lonely because of it she was a little worried that someone was aware of her in a way that she did not reciprocate. It had set her on edge for the night, even more so with the vultures staring at her. She knew that her natural beauty was causing more and more problems as time went on, and oftentimes there were days she wished she had the courage to take the knife to her face and remedy the situation.

Not having any female guidance didn't contribute to her situation either, she supposed. She had never known her mother. Josephine could only assume she had received her looks and personality from that bloodline because she couldn't be any more opposite from her father. They rarely spoke, and when they did, they were usually at odds. He didn't approve of her ferreting away her meager allowances and had threatened to cut her off altogether if she didn't stop her nonsense. A woman didn't make investments and had no property rights, and life was simple as that. And Michael never, ever spoke of her mother. Josephine didn't learn until age eight that she had died during childbirth.

At long last the meal subsided. The men were adjourning to the study for wine and cigars while the ladies retired to the drawing room. Josephine wasn't certain of what exactly she should do, so she followed the ladies, refusing to allow the stress to show a wrinkle on her face as they turned away from her, snickering behind their fans and casting anomalous looks in her direction. If it wasn't for the kindly glance of Mrs. Beasley, whom Josephine secretly deposited securities for, she would have broken down in tears for the frustration she felt. She wished her friend Brad was here. Brad made her feel like she could stand up for anything.

But he wasn't, and she was just going to have to make the best of it.

"Did I really hear you say you were interested in *investments*, Miss Beckham?" Madame Greenville asked pointedly from the divan across from her. Josephine did not miss the challenge in her tone or the murmur that swept through the drawing room. "How scandalous."

"I don't believe there is anything scandalous about a woman looking out for herself, Madame," Josephine returned. "After all, men won't do it for us in ways that benefit our own interests. I certainly think that in this modern age a woman's worth should be regarded by the content of her mind rather than that of her armoire."

Madame Greenville paled, her lips pursing tightly. "My dear, you are doomed to spinsterhood if you continue that line of bawdy talk. Spinsterhood…or perhaps the Pink House on Chalmers Street?"

The women in the room alternately giggled and gasped over the exchange. Josephine only flashed her best smile. "Are you referring to the same Pink House I saw Mr. Greenville entering last Tuesday eve?"

Madame Greenville went from white to a ghastly shade of red quite rapidly, Josephine noted, her cry of anger hardly stifled by her fan. Mrs. Oakley stood up, her teacup rattling as she set it to the table.

"Ladies, you will cease and desist this moment," she scolded. "And as for you, Miss Beckham, it is no secret that you are in company above your station and should not only have the decency to realize it but you should act accordingly."

Josephine did not feel the least bit contrite. "Pray tell, Mrs. Oakley, how did I come to be in such genteel company when this was, quite frankly, an invitation unsought? I do not mean to offend you, for you have been a gracious hostess, but I refuse to be trampled upon by others who seek to belittle me for having desires more affluent of integrity than their own."

Mrs. Oakley's lip trembled, her hand flying to her face to steady it. Madame Greenville seemed to be on the verge of going into a swoon. Mrs. Beasley winked at her from behind her own fan.

The door to the drawing room opened, and the room whispered with the rustle of skirts and petticoats as the houseguests turned to see who intruded. Mr. Oakley, Carter Seymour, and Josephine's father stood on the threshold. Michael Beckham fidgeted with the hem of his coat, his eyes everywhere but on his daughter as the man of the household spoke when it became clear that Beckham wouldn't.

"Miss Beckham, if you would join us for a moment," Dennis Oakley said, his eyes noting appreciatively the slight, rosy tint across Josephine's cheekbones. Seymour licked his lips; slight beads of sweat dotted the upper rim. His eyes, though a pale blue, seemed nearly black, and they were sporting erratically across her figure. His nostrils were flared, and the slight heave of his breath could be heard in the still room.

"What is this about?" Mrs. Oakley barked, not liking the way her husband had acted all evening, and with the latest developments, she was not going to be shut out. "This entire evening has been a strange charade, and I am weary of it, sir!"

"You can consider this dinner party an informal engagement celebration," Seymour announced. "For I have gained permission of the bride's father, and I intend to marry my betrothed come the fair month of May."

2

*F*ive hundred pounds.

Royal still could not believe the sum, even after he had seen the authorized contract with the official seal of South Carolina stamped upon it. Five hundred pounds would be the most money he had ever seen in his lifetime, and it would be more than enough to pay off his creditors. He could expand his fleet, upgrade to a larger office. He could buy a new home or maybe a horse. The options were endless, but Royal knew the task that accompanied the coin would need to be conquered first.

Royal had spent the two weeks since his conversation with Rembert anxiously awaiting *Stormchaser.* Energy that he thought had been drained from him burst out of nowhere. Even his senses seemed heightened. The sky and the sun were clearer, brighter; the scents of flower and grass and sea were pungent in his nose. The days were warmer than average for the onset of May, and the heat of summer could already be felt.

He had been spending more of his evenings in the taverns, ingratiating himself with the rough seamen who sought refuge there. It wasn't difficult. A few he even knew by name. Having spent most of his life at sea among the rigging of privateer ships rather than a passenger ship's plush cabins, Royal knew full well what was taboo talk and what wasn't, and it was only a slight tax of patience before petty thieves and pirates trusted him implicitly, relaying with glee the tales of their latest accomplishments in the sweet trade.

From what he could gather, Blackbeard had met up with the "Gentleman Pirate" Stede Bonnet at the Bay of Honduras. Accounts varied as to whether or not Blackbeard had stolen Bonnet's ship or if they were working together, but both Blackbeard's *Queen Anne's Revenge,* as he had renamed the *Concorde of Nantes,* and Bonnet's *Revenge* were in tandem, and reports had their course set in a northerly direction.

Royal knew this was bad news. While chances were slim, they were still apparent and altogether real that the pirates may intercept *Stormchaser* on her way into port. Without the flute, it would be impossible for him to even begin his task, especially with how badly he needed the purse she carried with her. If he had to wait another month for *Navigator* to arrive it would be folly; he was running on a thin timeline as it was.

The morning sun played hide-and-seek, and as the day drew on, it grew overcast and humid. The heavens became pregnant with rain and the waves had changed from a lap against the point to a lash. Royal had been pacing the docks consistently for nearly a week, attempting as best he could to quell the anxiety that had grown with each day *Stormchaser* was late to port. Five days overdue and he was trying not to lose faith. He had been hoping against hope every time a mast appeared between the peaks of the churning gray waters.

It was with nearly a bellow of relief that his head, with its rich mahogany hair tousled by the wind, snapped up as he saw at long last the familiar blessed bowsprit of his ship through the spyglass. She split the waves under full sail with solid determination, the momentum of both current and breeze propelling her forward. His chest swelled with quiet pride at the sight of her. He had worked long and hard to be able to acquire such a fine ship, and though he had far to go, Royal had never been as proud of anything as he was *Stormchaser.*

As she drew closer, he could make out the scurry across the planks as the crew prepared to dock. Yards were dropped to furl in the mainsail. Closer still, he witnessed Captain Everett Lawrence barking orders and pointing this way and that. Royal counted fourteen crewmen in all, and this was a good sign; every man was accounted for.

Though Royal had few means, he always made certain the crew left with good, hardy provisions and fresh fruit to prevent the plague of scurvy. It was an order direct that such things should be purchased in moderation at each layover. Too much would only spoil; too little and the crew's health could suffer. He also refused to allow the men to relieve themselves in the bilges, instead constructing a small, separate room with a trap door portal for the men to use. Never would he allow his ship to reek of defecation, and Royal made it clear that if any man were to violate this direction they were to be set ashore.

The cable was lowered, the anchor poised to drop. Men scrambled double time to slow the speed of the ship under Captain Lawrence's command. She responded well to their ministrations, and *Stormchaser* crept smoothly into the slip, gently bobbing to a halt in the chop as men on the docks helped to pull her ropes taut.

"Ahoy there!" Royal called up to the quarterdeck, his mouth split into a grin, his even white teeth flashing in the tan of his face. "Welcome back, captain!"

"Ahoy yerself, captain," returned Lawrence. He leaned to his mate, briefing him on last minute instructions before the weathered old salt made his way to the rope ladder and tossed it down. "I'm trustin' ye'll indulge an old man and come aboard. It's been rough goin' the last few weeks an' I don' quite trust me land legs yet."

Royal grasped a firm hold on the damp hemp ropes and shimmied up. The crew greeted him with curt nods and a few timid waves of the hand. "Everything aright?" Royal asked as soon as his boots made contact with the deck. His eyes scanned across the ties and portals.

"Everythin' went fine, Ash," Everett laughed, lighting a cheroot. The wisps of smoke curled around his grizzled face before dissipating into the wind. "Yer girl can move with the best of 'em. Dinna have a spot a trouble other 'n tempests the whole way to England 'n back. Not a leak or a ripped webbing ta be found." The old man paused and looked at Royal askew, an impish smile on his face. "Well, I'd best be stayin' quiet about how good she is tae me, Ash, or I'll have ye on me backside, crazed with jealousy that I was able tae deflower her. I've got yer purse below."

"Excellent. The crew has been paid?"

"Ayugh, took care of it as soon as we sighted land, just like ye asked."

While nearly all crews were paid after putting in to port, Royal remembered the times he had to wait the better part of a month before his share of the earnings had jingled in his pocket. He knew this small favor of esteem was what kept many of the crew loyal and content. "Ledgers all to date?"

There was a slight smack of Lawrence's lips on the cheroot and another puff of smoke. "Ye think they wouldn't be?"

Royal grinned. "We go through this every time, captain. One would think you know better by now."

"Humph. Who should know by now?" Lawrence's eyes sparkled. "So when do we set out again, Ash? Ye got another order lined up?"

Royal's smile faded. "Nay, there has been a slight change in plans."

"Something afoot?"

Royal leaned against the polished rail, looking out at the churning ocean with an obscure light in his eyes. "The next course is a complicated one. Unfortunately, it requires a bit of subterfuge, even where the knowledge of the crew is concerned. We will need to disembark immediately, though it is a local sail only. We're going to be chasing demons, Lawrence, and though I wish I could say more, my hands are tied. Yet I need to ensure that the crew will not desert me if faced with danger. I cannot afford it now."

Lawrence laughed. "Come now, Ash…the life of a seaman has always been a life of peril. Just because yer searchin' out different booty don't mean nothin'. The boys may be a tad sore 'cause their shore leave is so quick, but with sailin' close to home it won't be too hard on 'em. Hell, they may see it as a bit o ' sportin' adventure. An' ye don't need tae tell me nothin'. I've been at this game long enough tae know when somethin's askew."

"I need them to be completely convinced that I have turned my eye to a different prize, Captain Lawrence, though I don't perceive that as being difficult seeing as they are convinced I am the devil already. Though I have the utmost faith in you, Everett, this is one job I need to oversee personally. If I succeed you will not be forgotten."

"No 'ffense is taken, Ash. An' ye know yer secret is safe with me. Ayugh, a nice month or two with the missus. Jean'll be happy as a clam."

Royal did know. Everett Lawrence had been with him from the outset, had not said a word when times were almost rougher even than now, when pay was overdue and rock bottom to begin with. When he thought about it, Lawrence was the closest thing to a father figure that he had known through his pained growing years.

"I'll see to it that yer crew follows ye as they would me, Ash," Lawrence reassured. "Alls I ask is that ye give 'em a day or two tae rest."

Royal sighed. "I'm pressed for time, but I suppose there is no help for it."

"Mark me words, Ash, the boys will be ready. Otherwise, they'll have to contend with me." Lawrence laughed, his eyes bright as he looked into the darkening southern sky. "Devil? Hell, Ash, you ain't seen nothin' until ye seen me mad."

3

Josephine trembled, trying to keep from retching, as the maid, on loan to her from Seymour's staff, fastened the veil to her hair with pins. She looked into the mirror, realizing she looked about as good as she felt. *Whoever said all brides are radiant on their wedding day hasn't met me*, she thought bitterly, noting how sallow her skin was and how thin she had become. She had lost weight in the last few weeks, unable to eat or sleep. And, like it or not, the day she had dreaded came, entirely too quickly.

She had begged Brad to help her run away, and though he was sympathetic to her plight, he had refused. He had tried to reassure her, telling her that she could be worse off by far; even if Seymour wasn't a man she loved, at least she would have all of the finest comforts a lady could ask for. He had regretted his words as soon as they had come, and after apologizing, he had let her cry on his shoulder the rest of tea time. Josephine knew he would have married her himself to protect her if he could, but Brad was madly in love with and engaged to a girl named Rose, and knowing what a wonderful spirit Rose was, Josephine knew better than to even ask.

Seymour had only called upon her once since the dining ordeal. Josephine had never feared much of anything in her relatively short life, but she feared the look in Seymour's eyes. She had heard all about what went on in the marriage bed and she wanted no part of it, especially with the sluglike Carter Seymour. He had apologized that he couldn't marry her sooner but he had a prior official engagement to take care of away from Charleston. The beast had actually tried to console her about the wait with a touch of his chubby, clammy hands. When she recoiled, he had grit his teeth and whispered to her, "When you are mine, you will beg for my touch. I'll tame that rebellious streak in you, Josephine."

She shuddered at the mere thought.

The door creaked as her father entered the chamber. Josephine reached impulsively for the washbasin. Without warning, it became a missile, flying across the room at him. It barely missed his skull, connecting instead with the wall behind him and spraying porcelain across the floor. The maid shrieked and ran from the room. Josephine was glad; she couldn't stand the mindless girl anyway. And she hated her father, hated the sight of him now. "How could you do this?" she demanded of him. "How could you sell me this way?"

"Josephine, calm yourself," he muttered.

"You sold me like you would a cow!" she railed, searching for another projectile. "Did you think I wouldn't notice the new horses, the freshly cut clothes? How much did he pay you?"

"Josephine!" Michael Beckham snapped. "It was past due for me to wash my hands of you, girl. You're lucky that the man wants you, acting like a spoiled brat! I've been far too lenient on you. Now come!"

She was half dragged to St. Phillip's church on the corner of Meeting and Broad by two of Seymour's couriers, her jaw set in clear defiance. Final preparations were made on the doorstep, a bouquet of flowers was shoved into her hands, and then she was pushed forward unto the aisle.

Josephine clenched her hands together, her head tilted proudly back. She was thankful for the veil cast over her ashen face. If the witnesses to the ceremony were to see her tears, they might mistake them for tears of joy. Her feet felt leaden as they trod across the rich carpet, dragging downward in protest. She stumbled and nearly fell halfway.

At the other end of the aisle, raised upon the dais, stood Carter Seymour. He was watching her assiduously, a silent warning passing across his glassine eyes. Her blood coursed in icy rivers through her, making her shudder. Her breathing had all but stopped, synchronized with her heart. Josephine prayed for panache, knowing she would turn and run if only Seymour's thugs weren't standing at the door, preventing that very avenue of escape. She glanced upwards at the stained glass cherubs, the watery light filtering down through tinted panes an array of melancholy color. She prayed continuously with all her soul. The dampness of her eyes blurred the holy images into a kaleidoscope as she neared the altar.

A sudden blast erupted from somewhere out-of-doors; a boom that didn't quite come from the heavens, but rattled the buildings just the same. When it came again a split second later, the congregation began to stir in confusion. Seymour motioned to the guardsmen with a stern cock of his head. One stayed while the other two left the church to investigate.

"Come here, Josephine," Seymour commanded. She remained rooted. His lip curled stiffly in response. "Woman, do not test me," he growled.

Long minutes passed, and Seymour was pressing the clergyman to continue before the portal flung open anew. "Pirates!" a guard shouted from the doorway, attempting to catch his breath. "The streets are filled with them! It is Blackbeard's flag that flies in the harbor. The port is blockaded and Charleston is under attack!"

Panic ensued. People jumped from the pews. Refined members of the crowd were on the verge of fainting as others urged them to move. Seymour paled, his face twisting. "Josephine, come here, quickly! I will protect you!"

Josephine knew an answer to her prayers when she saw one and didn't hesitate.

She turned and ran for the exit, the pell-mell uncertainty of the guards allowing her to press nearly through to freedom on the other side. One man came close to stopping her; Josephine whirled, instinct bringing up her knee to strike him squarely in the groin. With a harsh cry and a green wash to his skin, he released her.

Once through the door, Josephine turned her head, running all the while. She could see the glimmer in Seymour's eyes even from that distance and it sparked the challenge in her. Violent disgust loosed her tongue. "Go to hell, damn you! Come one step closer to me and I'll unman you!"

Josephine bolted across the thoroughfare, mindless of how her ivory gown dragged in the dirt, its hem and then the lower folds staining as she went. The entire trousseau could rot for all she cared. She could hear Seymour bellowing at her from behind, his voice echoing ever more softly as she gained distance. He was easily outrun, and though his henchmen were in better shape than he was, they too had been suffused with too many seven-course meals. That, and the chaos uprooted by the pirates, had made her escape from the nightmarish wedding entirely too easy. Josephine didn't know where she could go other than to Brad's, though as luck would have it, he lived in the very house to the north of Seymour's. She only prayed that Brad could help her. There was no one else.

Josephine continued to weave through the streets, circling back every now and again if she heard the rabble of angry and frightened voices. Though she tried to worm her way nearer to the Harding residence, she only succeeded in getting farther from her destination rather than closer. She had caught a glimpse of a dirty sailor armed with a cutlass through the oaks, but it wasn't until she heard the boom of cannons in the harbor again that she truly felt her vulnerability. Still, no amount of piratical power would change her mind. She would rather die in the dust here and now than be toted around with the overblown windbag she had narrowly escaped marriage to.

She rounded the corner off of Legare onto Tradd, heading west towards the Ashley, doing her best to stay pressed to the stone fences and wrought iron gates around the homes when a threesome of grimy, toothless buccaneers emerged from an alley and blocked her path. Their clothes were soiled, sweaty rags, and even from ten paces Josephine could detect the reek of their body odor. She skidded to a halt, her hands reaching out to the wall to steady herself.

"Well, well, lookee whats we gots, boys," one of them said, his mouth splitting into a wide grin. "Purty as a dove, and dressed up like one, too, just fer us."

Josephine's stomach clenched. She didn't wait to hear any more. Though losing energy, she garnered another burst and sprinted back the way she had come.

"Hold it there, lassie," they called, the trample of their feet on the hard-packed earth echoing loudly in her ears as they sought to catch her. "C'mon, what ye runnin' for? I gots a shiny gold piece for ye if ye'll let me have what's under that purty skirt of yers…"

Josephine's face was hot and her heart was a triphammer as she scrambled to get away, but these men were seasoned mariners in good physical condition and they had not just run nearly a mile as she had. Their footsteps grew closer and closer still. No matter how she pressed herself to run harder, her lungs burning in her chest, inevitably the pirates seized her.

With rough hands they slammed her against the rock wall. Josephine's head swam with stars as they turned her around, creeping yellow jessamine and coral vine rustling beneath the weight of her body and tickling her face. She felt biting fingers on her neck as one of them forced her head forward and held it, another pawing at her hips to pull her backside until she was bent over, her legs splayed out behind her. Josephine choked from the smell of them, kicking out as best she could, her eyes tearing as much from the knowledge that they intended to violate her in broad daylight as from the pain. And she had no doubt that it would be brutal. Greedy hands squeezed her breasts. Guttural hollers were followed by a barrage of slimy, sweaty kisses across her face, one man rubbing the cleft of her bottom as he steadied his prey for his friend's abuse.

"Yeah, gal, I ain't never had such a pretty piece, and one as young as ye, I'd be bettin' that yer pure or damn close," one of them heaved between clenched teeth. "I'm goin' first!"

"You went first last time, Sal," the one holding her neck whined.

"You two have that sickness ye gots tae take mercury for. I ain't catchin' that shit. I don't want my hair fallin' out in clumps. That's what happens when ye take any whore who's willin'."

Josephine kicked harder when she felt her skirts being hoisted to her waist, unrelenting even when he slapped her bottom. "Stop it, bitch, or it'll just take longer!" She felt the cold steel of a blade sliding beneath her undergarments, and the sting across her rear, ready to slice the fabric away to bare her for his invasion.

Then there was an odd, dull thud, and Sal's hands released her, his blade falling forgotten onto the earth. The other two men relinquished their hold on her a split second later, their hands moving to the arms at their belts when a pair of pistols fired in rapid succession, the exploding noise and smell of spent powder blinking through the air. Josephine wiped the tears from her eyes and looked down, her breath catching in her throat at the sight of the three pirates lying slain at her feet. Sal held a dagger imbedded between his shoulder blades and was lying face first on the ground. The other two nameless assailants were beside him, one taking his last gurgling breath before he joined his companions in the afterlife, both dead with well-aimed shots to their hearts.

Josephine began to wring her hands. She had never before wrung her hands but this seemed like the perfect time to do such a thing, and though she would deny it afterwards she felt like remaining in her seated position with her head on her knees and crying. She tried to avoid it, but the sight of the thirsty earth greedily swallowing the blood of the fallen men, along with the goose egg developing along her skull, made her stomach queasy, and the helpless frustration she felt kept the burning tears in her eyes. She could vaguely make out the shape of a tall, dark-haired man, and she guessed this was her rescuer. She attempted to murmur words of thanks, but they would not come.

Royal knew the woman was upset; hell, who wouldn't be after nearly being gang-raped by a bunch of ugly scrubs. But he knew that he had to get out of there, and quickly, before some of their comrades came along and decided they were going to take vengeance upon them both. "Get up," Royal growled, more out of urgency than irritation. When he had come down the street and seen what was happening, it enraged him. Men were supposed to protect women, not harm them. If a man couldn't receive a woman's favors by choice or payment, he had no right touching her. Royal hadn't minded dispatching the three pirates, not in the slightest. What he did mind was how she continued to sit there, shaking like a leaf. Was she daft?

"Get up, or something worse might happen to you," he said, more forcefully this time. She continued to shake, though she did make a slight attempt to right herself. It wasn't enough for Royal.

"Take my hand," he ordered.

Finally, he thought. She did as he told her, and though the first steps were shaky at best, she kept an iron hold on his hand as he towed her along. Long minutes passed as they ran down the street, relentless in their pace. Royal skillfully led her through a maze of twists and turns in conscious avoidance of the bandits that streamed from fissures in the undergrowth. As the scenery began to deteriorate, Josephine realized they were now in an uncertain, disreputable district, near to the docks, further east on Tradd. Ducking beneath the archway of one haphazard building in the row, they plunged into a dark, gloomy hall. The only thing she could recognize in the dusty black was the sound of her own breathing and that of the stranger's.

"Come with me, you'll be safe, I assure you," he said softly. His boots echoed slightly on the floorboards and steps as he led her up a rickety staircase, the boom of cannons in the harbor noticeably muted from the last round they heard. There was a tinny jingle of keys, the click of a lock, and then he was leading her inside.

The man said not a word as he locked the door again behind them. He went to the wall where he retrieved a blunderbuss and more ammunition for his flintlock pistols, his movements graceful yet methodical. He took up position next to the window, where he drew the shutters, keeping them cracked the barest inch with which to watch by. He sat one of the spent pistols across his lap and began the process of reloading, his fingers knowing every movement by heart, his eyes trained on the street below.

"I dare not light a candle, even," he said, not turning from his ministrations. "I have no doubt that pirates are marching through Charleston as we speak, searching for any sign of susceptible life they can feed upon. I do not want to draw attention to this place."

"Where are we?" she asked.

"My home," he replied, watching as two pirates strode boldly past on the thoroughfare below, their pistols dangling carelessly from their hands.

Her eyes had adjusted to the dim light, and it was not nearly so difficult to see as it had been at first. The room was a contrast to its surrounding area. It was clean, smelling of polish and wood smoke. There was a well-worn couch near the empty fireplace, and with the rustle of her silk loud in the room, Josephine went and sat down upon it. A small, neatly-made bed sat in the corner to the left of the window, the mosquito netting around it pulled back. A washbasin sat atop a pine table, as did a mirror and shaving kit. Beneath the table was a mariner's chest. Various other domestic amenities were placed in an organized fashion throughout the room.

Josephine was well aware of the precariousness of the situation, but she did not fear the stranger though his physical capacity could certainly challenge most any man and far surpassed her own ability. In the pale light she was able to study him. The window silhouetted his profile— broad shoulders with locks of nearly black hair curling to his collar. His arms were thick and well-muscled, which his shirt could not conceal. He had a defined jaw and nose, aristocratic in its appearance. He seemed out of place in his rough surroundings, as if fate had denied him something more.

"What is your name?" he asked her, startling her out of her wandering thoughts. "And what, exactly, were you doing running about like a mad hen in a wedding dress? Where is your groom?"

Josephine blushed, feeling her cheeks grow hot in the gloom. "My name is Josephine Adelaide Beckham, and thank you, sir, for saving me fr-from—" she couldn't finish, her eyes welling with suppressed tears. She despised them for the weakness she felt they signified. "I don't know what would've happened if you hadn't—" she choked, biting her lip to keep her shame inside, "—hadn't come to my aid."

He said not a word. He had the grace not to mention her near rape when he saw she could not, and she was silently thankful for that, too.

"My name is Royal," he said. His voice was deep, resonating in her ears, his apparent change of subject soothing her as much as his tone. But he hadn't given up. "And I'm still curious, Miss Josephine Adelaide Beckham, as to why you were traipsing through Charleston in a wedding dress during a raid. It's apparent the ceremony wasn't culminated, for your finger is bare of a ring."

She wondered how he knew that, for Royal kept his constant watch out the window, never looking over his shoulder even when the soft sounds of her weeping reached him. He could tell she was trying to conceal her misery; no doubt she was afraid and hurting. He admired her attempt. She had probably been separated in the mayhem from her fiancé, was frightened, and pining for the secure arms of her amore. "Lie down and rest on the bed if you like," Royal offered quietly. "This may take a bit of time. I can assure you that you need to have no fear of me nor the meager comforts I offer."

There was more elapsed silence before the rustle of her skirts and the slight creak of his bed alerted him to the fact that she had accepted his lodging. The faint scents of fruit and flower followed the wake of her movements and Royal did his best to ignore them.

Even as he kept a watchful eye on the street below, his thoughts couldn't help but focus on the presence of Miss Josephine Adelaide Beckham lying in his bed but paces away. Her near perfect beauty had been something he had noticed from first sight despite her assault, and it was extremely difficult to remove the picture of her striking qualities from his head. A score of different scenarios had already swept through his imagination, cresting and leaving in reckless succession, leaving his body tense and strained.

"What is going to happen, Royal?" she asked some time later, her butterfly voice turning his name into a caress. Daylight was fading now; a few more straggling men had crept through the streets during his watch, though thankfully none had even shown a modicum of interest in the building in which they resided. Despite himself, Royal looked over at her. In the pale illumination he could see her small fist curled beneath her chin. She was looking at him with curious eyes, the trust in them naked to his own scrutiny. It made him feel all the more beastly for the intimate wishes he was harboring.

"I don't know, Josephine," he replied, the need for formality somehow dissipating with the sinking sun. "I was on the docks when the ships began to appear off the bar. Four of them in all, their *jolie rouges* flying carelessly. Long boats filled with men streamed towards the point. I'd hazard a guess that there are easily three hundred pirates or more. I, like everyone else on the wharfs, did not stay to watch. I was en route to a friend's to warn her when I came across you. The pirates are led by the unmistakable Blackbeard, and with as much manpower and artillery he is boasting, you can be certain that we are in for a bit of a siege, until they get what they have come for." He sighed heavily, and then added, "Is someone searching for you, Josephine? I doubt you will be reunited soon."

Josephine swallowed, turning her face into the pillows. The scent of clean, crisp sheets mingling with the faint musk odor, ever slight as it was, comforted her. She clenched the coverlet between her fingers, her palms suddenly clammy, her body hot and cold at once. "No one I want to find me. No one at all."

She sniffed back another onslaught of tears, knowing there was nothing she could do, nowhere she could go for the moment; and even if she could leave, she wouldn't have an inkling as to where to begin. Josephine took a deep, calming breath, trying to expel some of the tension that had cramped her shoulders. "Thank you again, Royal. You saved my life today. If only there was some way I could repay you."

Royal exhaled between clenched teeth, surprised by her initial reply. "There is nothing to repay. I only hope that the man who allowed you to be separated knows what a bitter mistake he made."

Josephine could not suppress a sad laugh. "Oh, but I left him. He was a horrible, disgusting pig of a man. My father gave me, nay, sold me to him. I'm almost thankful to the pirates. They created the diversion I had needed so desperately. Otherwise—" she trailed off, staring at the ceiling.

You would be in his bed instead of mine, he couldn't help but imagine. Lord, he had to stop this line of thinking. "Rest now," was all he said.

"My head hurts," she whined, more to herself than to him. "The curs slammed me into the wall."

With resignation, Royal set his weapons down, moving to the bed. He made his pace slow, as not to frighten her. "Let me see it, Josephine."

His strong, gentle fingers probed her scalp, his touch becoming feather soft when she gasped. He pressed his lips together as he felt the sizable lump forming there. "They got you good, didn't they?" he breathed.

The same musky fragrance that clung to his sheets intensified with his nearness. She felt hot, her head tingling where he was touching her. "Am I going to be aright?" she asked.

"A lump has formed outward. That is a good sign. If you were hurting and there was no swelling, it would mean the pressure was building inside rather than out, pushing against your brain. You may be sore, but you will live." He dropped his hand, and she felt chilly. "Now, please, get some sleep."

He was but paces from her side when her voice came again. "Royal?"

"What is it now?" His voice was rough. He wouldn't turn from his perch and face her. Josephine swallowed, sensing his patience had worn thin.

"What is your full name? I mean…your given name…it's not all that common, and it seems familiar to me."

Silence.

And then, "I am Captain Royal David Ashhurst. You, perhaps, would know me better as the devil of Charleston."

Josephine caught one side of her lower lip between her teeth. She knew *that* name. She had first heard it in her growing years at the academy. Her fellow roommates had gasped and giggled over the tale they had heard about the ghost of a fabulously rich shipper's son that had come back to haunt Charleston. Not a ghost so much as an undead, zombie-like creature, the story told that he was a gruesome, cruel specter who had come back to challenge any and all who may have been responsible for his death and the deaths of his family.

It was a sad, though romantic, story. Josephine had doubted that there was any kernel of truth to it at all, especially when the schoolgirls changed the devil from a horrible monster to a dashing hero hell-bent on rescuing the woman he loved to suit their girlish fancies. Everyone of older years knew of how prominent Benjamin Ashhurst had been killed by a crazy, nomadic former employee out of a sense of twisted jealousy, who then proceeded, unceremoniously, to dispatch himself with a load of grapeshot to his head. Ashhurst's wife and child were reported to have met an odd sort of doom themselves not long after that first dreadful scene, though rumors as to how were varied and contradictory. After hearing these stories in childhood, it was with some surprise in her adulthood that she had heard the name again from her father's mumblings.

Just as she was surprised now at how accurate the reconfigured academy lore was, at least in regards to the dreamy proclamations of his attributes.

"Shall I continue to call you Royal, or would you prefer 'the devil'?" she asked.

Royal looked at her with near amazement before he threw back his head and laughed. The sound was a rich tenor, echoing in the small room. "You surprise me, little one," he grinned.

Somehow, the term seemed to be endearing rather than demeaning coming from him. Josephine smiled in return, thinking of how peaceful this moment seemed after weeks of uncertainty.

More cannon fire resonated from the harbor, and both their smiles died away. "Come the morning, I am going to venture out and see what is afoot," Royal told her, seeming restless as he caressed the flintlock in his palm. He didn't feel right about leaving her with the situation as volatile as it was, but he had little choice. "I want you to stay here."

"Quite honestly, I have nowhere else to go," she told him. "The only choice I really have is my friend Brad, and I'm not certain how much help he can be to me now. Both my father and my fiancé knew he was my closest confidant, and logically, the person I would run to."

The muscle in Royal's cheek flexed, unnoticed in the darkness. "Is Brad your paramour? Is that why you left this hideous fiancé?"

Josephine snorted good-naturedly. "Nay, Brad is simply a dear friend, in love with an equally dear woman," she supplied. "But he would help me if he could. He knew I didn't want to marry that beast in man's clothing. My father knew it, too, but he didn't care. He said he was happy to be rid of me. I dare not think of what will happen if, or when, Seymour finds me. He had an unparalleled look of nastiness in his eyes that perturbed me from the moment of introduction. My father, on the other hand, does not intimidate me in the slightest. He is weak of heart and even frailer of spine."

"Do you believe Seymour would hurt you?" Royal asked quietly, failing to realize that Seymour was a last name and not a first. "He must be very angry with you for leaving him. You're a very beautiful woman, Josephine, and undoubtedly an accolade most any man wouldn't let go without battle."

She blushed, finding her breathing slightly constricted by the blunt compliment. "Considering that I publicly embarrassed him, I highly doubt he would fight for me now, and I'd be most appreciative, mind you, if he didn't. The only problem with this whole fiasco is that I have no belongings, no money, nothing. If I can get a note to Brad, I'm certain he would find some way to help me. I have means, just—not presently. I could go to North Carolina. He has friends there."

"So it is impossible for you to stay?" Royal found himself asking. "The rift between your father and yourself has become so wide that it could not be sewn back together?"

"He works for Seymour, at the underwriting firm he uses. To put it plainly, if I had married Seymour, I would have been jumping far above my station. But the estrangement to my father goes much deeper than that."

"So your fiancé is a rich man, is he not? Most women would clamber to wed money, despite the way they felt about the man," Royal mused aloud. "Not to mention rich men are powerful, and powerful men do not like to lose, especially to a woman they may deem inferior."

Her forehead had creased into a frown. He could see the slight reflection of her alabaster skin in the translucent light of the moon peeking through the shutters. He could sense her distress as well, that something more was bothering her than she was letting on. "I'm sorry, Royal, I don't mean to dump all my problems onto you," she said then. "Please believe me when I say that I'm not fishing for assistance or expecting you to help me rectify this mess I have found myself in."

"I never thought you were."

The room fell silent save for the odd chirrup of crickets, the riot outside somehow seeming to skip over their tiny portion of the peninsula. Josephine lay snuggled in the covers of his bed, her eyelids drooping as Royal continued his watch despite the magnetic pull he felt to lie down beside her. The moon caught the sheen of her dress, and he could have sworn that the heavens would have wept for such a lovely sight. "Just answer me this, Josephine, and truthfully," he said, his voice nearly inaudible. "Do you fear that Seymour will harm you?"

Seconds ticked by into a minute. Royal had assumed she was asleep when the response came. "I think he is capable of anything."

4

Josephine's eyelids flickered open, her gaze widening to catch the placid morning rays of sunshine that crept through the cracks of the shutters. It took a moment to recollect what had happened the day before and somehow things seemed to be less clear for her than they had during the night. Royal still sat at the window; he turned when he heard her stir.

Josephine had her first unmistakable look at him as they locked gazes across the room. She could feel her cheeks grow warm as she continued to look, unabashed, into the depths of his eyes. Though circled with dark rings, belying his lack of sleep, the rich, deep, blue-green color of them awed her, drawing her in. His dark brown, almost ebony hair was glossy in the morning light, catching highlights from nearly purple to blue to golden. A day's beard covered his chin and jaw, creeping to his upper lip. He was incredibly appealing, even in his disheveled state. Long seconds passed before she could even think of a thing to say.

"Good morning," she managed at last.

"Good morning," he replied roughly. "The streets are eerily quiet."

"Do you think that the pirates have left?"

Royal grinned, though the humor did not reach his eyes. "I doubt it. Normally the city would be filled with clamor at this hour."

Josephine sat up, stretching her limbs and rubbing her neck. She knew she looked an awful mess, not to mention she hated the wedding gown she still wore and the reminder of what it represented. She ran her fingers through her hair, combing out the twisted copper strands and searching about for the pins she had lost in her sleep.

"I'm sorry I slept so long," she murmured. "Let me keep watch at the window while you rest. I am quite adept at the handling of a weapon."

"You certainly may wish to do so while I'm gone," Royal replied, and though he seemed skeptical, he said nothing. "As I mentioned yesterday, I must go and see what sort of damage has been done and see what may have befallen my ship, *Stormchaser*, moored in the harbor. I can only pray that they have left her be, for I will have nothing without her. Are you skilled at reloading?"

Josephine nodded. She often had target practice with the ill-shooting blunderbuss and flintlock when she could find nothing else to do, being careful to go deep enough into the salt marshes or find adequate cover beneath the live oak and magnolia canopy to avoid detection. Rounds of earthen jars had shattered beneath her aim and even once her father's eyepiece. He never knew, had thought he had lost it, and it was Josephine's adolescent smug comfort when their battles had become heated.

"You need to have no fear. No miscreant will breach this house," she told him with confidence. She heard her stomach growl loudly and she pressed her lips together. "I do apologize, Royal, but I am quite hungry."

"That was on my list to do as well," he smiled, his eyes losing a bit of their hardness. "That, and finding you something to wear other than your wedding gown, though I must say the style does become you."

"This gown is horrid, and I will entertain no other mention of it," she scowled, the rustle of the fabric loud in the room as she stood up. Her chin was high as she looked over at her companion. "Indeed, sir, I would remove it this very instant if there were but something else suitable."

Royal's dark brows arched together, the corner of his mouth turning slightly up. It was funny, he had just been thinking something along those lines, except the part about finding another item that was suitable. His imagination had been more than aroused with the slight peek of stockings shimmering across her legs he had seen over the course of the night. What made him grin all the more was that it was becoming plain that she had no inkling of the sort of image her words were conjuring.

"Well, I will certainly endeavor to remedy that in short order," he sighed with a slight flare to his nostrils. "Though the attire I am able to provide you with may not be palatable to such a fine taste."

"Anything would be better than this," Josephine stated, her words biting like cold steel. "Fine taste, hah! A fine reminder of everything I have come to deplore about society as a whole and certain people in particular."

Royal could not suppress a chuckle. "Come now, you cannot say that a beautiful home and expensive clothes aren't at the top of every woman's wish list. If that were not true, all the lovely ladies of Charleston would be vying for the hand of Thomas Crowder, a very poor farrier who is stout of heart even if not of purse. I have been an acquaintance of the man for four years and not once have I ever known him to have female companionship."

Josephine's eyes flashed at him. "You have a lot to learn, Captain Ashhurst," she confirmed. "You may be correct in the assumption that many women are blinded by their pursuit of pretty, petty things—but not all. Not by a long shot. There are, believe it or not, some women out there with a head on their shoulders whose pursuit is to have these things—and much more—on our own and without any help from the masculine segment."

"Well, I have yet to meet any," Royal stated mildly, leaning against the wall, his shirt taut across his shoulders as he crossed his arms.

Josephine's lips tightened. Was he purposely goading her, or did he really think she was a fan of foppery? "Wrong again, Captain Ashhurst. I would be quite happy running about in a rice sack if it were on my own plot of land."

He laughed outright at that. "I'm sorry," he apologized at the barbs shooting from her charming face. "I'm certain that the rice sack would be most fetching, princess, but I have never heard of a woman owning land in the colonies, let alone Charleston, unless it was a house of ill-repute. You're not thinking of going that route, are you? If so, I could make a few discreet introductions for you."

Her face had turned a dull red. It really was quite amusing, Royal thought. Josephine didn't agree. "Really, Captain Ashhurst. I do believe my opinion of you is beginning to change."

"Ah, for certain?" he volleyed, his eyes catching a ray of sunlight and shining a radiant green. Goodness, they really were amazing. As annoyed as she was, she still could not resist staring into them. "I couldn't help but notice how quickly you've reverted back to the proper use of my surname. Perhaps you are seeing me for the devil that I am, Josephine."

"Rubbish." She raised her chin and did her best to look down at him even though he stood a good foot taller than she. "I do believe that you are trying to get rid of me. And you will, Captain Ashhurst, as soon as possible, but I am afraid that we are, for the present, stuck."

"At least you are, princess," he grinned.

"Why do you call me that?" she complained, stamping her small foot involuntarily. "I am no porcelain ninny."

His eyes raked over her, the scene of her attack overlapping the image before him. It was true that she was no brainless chit, but for all her bravado, physically she was as close to helpless as one could be. He knew better than to rub her nose in that fact, however, and kept the smug comeuppance to himself.

Royal gave her a quick no-nonsense good-bye without answering her question and left her, the grin dying from his face as he stepped into the oppressive humidity the break of day in the Lowcountry had to offer. So-called because the majority of land sat at or below sea level, the Lowcountry stretched from the edge of the foothills of the Blue Ridge Mountains east to Pawley's Island and then southwards to the sea islands of Georgia. Keeping Charleston out of the clutches of the Atlantic Ocean was trying at times as the waves lashed at Oyster Point, attempting to reclaim the thin strip of land. There was a bit of a joke that stated the Ashley and Cooper rivers met here to form the ocean, but what Royal saw in the harbor as he made his way closer was no laughing matter. He made himself as inconspicuous as possible, loosening his shirt and picking up an empty earthen jug from a snoring pirate who had found some shade from the heat beneath an arching oak.

The port was a dismal picture of passed-out sailors and ransacked ships. His own *Stormchaser* had been stripped of her mainsail, but otherwise appeared untouched. Anger boiled deep inside him as he surveyed every inch of her from a distance. She sat at the end of a long line of merchants, smaller by half and therefore less of an enticement for the burglars. Royal was thankful for that, but damn it all, procuring another mainsail was a secondary nuisance he could have done without.

If Rembert wanted him in league with the pirates, then the blockade could possibly be a blessing in disguise. Royal wondered now what angle they would attempt; without question, the existing plan would need to be altered or scrapped altogether. Charleston was dealing with a seasoned armada, not some naysayer who was traipsing about with colors and a cutlass. Blackbeard was delicate to handle on his own, and while rumors did not place Stede Bonnet in high esteem as far as his pirating skills, he had money and resources and that was more than enough to make Royal's job insurmountable.

It was not his duty to take down the pirates by force, but to secure sensitive information that would allow South Carolina to organize and trap the villains—routes, numbers, weapons, and contacts. Enough knowledge of each was needed to secure imminent disaster for the colony's prey. In effect, spying on the pirates was almost a worse assignment than attacking them directly. Punishment if he were discovered would be nothing short of base, endless torture.

Charleston seemed to sag beneath the sky, with low-flying scud clouds and a blazing sun casting eerie light across the ground and trees. The sweet scent of the magnolias was heavy across the alleyways, the wind quietly wrapping her arms around the beleaguered city, as if to comfort her and let her know that not all hope was lost. Charleston seemed almost alien to him, her beauty and majesty as the premier port of the American colonies almost a laughable idea as sailors broke through windows and looted what they would. Even the walls put up in 1704 had done little to curb the flow of pirates or help otherwise in defending the maiden city; in recent years, population growth had made them nearly obsolete. He forged his trail along the depreciated fortification, a segment of which had already been torn down.

He made his way over to the magistrate's office, feeling the pulse of fear before he even stepped foot inside the building. Jonathan Rembert's office was the first on the left, and Royal quietly rapped on the door with his knuckles. He was allowed entrance by an aide, and as Rembert's cautious, wise eyes met his own, Royal knew there was trouble indeed.

5

Carter Seymour stood in the kitchen of his townhouse, his face red with exertion as he set his whip time and again against the back of the serving boy who had tripped over his own gangly feet and shattered a crystal decanter. Two other slaves held the boy's arms, their faces masks of barely concealed hatred. If they didn't show him some respect, the niggers would be next in line. The rosy marks of his crop had easily given way to ribbons of scarlet, the criss-cross pattern smearing into a mess of bloody, tattered flesh.

Seymour hardly saw the boy he beat. Nay, all he knew was how good it felt to swing the whip, how once he had started he found it hard to relent and how even after a second check of conscience he had lost every measure of control and could not stop.

Josephine. That unholy bitch.

"Massah! You be killen 'em iffen ye keepun," one of the slaves was begging him in rich Gullah tones and had been for some time. Seymour finally realized what the distant murmur in his ears had been. He let the crop fall once more before he noticed too that his arm was sore and blood from the slave had spattered back on his neat white cuffs. The victim of his abuse lay limp in the arms of the crying servants, having passed out long before the end of his punishment had come.

"Take him to his quarters and see to his wounds. I'll not have him die. He's too expensive to replace," Seymour ordered, knowing without remorse that he had gone too far and it was likely the boy would die.

Go to hell, damn you!

The hatred in her voice, the icy reflection of that feeling in her forsaken eyes…

Go to—

"No!" Seymour snapped, his arm swiping the polished silver serving tray that sat fully loaded on the nearby cart clean, glass and imported crystal shattering across the stone floor. He had done ten times over the damage the boy had, but still he held no repentance. Carter Seymour held nothing in his heart or mind at that moment other than pure, unbridled rage. She had shamed him, made him a laughingstock. With what was spinning around him already, his nerves were on but the edge of a knife.

He was due to meet with the governor. He knew he was late. He didn't particularly care. Charleston was a riotous mess at the present time, and the pressure Blackbeard was exerting on them all was not only an excuse but the bloody truth. The courier had brought him notice two hours ago that the pirate was holding Samuel Wragg and his four-year-old son hostage. Though Wragg was a favorite councilmember of Governor Johnson's, Seymour couldn't stand the man and couldn't care less about his brat. How they had been taken was a mystery, but regardless, the end result was that the pair was being held for an undisclosed amount of ransom.

The siege had continued through the night and well into the day; now it was late afternoon, terribly hot and humid with the sun beating down mercilessly. Seymour was sweating, his face puffy and red as he coerced his horse into action. The never-ending boom of cannons went off with the hour. Streets were mostly deserted other than the occasional laborer or slave with worried looks plastered on their faces, or any number of rough, devious-looking pirates that eyed his expensive horse and clothes with envy. Broken glass and smashed woodwork littered the alleyways. When he passed a popular dramhouse on Cumberland, boisterous laughter bubbled out the open doorway, mingling with hysterical screams from a serving wench who was suffering from some unseen maltreatment.

Jonathan Rembert met him on the doorstep of the magistrate's office, his quizzical brow smoothing somewhat as Seymour tossed the reins to the waiting liveryman and waddled towards the secretary. "We were going to start without you," Rembert said by way of greeting, not missing the specks of reddish-brown across Seymour's dress. "I must say I'm interested to hear the reason of your tardiness, but we don't have time for it now. Though you may, Seymour, wish to wipe your face."

Seymour turned a bit darker red, but as he complied with Rembert's advice, he caught a glimpse of a coppery smear on his white kerchief. Damn, the darkie's blood had spattered up higher than he thought. The fact only prickled his rage further. "I really don't see how this business concerns me," he spat.

"This business concerns us all, Seymour," Rembert produced without a flinch. "If Charleston were to be taken, you would lose everything. You've already lost your ship *Destiny*, or haven't you heard?"

"What?" Seymour stopped short, his eyes glowing. "She set sail just before the attack—"

"Apparently she didn't make it far," Rembert interrupted, holding the door and directing Seymour to precede him inside. "Her name and figurehead washed up unto Oyster Point this morning, burnt to cinders."

Seymour was still reeling from this announcement as he and Rembert entered the officer's drawing room, where the entire council and numerous upstanding members of Charleston society lingered, smoking cigars and cheroot, their faces reflecting the same air as those on the streets. Tension reverberated through the room and Seymour added more than his own fair share. Johnson himself paced back and forth, rubbing his neck.

"It appears everyone who is coming is here," Rembert announced. "Drayton was unable to be reached at Magnolia Plantation and I fear we must continue without him."

Governor Johnson cleared his throat and made eye contact with each man in the room in turn. "The day we have all feared has come," he addressed them. "Blackbeard and Major Stede Bonnet have teamed together, and Charleston is under attack. Some of you know that Samuel Wragg and his son have been taken hostage; the rest of you, consider yourselves informed now."

Murmurs flitted through the drawing room—garbled voices jeering the pirates and anxious whispers concerning the council member and his child. "In addition, several private merchant ships have been raided or lost. Livingston's *Tradewind*, Caldwell's *Pride of Charleston*, and Seymour's *Destiny*—all within the last twenty-four hours. Now Wragg has been taken and we have yet to receive a ransom note. We don't know whether or not he and the boy are still alive. Steps have been taken in recent weeks to curb the pirate activity, but unfortunately, they have come too late." Johnson's gaze flickered to the corner of the room momentarily before he continued. "Alas, I take sole responsibility for this, for I should have acted sooner. However, it is up to us, as a collective whole, to remedy it from here on out."

"Where is the Royal Navy?" someone interjected. "Why isn't Mother England protecting us?"

A rousing cheer of agreement followed, which Johnson promptly quelled. "I have petitioned the Queen and Parliament, but so far there has been no response, and we cannot wait any longer."

"What are we supposed to do?" another asked. "Stand back and allow them to take our property? Our families?"

"I had set in motion plans to have a spy infiltrate Blackbeard, though this changes things drastically," Johnson stated. "Of course, Blackbeard seems to receive pardons every other week from that damn Governor Eden; yet Spotswood of Virginia and I are together on the fact that if we have to, we will hire our own private entourage to take care of the bastards. Private donations would help immensely in speeding things along."

"And if we don't?" Seymour asked. "I've already felt the loss of one ship. Don't you think that's donation enough?"

Johnson's smile was bland at best. "If that is your reasoning, Seymour, be prepared to donate a lot more from that avenue." He inhaled deeply before he continued. "For the present time, at least, it appears that the pirates are leaving the ships moored in the harbor alone, finding more pleasure in looting the town brothels and imbibing of liquor stolen from the pubs. Perhaps this distraction will allow us to find a way to see if Wragg is indeed alive, and what Blackbeard wants for his safe return. For this, I have found a volunteer. Captain Ashhurst?"

Royal had been standing in the shadows of the drapery for the last hour, calm on the surface despite the odd looks he had been receiving from the rest of the assemblage. Irritated to begin with about Seymour's mere impending presence and then with his lack of punctuality, the stare he was receiving now made Ashhurst want to lash out a solid fist and knock the overgrown blob of a man into the wall. He felt a rush of power surge through him, and it took every ounce of self-control he had to maintain civility. Years of hatred boiled his veins but Royal refused to show it. He knew Seymour, knew his methods well, and Royal would not betray himself nor his intentions until he was ready to do so.

"Thank you, Governor Johnson, and the rest of the congress here," Ashhurst began, his voice flowing evenly through the room before it was chopped off harshly by Seymour's outburst.

"What the hell is he doing here? The devil of Charleston? Governor Johnson, this is a disgrace to us all!"

No one said a word.

Governor Johnson clenched his teeth. Leave it to Seymour to cause a scene. He knew that Seymour once had been Benjamin Ashhurst's friend, or partner, or something of that nature eons ago, taking over his business after his death, and wondered at this vehement hatred he harbored for Ashhurst's only son. It was no secret that there was debate over the right-ful ownership of the company, though Seymour claimed it in legal rights during some surreptitious trial a few years back. And as for Royal—no one had heard anything at all about him for the twenty-five years previous. It was little wonder people couldn't help but be suspicious of the man—especially after the nasty little scene he'd staged while inebriated.

"Who better, then?" he replied sternly.

Royal simply watched Seymour with a faint, amused expression on his hard features, his arms crossed across his chest. He stood a good bit taller than Seymour and was not nearly as thick through the middle, though his shoulders were much broader. Royal sensed rather than saw Seymour's intimidation, and it only made him smile all the more as he took a few paces forward. "I should think you know all about disgrace, Seymour," he breathed softly. "But with discretion being the better part of valor, now is not the time and place to accurately describe why."

"Miserable whoreson," Seymour muttered to himself, though he backed a step.

"Gentlemen, please," Rembert interceded. "We must be united now or we will accomplish nothing."

"John has a point," supplied a rotund merchant. "Though I myself am skeptical of Ashhurst's intentions. How do we know he isn't in league with Blackbeard?"

"Yes, I recall seeing *Stormchaser* dropping anchor the day of the siege," another merchant cried. "'Tis a bit fishy his ship made it in when mine did not, though *Proud Molly* was due in a week earlier."

Royal clenched his jaw, looking his accusers straight in the eye. "*Stormchaser* is smaller and faster than the East Indiaman you await, and quite frankly, if I were Blackbeard, I would prefer to take the cow rather than the calf." He paused, awaiting further challenge. When none came, he continued. "I am willing to befriend Blackbeard and his crew. Tonight I shall search them out in the taverns they have overtaken and petition to hear their captain's price for the ransom, according to the common and accepted standards of parley. Perhaps I will learn something useful in short order. On the other hand, I could be killed and none of you would be the worse off." His aqua-tinted eyes narrowed on Seymour. "Not that it would be of any concern to certain parties."

Seymour's lips were pursed tight as he volleyed stares with Royal. "I still don't like this, governor. I am not about to contest your decision, but I say someone else must accompany him in order to check his movements."

"Are you willing to accompany him, Seymour?" Johnson countered, noting the blanching of the rotund man's face. "I thought not. Besides, Captain Ashhurst would be better off alone. Any hope of subtle reasoning may otherwise be lost."

Royal didn't trust Seymour not to betray him. This was the perfect opportunity for him to do so. Yet he knew Seymour wasn't stupid enough to go against the governor, and he could only hope that Seymour's greed for power and prestige would get him to adhere to the plan. It was a strange, heady feeling to have the governor of South Carolina at his back. "Can I trust that no one in this room will interfere with, or sabotage, this arrangement?" Royal questioned the conference. "Any disruption of this, no matter how slight, could bring down the wrath of hell upon us all."

"Well, answer the bloody question," Johnson scowled when no one replied. Instantaneously nods of agreement abounded. "You have everyone's word, Captain Ashhurst."

"Do I?" he objected mildly.

Johnson was wise to the scuttlebutt in the room, and he was growing sick of it. "This grudge of yours will cease and desist this moment!" he bellowed, slamming his fist on the table. "Damn it all, there are other things to worry about now!"

Seymour swallowed. Royal's face was void of emotion. "You have my word as well, governor," Seymour coughed, barbs of poison shooting from his gaze at the son of his dead friend. "Now if you will excuse me, sirs, I find the contemptible company I am in has made me quite ill." Seymour spun on his heel and quit the room.

"He looked a frightful mess, didn't he?" someone commented. "Was that blood on him?"

"We will leave you to your own devices, Ashhurst," Lockwood, who owned one of the largest fleets in Charleston, stated blandly. "But it is no secret that few of us trust you, and if you betray us, you will pay."

"Your venom is unjustly placed," Royal countered, his blood hot in his veins. "One day you will apologize for that, Lockwood."

Josiah Sandall, who managed the overland shipping for over half of the colony, including Royal's, spoke up. "I believe that Ashhurst's interests mirror our own. I find it highly unlikely that he is exactly the devil he has been labeled as. Most of you all were friends with his father, for Christ's sake!"

"Thank you, Sandall," Royal acknowledged stiffly, touched again by the unexpected public support. "It is no secret, of course, to anyone here why Carter Seymour and I are on opposite sides of the fence, but the council is correct that the issue will be moot if pirates are allowed to overrun Charleston. I beg your pardons, sirs, I must try to rest before the evening comes."

Royal walked with an assured pace to the exit, his mind distant from the rest of him, thinking of how it was rather odd to have his voice heard, when he caught a comment in the distressed babble of the room that he wasn't even quite sure of at first. Talk of the day he had come back to South Carolina and in a drunken stupor heatedly challenged Seymour on the docks—like a blazing fool—mingled with suspicion and surprise regarding the strange plan, nearly burying a certain, slight, softly-worded bit of gossip.

"Seymour is at his wits' end, obsessing over that girl. Left him at the altar, causing no end of embarrassment. You should have seen it, Pierce..."

Royal froze, casting a sideways glance at the group holding the conversation. "Seymour was left at the altar?" he asked dumbly.

"By some red-headed chit, a clerk's daughter, Josephine, I guess her name is," a young eyewitness revealed. The stout dandy was all too eager to share the juicy bit of news with Seymour's rival. "Happened the day the blockade started. Beautiful piece, though completely unrefined. Probably dead in the gutter now, the silly wench. She's been missing since yesterday afternoon. Seymour was nearly crazed with lust over her when he met her, and now he's gone barmy without her."

"Josephine?" Royal repeated. The man mistook his shock for confusion.

"Do you know of her? By all saints, the creature would make even the most devout man think of forsaking the cloth in order to bed her."

"Can't say that I do," Royal replied and walked on.

6

Royal counted himself lucky when he found, hanging on a line just past Dock Street, several dresses that were approximately Josephine's size. While it was true they were well worn, the material was clean and not tattered; and though they were made of simple homespun cotton rather than extravagant silk or chenille, he was of the notion that Josephine Adelaide Beckham was not going to mind. Lord knew she was probably more anxious to get herself out of that wedding foppery than he was—and he was damned ready.

Darkness was sweeping its velvet cape across the Lowcountry when Royal drew near his modest home, the faint glimmer of red and purple from the sun setting behind the trees and lacy Spanish moss succumbing to black. The air had grown oppressively thicker in the last hour. Moisture clung to the sides of buildings and cast a hazy aura around the light thrown from the gas lamps, one by one, as the lamplighter went about his duty, humming a soft tune to himself. The usually unceasing breeze from the Atlantic was still. Royal was aware of every sound and movement in the blocks around him, not trusting the shadows. While he did not intend to live his life looking over his shoulder, he did intend on keeping a wayward dagger from between the blades of his back.

The stakes had been raised. Royal's mouth twisted into an engaging smile despite himself as he mounted the steps to his loft, his mind of a sudden quite detached from his mission. He wondered what Josephine had done all day. His smile died away as he realized that she would have to go somewhere else, for his residence very soon would, without a doubt, be probed by unfriendly eyes. He had begun to like the idea of someone waiting for him at home, as short lived as it was.

He inhaled deeply as he reminded himself that she was far above his league, though perhaps frowned upon by Charleston society at the present time, the gaffe would pass, being second nature even now to Blackbeard's blockade. There would be hundreds of rich, stable suitors, English and colonist alike, pounding on her door. Even if she didn't come from extravagant means, her beauty alone would secure that prediction. Why her father had given her to Seymour was a mystery. Though somewhat powerful and quite rich, the man was a monster who would have rutted on his daughter without mercy, eventually stamping out the fire, the lust for life that made Josephine the intriguing mixture of angel and devil that she was. The mere thought of that swollen globe of a man doing private, erotic acts with Josephine was enough to make Royal's stomach hurt and temper flare. What soothed him was that she hadn't allowed the blindness of wealth to subdue her—she had refused Seymour, and in a laughable fashion that would keep him grinning the better part of the next several months, regardless of anything else that may occur.

He opened the door with nary a creak, but Josephine still sensed his presence as she looked up from the table. She had drawn it to the center of the room, hugged on either side by the pair of haphazard chairs. Though bare of a tablecloth, the wood was smooth and clean. Shiny carved bowls sat pleasantly together next to a small iron cauldron that held something aromatic and steamy. Though the room was warm, it did not feel as stuffy as outside; the fire helped to alleviate the humidity.

The orange glow cast her soft skin in an impassioned hue. He could feel the radiance and comfort of her cheek beneath his fingertips as surely as if he were touching her. His palm itched and he clenched it dazedly, squeezing his eyes together tightly for a moment, waiting for the vision before him to disappear. His other hand mindlessly felt the roughness of the dresses slung over his shoulder, as if expecting to conjure the curve of a hip. She was smiling at him, all angel now, her delicate brows smoothed evenly across her forehead. Royal noticed that her forehead was a bit higher than average and her copper hair came down in a widow's peak. The minor flaw had gone unseen before, but it endeared him somehow. She had bathed; her hair still had damp tendrils curling rebelliously out from her prim bun.

"Josephine—?" he didn't know what else to say. It came out harsh, even to his own ears.

Her smile faded. "Is something wrong?"

"No, princess. It's just—this is a surprise. A pleasant one, though," he added lamely. "I'm sorry, I forgot about the food..."

"Do not worry, I was able to make something from what you had." She was looking at him softly. He found it hard to speak and forcefully cleared his throat.

"I got you a few dresses, though nothing that's worthy of you."

The smile returned. "Oh, thank you, Royal. Where did you—?"

He was shaking his head. "Does it matter?"

"No."

He still hadn't moved from the doorway. He was thankful for the length of the dresses concealing his arousal. With extreme will he entered the chamber, closing and locking the door behind him. The intimacy was so pronounced that it nearly ran a chill down his spine. "Where did you get the fresh water?" he asked.

"From the well around the corner. I saw it out the window." At his hard look, she assured him, "I was very careful, Royal."

He highly doubted it. She didn't seem the least bit contrite. "The pull in the corner will draw water from the roof," he informed her. Her erroneous actions seemed not to register and the frustration he was feeling elsewhere found its outlet. "Well, it's your hide," he scathed. "Why don't you leave and go to Brad's, seeing as you have such little concern for yourself."

The steel in his words did not pass amiss but Josephine ignored it. "Because Father and Seymour would look for me there," she stated matter-of-factly.

"So you do not think that being alone outside my home would allow them to find you?" He shook his head. Josephine flushed, knowing he was right about that. She could sense his irritation and she knew it was because he hadn't asked for this, not by any stretch of the imagination.

"I'm sorry to be a burden, Royal. Brad said before he would find a way to help me if I needed it, but it will take a little time."

"I didn't mean that you were a burden," he interrupted softly. He was but inches away from her now, his senses electrified. "In all fairness, Josephine, this is the most beautiful homecoming I can ever remember having."

His pacific eyes were haunted as he looked down at her, betraying flashes of deep torment. She swallowed, looking away. "Eat now, before it gets cold," she directed.

She sat across from him, both of them quiet and deep in their own thoughts as they ate. When they finished and the dishes had been wiped out, Royal exited the chamber to allow her privacy in which to change, brief apologies about the possible fit unnecessary in her relief. As he stood outside, the rumble of distant thunder high above masked her movements, but the want of her he didn't feel any less. The floor was going to be hard and lonely tonight. He wondered if he would even be able to sleep.

When her sing-song voice bid him entrance, he saw the dress was even worse than he had imagined. The bust was too small and Josephine was nearly coming out of it, the curves of her breasts full and high, her nipples taut beneath the fabric. Though the hem was short and he could see her bare feet and ankles, and the waist and hip were just a fraction too loose, she looked better than any woman he had seen in her evening finest. Maybe it was odd, but seeing her again for the first time, he had hated the way she looked in that wedding dress.

"You are very beautiful, Josephine," he said simply.

She blushed and bit her lower lip. That was even more provocative and Royal stuffed down the urge to pull her to him and kiss her until she was crying with the same needs as he.

"I must confess I am infinitely more comfortable," she sighed, and then proceeded to stifle a yawn. Her eyes cast upward at the growing reverb of the heavens; her heart was pounding and she was certain Royal would hear it if it wasn't for the thunder, and she was thankful for the distraction. She marveled at this man, how a simple pot of stew was so much to him when it was probably no better than what was served to Seymour's slaves. He seemed so shadowed, she ached to go to him and caress his troubles away. "Royal, I have found myself indebted to you, and I don't even know you."

"You will need to be moved on the morrow," he stated rigidly, yearning to change the subject. Her apparent gratefulness and self-quoted liability to him was stabbing at his side. "Do you have somewhere else to go? Anywhere at all?"

Josephine's lips tightened and her chin jutted out ever so slightly. "I will be able to manage whether I do or not."

"I take it that's a no."

She glared at him, though it was not all that venomous. More pride than anything, he supposed. "Don't worry, Josephine, I have another place I can stow you away, if need be."

He ran a hand through his dark hair, careless of an unwitting lock that fell roguishly over his tanned forehead. His eyes reflected green in the firelight, his arrogant nose cast in stark silhouette. "Josephine, there is something you need to tell me."

"Anything." She had no fear, no reservations as she looked at him squarely.

"This…Seymour you speak of," he worded carefully, watching her eyes, "is Carter Seymour of Seymour Transport, is he not?"

Josephine couldn't recall if she had told him that or nay, but she supposed in his business that the guess wouldn't be much of a stretch. "Yes, he is. Why?"

"I was at a meeting today, held by the Charleston committee, where I was discharged with certain duties that I will not detail here, but Carter Seymour was there, and rumors of what happened at St. Phillip's were flying about the room as I left. In fact, one of the congress asked me if I knew of you."

Josephine's eyes widened slightly but otherwise she gave no outward sign that her heart had begun an instant triphammer beat. Royal was studying her, she could tell. Her nerves tingled and her stomach turned as she thought of the possibility that he had decided to turn her over to Seymour, and then tense relief as she disregarded the notion. "How did he look? And what, may I inquire, did the rumors consist of? What did you say?"

"He looked like a man obsessed." Royal clasped his hands together behind his back to prevent himself from reaching out for her. "And the rumors, well, were nothing but the truth from what you have told me. How you, akin to an untamed lioness, left him standing at the altar and he's been a hunting madcap since. By the attitudes of the gossips in the room, Josephine, you will have nothing to worry about if you seek to replace Seymour—there will be waiting suitors, though I suppose the question is if Seymour will allow it. And what did I say? I acted as if I did not know you."

"If he allows it? Bah, he has no say in the matter," she informed him, rubbing at her temple. "The only reason things progressed as they did was because I feared what would happen if I had no home to go to. But since that has already come to pass, I realize that a month or two—or as many as it takes—of uncertainty cannot compare to a lifetime of atrociousness, saddled with such an ogre. It was a bit of a revelation to me as I stood at the end of the aisle."

"Carter Seymour is a ruthless, cold-blooded man," Royal worded softly. "He will stop at nothing to get what he wants."

"And neither will I," Josephine confirmed, her eyes flickering toward the window, the likes of which was illuminated by the advancing storm. "I want a life where I can pursue what I want when I want, with no one telling me that my desires are unacceptable or unladylike. If I had to sew needlepoint all day long and entertain with fancy tarts and tea, I would go mad by the ripe old age of twenty-five. I don't believe that's being cold-blooded."

"You realize that he would not think twice about killing you for this humiliation," Royal pressed. "Perhaps you should find a place for yourself far from Charleston. You don't know him."

"Charleston is my home," she defended. "I have as much right to be here as he does."

Royal admired her panache, even if there was little hope in it. The corner of his mouth curved into a wistful expression. Unable to resist, he reached out a hand and brushed the knuckle of his forefinger across her cheek, teasing a tendril of her copper hair away from her face. It pleased him that she didn't shy away. "Sometimes life doesn't turn out the way it was planned, does it? Yet it still goes on."

"It sounds like you know it from experience."

"If only you knew," he said, dropping his hand.

"You could tell me," she countered, the green jewels of her eyes sentimental.

"It's a long story, and it happened a long time ago." Lord, why did he feel like weeping?

"It seems to affect you greatly."

"Please, Josephine." Royal's voice was nearly hoarse. She was so young, too young to understand. He moved across the room to stare out the slits of the window, leaning his head on his forearm. "Let those bones rest."

Josephine felt the raw anger and hurt in him. It blazed from every limb of his body like a torch. She knew she shouldn't pry, but the question stayed on her tongue and wouldn't abate. "Royal, you can trust me," she breathed.

"Damn it, Josephine! I said let it go!" he roared, his fist leaving its imprint on the wall, bits of dust falling to the floor in its wake. Even the clamor of the night sky could not wholly conceal the explosion. His eyes glowed with hot rage as he turned on her. "It is not an issue of trust, girl, but of pride. I am not proud of the fact that I have nothing other than my three small ships. I am not proud of the fact that I have been unable to establish my name and holdings that were ripped from under me when I was very young. I am not proud that I have been unable to avenge the deaths of my father and mother. But, by all that I hold sacred, I will in time. And when the day I slowly extract revenge on the son of a bitch who did this to us comes, even if I could kill him a thousand times over it still would not be penance enough for what he has done!"

His acrimony hung unchallenged in the room. Josephine bit her lip, knowing that he was upset with her now and it was her own fault. "Royal, I'm sorry, I didn't mean—"

"Save your apologies," he snarled. "You got the answer that you wanted, did you not?"

She wanted to say no, because she still didn't know the whys and the wherefores of it all, but she thought better of it. Even though he was angry, and no doubt at her, she did not fear he would hurt her.

"Then there is nothing I can say," Josephine replied. "But know my apology is honest."

He seemed to relax. There was a long moment of silence. Josephine put another small log on the fire.

"How is your head?" he asked suddenly.

"Oh, fine," she told him, reaching for the volume *A Mariner's Guide* she had found on the shelf earlier in the day. She knelt by the fire and thumbed to the page she'd left off at earlier. It was a fascinating work; specialty knots, rigging, and sails she had already covered.

"Josephine, I didn't mean to snap at you."

"It's quite all right," she said. "I had no right to press you for any personal information."

Royal sighed. Another long moment passed, and then, "Try to relax, princess, yet keep your wits about you, I'm going out for awhile. The more I think about it, the more I want to move you to another locality as soon as possible."

"Why? No one has come near here," she argued, hurt a little inside at his callous tone.

Not yet, he thought. Did he want to take his chances with the pirates or Seymour? He wasn't certain. He would be finding out the former's threat tonight. He already knew the extent of the latter.

"Just trust me, princess."

Royal tore himself from the window. He knew he would be soaked the moment he left; he could have easily avoided it. He just hadn't wanted to leave. He still didn't. "Do you still have the weapons handy?"

"Yes." She dropped the book to her lap and faced him. "Royal, do you have to go?"

The words came without thinking. She cringed inwardly at the neediness in them. Josephine blushed, thankful for the reddish tint of the fire.

"Don't worry, there's enough supplies to see you through the siege if I don't return," he said gruffly, collecting his pistols, checking them and hiding them beneath his coat.

"I'm not worried about that," she protested, frustrated. He was nearly to the door when she came to her feet and hurried towards him. Surprised, he stopped and turned. She crashed into his chest.

"Oh!" she cried. "Excuse me, I didn't mean to—"

His arms were loosely circled around her waist. Being so close, his height advantage was much more noticeable. Her head could very likely slip under his chin without any trouble at all. Lord, he really was big. His shoulders didn't seem to end. And he was grinning at her. He was very handsome when he did that. Almost too good-looking. Her eyes cast down from his face only to see that her small hands had gripped a hold of the flaps of his cloak in tight fists. Instantly she released them, smoothing the wrinkles out of the folds.

"What did you mean, then?" His eyes twinkled at her. He still hadn't let her go. Josephine also noticed she didn't mind.

"Well, I—"

Thunder cracked and peeled the sky above them, making her jump. His lapels crumpled a second time.

Josephine felt his hold on her tighten. She was pressed against his chest now, her ear catching the solid beat of his heart that sounded through the shield of his clothing. The warm musky smell of him tingled her senses and sparked small fires at her fingers, toes, and spine.

"You were saying?" Royal prodded, his voice playful. The lightness in his tone belied the desire that was running rampant. Christ, how could he concentrate on what he had to do when Josephine was snuggled up to him?

He wasn't going to release her until she gave him an answer. Lord, he was difficult. She could see it already.

"I just—wanted to tell you to be careful," she managed, her rosy lips parting into a tender smile. "Though as easily as you dispatched those three pirates I guess I shouldn't worry."

It only took a moment's memory to cause the smile to fade into a frown. Royal sensed her withdrawal and loosed her, bringing a finger under her chin to lift it gently so he could look her in the eye.

"I want you to know that I don't take killing a man lightly," he told her. "Death is an irreversible punishment and not given by my hand without extremely good cause. When I first saw you I knew that I would have no choice but to kill them all or find myself dead otherwise for interfering."

Josephine nodded. Her eyes were wide as he looked into them. So innocent and expressive, he felt akin to lost. His thumb traced her jaw line several times, her skin smooth and warm beneath his touch. Royal sighed heavily through his nostrils, his cheek flexing. His hand felt heavy as he dropped it.

"How old are you, Josephine?" he asked, crossing his arms over his chest, looking down at her, telling himself she couldn't be but a day past sixteen.

"I turned twenty scant weeks ago," she replied self-importantly. "I am no child, Captain Ashhurst."

Of that he was entirely too aware; but to a man of thirty-four, she was also entirely too damned young. His teeth clenched tightly together without his even knowing it as he exhaled heavily. "I will see you in a few hours, princess," was all he said.

Josephine felt empty after he was gone, her skin warm and overly sensitive. She was far from tired as she listened to the storm, the rain pounding down, the thunder clapping. Captain Royal David Ashhurst intrigued her. She tried to tell herself that the attraction she had for him was due to the craziness of the situation, that it would pass. She blushed to herself at the wild fantasies racing through her head even as she tried to push them away.

She sensed, too, that he was attracted to her as well, but he was a deeply complicated man and seemingly more reserved than herself. Josephine was glad then he hadn't kissed her, though the idea of it had been the only thing on her mind when he had held her. She resolved she would have to be more careful to keep her distance in the future.

Her thoughts strayed to Carter Seymour. Subconsciously she drew the blunderbuss a little closer, shivering at the image of him that blinded her mind's eye. She had never understood the way he looked at her—

lust, yes, but it was a depraved thing in him, a chilled glow in his expression. The fact he was old enough to be her grandfather made it even more unpalatable. And she feared Royal was right; she had even said it herself. Seymour was capable of anything.

Still, the reality seemed so detached, at least when Royal was there. Josephine wondered as to why he thought his quarters weren't a safe place to hide. After all, what chance was there that Seymour would look for her here?

7

Royal paused before he entered the pub on Union Street, water dripping down his cloak to form puddles in the sodden earth at his feet. Whale oil lamps flickered from dynamic currents of the spring zephyrs that edged their way around the finely-wrought iron and glass, the echo of raindrops across their hoods creating an orchestra in the night. Among this sweet music, a raucous roar coming from the establishment signaled that the criminals were having an immensely good time inside—and he did not doubt that it was at the owner's expense.

He pressed his way into the crowded tavern with resolve, observing the horde with a practiced eye. Some turned their steely eyes towards him, sizing him up as they had all newcomers that evening. But most gazes fell away a short time later in disinterest, finding escape from their burdens in either the bottoms of their pitchers or in the serving wenches who brought them.

By luck and chance, a patron moved from his stool at the bar with the assistance of his companions. Judging by the sheer girth of the man, it was taking the other drunkards every bit of sobriety they had left. Royal deftly shot his way onto the seat as he ordered a mug of ale from a flustered looking barmaid, doing his best to ignore the fact that she was being mauled from all sides. Now was neither the time nor the place to intervene. Being taller than the average sailor helped immensely in certain situations; his cerulean eyes scanned the crowd for the possibility he may recognize someone, or be recognized in return.

He didn't have long to wait. A burly black man, in his forties and nearly as wide as he was tall and sporting a beard down to his torso, called his name from the end of the rail. It took Royal a moment to recall him; time had made him not so easily placed. "Well, are ye just gonna gape at me or buy me a drink?" the man demanded. The people between them subconsciously leaned back at the snarling tone, waiting for an explosive fight to break out at any moment and preparing themselves to launch out of harm's way if fisticuffs did indeed ensue.

"I'll buy you a drink when I'm ready and not a damn minute sooner, Kingsley," Royal shouted to make his voice heard across the rabble. He grinned widely. "I'm still waiting on my first."

The big black man moved next to Royal. "Ye've slowed down in yer old age, Ash," Kingsley snorted. "How long's it been, six, seven years? Last time I saw ye, ye could swill 'em with the best of 'em, and ye were long past yer first by the nooning meal."

"I decided that the unpleasantness afterwards wasn't worth the trouble," he replied.

"*Unpleasantness?* Is that what ye call it, now? Ayugh, I didn't know that bein' a downright surly cuss with a sharp tongue an' quick fist was called that nowadays," Kingsley chortled. "Of course, ye always picked a fight when it was the worst odds, an' somehow, ye always came out on top with yer handsome face bruised but not busted. Ye still chasin' demons, me friend?"

Royal's face darkened. "Are my years showing that well, then?"

Kingsley shook his head and took the last pull of his mug, wiping foam from his beard with the flick of a wrist. "Nay. Ye just have the same light in yer eyes that ye did back then. An' the mannerisms that made ye different, like ye didn't quite fit in—that ye were cut from a different cloth than us barnacles. But of course, this ain't nothin' new to ye. We've had this conversation a hundred times over. Seems like yesterday, doan it?"

"Well, to answer your question, I haven't done much of anything." Royal had to shout his words over the noise of the room. "I've done some labor here and there, and I currently oversee a very small operation. But the money isn't quite what I had hoped for. If anything, Queen Anne's War had done me better."

"Yer mind is fogged if ye think pirating is where the holy grail is," Kingsley reminded him. "Do ye remember the sour food an' low wage we got privateering?" At this point Kingsley gave up his seat, moved over to where a young man, more of a lad, really, who was thin as a pole, was sitting to Royal's right. Kingsley simply looked at him with a big grin and within moments, the elder mariner claimed the spoils for himself. When he spoke again, it was in a loud whisper. "Well, the sweet trade ain't a whole lot more than that. But fer blokes like me, there ain't much else out there waitin'." His shoulders stooped so slightly that Royal almost didn't notice. "But Cap'n Blackbeard, he's as fair as they come with the treasure, despite what may be told about him. Caught the quartermaster keepin' an extra share fer himself out of the last stuffs of booty we took in the Indies. The entire crew was ordered above deck; ol' Jim was tied to the mast. We were ordered te watch as Blackbeard cut off each finger, one by one. He was lyin' haggard in a pool of his own blood with the flies swarmin' about him when cap'n sliced off his eyelids, lettin' the sun burn his eyes 'fore the birds got 'im. He held on for near an hour before he passed. I almost felt sorry for 'im, but he was about as nice te us as the backside of an ass, an' he smelled about the same too. He got what was comin' te him."

He and Kingsley drank a few and reminisced about the days they had shared aboard the *Dancing Dolphin*, which in Royal's memory was the most awful privateer ship he had ever sailed on. For the seven months he had been in its employ, he had kept himself half-drunk simply to avoid reality. In circumspection, it had probably been his worst time, monetarily and emotionally. Only Kingsley and the liquor, it seemed, had understood him at all. Luckily, he had managed to meet Johannes Wylie while on layover, and with a short good-bye to his friend, he had set a different course and never looked back.

Privateering had been his life for so long that the transition to life upon land had not been easy despite the lessons he had tried to learn by observation. Prosperity, he had seen, could be won and lost over a simple game of dice or cards. Royal had visited distant lands that most people would never have the lot in life to see. He had been appreciative of those small fortunes, been grateful for the exposure to languages and cultures far removed from the American colonies. He had forced himself to grow intellectually in a cutthroat world that inhibited self-enlightenment. He refused to act, and therefore be, the poor and downtrodden. He acquired tastes for art and music and life's small pleasures.

"Is there any way you could get me in contact with your captain?" Royal asked some time later. The tavern had emptied somewhat, and those who remained were half dozing at their tables. He had already bought Kingsley four rounds to his two, but he didn't begrudge the coin. It was hard for Royal to imbibe of spirits, for once he started, there was a little part of him that told him he did not want to stop. It had taken years to force that demon to submit.

He artfully wove an embittered tale that barely separated truth from fiction. The stack of creditors knee deep. The difficulty he'd had procuring honest work. The sniveling portrait he'd painted of Rembert and the council asking him to negotiate because they really believed he had active ties with the pirates. Royal almost felt guilty about his comments on Rembert. He honestly liked the man.

"So I came here, hoping something would come up. I never would've thought it would be you, though, Kingsley—but I can't say I'm disappointed." Royal raised his mug slowly. Though he had been careful with his timing, he could feel the mead's fuzzy, warm effect.

Kingsley belched loudly and looked at him through bleary eyes. "So ye need tae meet with the cap'n, eh?" he queried in his rich seaman's brogue. "I think that can be arranged. On his terms, of course. Lemme see what I can do fer ye, Ash."

Kingsley stumbled away from the bar and went to a table in the far corner where three men were positioned in varying slumped forms. Royal's brows arched in skepticism at the possible results of this plan, but there was nothing more he could do short of swimming out to the *Queen Anne's Revenge*, a course of action that would undoubtedly succeed only in getting him pummeled by loads of grapeshot. After some deliberation and nodding, Kingsley approached him once more, a grin on his burly face. "Boatswain says ye got his ear tomorrow, Ash. Noontime, dockside." He yawned, and a sour plume of breath met Royal's nose. "I best be bunkin' up. Long day tomorrow, I'll bet. It was good te see ye, Ash."

Royal turned towards home four hours after he had left it; dawn was still some hours away and the storm did not appear to be losing strength. The rain was coming down in a steady, rhythmic beat on the stone and earth, the skies a battlefield of cosmic wizards. Shadows changed shape before his eyes. The rumble of thunder covered all other sounds. Yet the night held with its magic a darker secret he felt rather than saw. Instinct snapped back the veiled haze around his senses and he concentrated on the edifices and elegant courtyards, searching for any sign to explain his disconcertment.

He ducked into an alcove just past Chalmers Street, his nerves strained. One shadow did not change in the flashes and Royal reached out for it. He caught the man in a chokehold, spinning his stalker around and slamming him into the wall. His head was balding, shiny with rain, the ring of fading hair around it plastered together.

"Why were you following me?" Royal demanded, using all his strength to keep the man under control. "Who paid you?"

"The hell with ye," he grunted, wrestling away.

Royal snapped out an arm and caught him alongside the jaw. The man fell to his knees, the thud of his weight upon the ground shaking the earth between them. Mud splashed up and spattered them both. The two exchanged blows as the man tried to escape and Royal subdued. Then the click of a pistol, as faint as the sound was in the angry night, silenced both their movements.

"Start talking," Royal commanded.

"I don't know nothin'," the man spat. He nodded at Ashhurst. "Go on, boy. Let's see if yer serious."

The man lifted his own pistol and fired, yet it was too late. Royal had already shot him through the heart.

His breathing heavy, Royal scanned the area and then the dead man, his fingers searching for any sort of clue to identify his assailant. There wasn't one. The man's skin was still warm to the touch despite the pouring rains, but there would be no retelling of any secret he may know. Royal clenched his jaw and pushed himself away, leaving the body flaccid in the muck as he ran down the street, his eyes blurring with trepidation and fury.

It wasn't until he was out of the rain that Royal realized he hadn't gone unscathed. His shoulder was burning, and it was with a bit of surprise that he touched it and his fingers came back sticky with blood. He made his way up the stairs, his heart pounding in his chest as he thought of what he might find. A thousand possibilities could greet him on the other side of the door, and he swore that he imagined each and every one of them as he made it to the head of the stairs. A brief examination of the lock had shown nothing amiss, yet that didn't alleviate the worry.

He didn't even remember how he'd gotten home. Royal turned the key and slipped in, his one unfired pistol before him. Quickly he viewed all corners of the room, his throat catching as he saw Josephine's telltale figure slumped on the rug before the dying embers of the fire. She didn't move as he locked the door and with one eye on the window strode to her side.

She shrieked softly as her eyes flew open. The back of her gown was already cold and wet from his sleeve; water dripped from his hair onto her breast. His face seemed evil in nature's unpredictable glow, his dark brows tightly knit, his eyes squinted. She clutched at his shoulder to push him back.

Royal grit his teeth as she caught his wound. He let her push away but caught her wrist before she rubbed her forehead with the same hand, wiping it clean across his sodden cloak. "Come with me," he growled, turning away to retrieve his other cloak. It was not as heavy, but for the moment dry, and he draped it around Josephine's shoulders.

"What's wrong?" she asked as she stood, responding instantly to the alarm in his voice. She pulled the cloak closer and picked up the blunderbuss she'd kept company with while he pocketed more ammunition. He barely cast her a glance as he checked the door and then the hall before he led her outside into the violent night.

Charleston swallowed them unseen as Royal led her down strange, hidden lanes, the dancing fans of the palmettos glossy in the rain. The wind pushed at their backs and then their fronts in turn. They made an arch through the city, through avenues that did not seem familiar at all. Vaporous, whispering breezes tousled Josephine's hair beneath the hood of Royal's oversized cloak, the strands catching droplets of water and plastering to the flushed skin of her cheeks.

At last they were hidden beneath a mass of azalea and rose, lilac and palm; Royal's knuckles softly rapped a board and Josephine realized they were at some sort of entrance. A tiny beam of light shot out through an equally tiny peephole, though covered as it were, there was no trace of it to the outside world.

"It's Ashhurst," he rasped.

The light snuffed out and the door opened without a sound. Her hand had found Royal's some blocks ago but it was only now that she noticed, their fingers slick as they intertwined. She moved to release her grasp, but he held her firmly until they were well inside the structure. He led her with confident strides, the length of his legs a distinct advantage she had to scurry to keep up with. They entered a small enclave where the air was warm and quite perfumed. Josephine sneezed and began to shake.

"Poor thing," she heard a woman coo. "She's caught cold already."

Josephine wanted to comment that it wasn't the rain, it was the scent, but she didn't think that now was the time to be rude. She was, however, soaked to the bone and ready to find out what was going on. They were inside a small room, opulently furnished with silk wallpaper and a gilt-edged settee and chair. The colors, a deep rose and gold, were fashionable yet almost gaudy in their brightness. Incense burned from a small cauldron in the corner. An erotic painting on the wall—a portrait of two nude women doing explicit things that Josephine couldn't even find words for—caught her eye.

"Don't fret, princess, you haven't been sold into bondage," Royal reassured her. Her eyes were as wide as dinner plates. "If I may introduce you to Madame Kirkpatrick."

Madame Kirkpatrick ran the most elegant bordello in the Lowcountry. That much Josephine knew. She had seen the woman before in passing; buxom and bawdy, with a pale blonde wig and an extraordinary amount of rouge. She was smiling genuinely enough, yet Josephine felt an undercurrent of hostility. "Pleased to make your acquaintance, Madame Kirkpatrick," Josephine managed.

"Bah, no woman is pleased to know me," Kirkpatrick returned, "unless she is in a tight spot and needs a job." Then she laughed and rang a little silver bell. A small oriental girl with ivory features appeared and bowed. "Fetch the girl something from Elizabeth's closet, Mi Lin. They seem to be about the same size. And something for Captain Ashhurst from storage." Mi Lin turned with another bow to see to her mistress's bidding. Kirkpatrick winked at Royal. "Those clothes you left here have come in handy after all, Ash."

"No one must know we are here," Royal returned without preamble, peeling his overcoat from his body and letting it slump to the floor with a squish.

"My staff is loyal to me and me alone," Madame Kirkpatrick replied. "You know that, love—oh my goodness! You've been shot!"

Josephine's eyes widened as she saw the torn flesh of his shoulder, crimson blood oozing from the wound and staining rivulets down the whiteness of his shirt. The bullet had grazed the outer curve of his bicep, ripping a shallow u-shape through the tissue. Madame Kirkpatrick hurried to his side, her makeup creasing in worry lines across her forehead and around her pale blue eyes. Josephine stood back, her lips pressed together. Her eyes met his; they were dark and brooding. His gaze seemed to pierce right through her. "Are you all right?" she asked dazedly.

"I'll live." His eyes did not waver.

Madame Kirkpatrick was busy unlacing his shirt and then pushing it down his body until it, too, joined the wet cloak. Josephine couldn't help but stare at the masculine beauty of him— broad, thick chest with soft hair curling across his breast, only to taper down to a line across his stomach, which resembled a washboard. It quested lower still to disappear beneath the waistline of his breeches. She didn't dare look lower; seeing him gave her that warm, tingly feeling all over again, only a thousand times more intense than it had been before. She looked up hastily and it was then she saw the odd smattering of scars across his skin. Raised scars blighting his side; purple scars across his stomach. He bore a lifetime of battle upon him, the marks of a warrior profoundly experienced.

Josephine noticed, too, that she didn't care for the way Madame Kirkpatrick was touching him with such familiarity, either—or her free use of endearments. Now she was caressing his arm. Josephine looked at the smoldering pot of incense and sneezed.

"Do tell me what is afoot, Ash," Madame Kirkpatrick pressed.

"Headhunters and pirates." His face barely tightened as she dabbed at the wound with her handkerchief.

Mi Lin re-entered the room carrying all the requested items on one arm and a tray holding a decanter of wine, cheese, and fruit on the other. She placed them on the table gracefully, her eyes in turn, too, straying to Royal's naked chest. Madame Kirkpatrick gave another softly spoken order for hot water and bandages, and with a secondary bow, the translucent girl excused herself.

"You know I hate imposing on you, Isabella—"

"Do not fret, love. You know you can always find sanctuary here."

"It is not I who intends to stay, Madame," Royal replied, sorting out the masculine apparel. "I am asking that you give Josephine haven."

Josephine felt her limbs tighten. Madame Kirkpatrick looked only mildly surprised, though there was that same, mysteriously accusing glint to her eyes when she looked at her. "If I'm going to grant your request, I should at least know the nature of her sin."

Josephine swallowed. "There is no sin I have committed, Madame Kirkpatrick, unless refusing an unwanted marriage is to be considered one."

"Well said," the prostitute nodded, though she looked mistrustfully between Royal and Josephine. "But I do have to say that there is one sin I suspect you are guilty of."

Josephine's cheeks burned hot despite the cold, dripping clothes she wore. Her unconscious shiver saved her from having to find a suitable reply as Royal's deep voice came, "Josephine, there's a room through that door in which you can change."

"Thank you," she murmured, unable to meet Isabella Kirkpatrick's knowing look. Royal was holding a fresh dress in an outstretched hand. Her eyes strayed to his wound and her face fell. It was bleeding swiftly. "Oh, Royal," she sighed. "Are you certain you are all right? You need to get that bandaged and—"

"I'm taking care of it," he interrupted gently. "And I would like to change out of these clothes but I'm not going to do that while you're standing here in front of me shaking like a leaf."

"I shall hurry, then," she said.

Josephine went where she was directed. Royal watched her go.

"You're going to bleed on my floor if you don't take care of that, darling." Isabella was shaking her head though the concern was strong on her face. "The girl is not going anywhere. There is no way for her to escape."

Royal wiped away the fresh blood and cleaned the wound himself with a damp square of linen, then patched it with another. "Do you think it needs a sew?" he asked offhandedly.

"Nay, it looks worse than it is," she assured him. "I've seen enough to know. So have you." She leaned back gracefully on the settee. "Is this because of the girl?"

"Yes. No. I don't know." He raked a hand through his hair, a strange grin on his features. "I believe Seymour has something to do with the attack on me, but for the usual reasons, not Josephine. I know he was to be her husband. Life is a bitter circle, is it not?"

"Indeed it is," the prostitute confirmed. "It's been all the pillow-talk, Ash. This is the girl that belongs to him—"

"Only in his mind," Royal snapped. He took a breath and softened his voice. "I met her as she ran from the wedding, just as Blackbeard began the blockade." Royal secured the bond around his arm and tested his movement. It was starting to burn mercilessly. "Josephine has no one to turn to. Her father sold her to that bastard. As far as anyone knows, she could be dead."

Isabella Kirkpatrick listened quietly. She knew full well what a monster Carter Seymour was. He had thrown her girls around before; none of them enjoyed the prospect of bedding him but he always paid double. Just yesterday, however, he had gone too far, leaving bruises on poor Benzenia's neck. She was the only redhead in the house and was popular because of it. She wouldn't be working for nearly a week now. The girl had cried for an hour afterwards, and Kirkpatrick was considering refusing him future service. Now she could see the reason behind his volatile behavior, and she told Royal explicitly of what had occurred.

As he listened, his lips tightened and his eyes grew cold and distant. "Despite all of this, Isabella, you cannot refuse him. Anything he says may be of use to me and I don't want him suspicious."

"Does Josephine know of your past?" she asked.

Royal was pulling on the shirt. That, at least was dry. He faltered, then moved again with a snap. "Not much."

"Not Seymour?"

"No. She knows my family was ruined, but I don't think she understood at the time I was talking about Seymour."

"Royal, you must tell her!" Isabella protested. "I can see you are already too involved not to."

The slight creak to the door caught his attention, and then the sight it had been a precursor to. Josephine had loosed her damp copper hair to flow freely, the delicate waves of fire lapping at the small of her back. The gown of deep sea green was meant to be enticing—and it did its job all too well in his estimation. It hugged her body, off the shoulders with a low, scooped bodice pressing the curves of her breasts up, the expansive mounds of ivory flesh bare to his fantasies. It was made of a light, airy fabric that clung to her hips and buttocks.

Royal silently watched her advance. "I hope I didn't take too long," she said. The sparkle of defiance had returned, though he could not place where it was coming from. All he could focus on was how badly he wanted her, and he was having a hard time concealing it. Lord, her hair was begging his hands to lose themselves in it.

Royal said nothing as he went into the connecting room, the door closing somewhat forcefully. Josephine's mind was spinning with all the different emotions and she was suddenly very tired and frustrated. She could feel the assessing glances of the prostitute and envision all sorts of scenarios involving Kirkpatrick and the captain.

"Royal told me a bit of your tale, Josephine," Madame Kirkpatrick informed her. "Please, have a seat, and know my sympathy. Carter Seymour is an unpredictable danger."

"You know him?" Josephine's heart turned over, and at Isabella's hidden smile, Josephine felt silly. "Of course you must. Please, you mustn't tell him—"

The blonde waved her hand. "Do you really think Royal would bring you to me if he wasn't certain of the safety? I can see how he looks at you; like a wolf. Yet he is honorable, despite what may be said of him."

Josephine's mind hazed with a rapid secession of remembrance; Royal delivering her to safety first from the sick hands of the villains and then shielding her from Seymour, which brought them to their present state of affairs. He had asked for nothing from her, and though she could tell his means were small, he was extremely proud in spite of it. She could sense that asking someone for help was something that Royal was loathe to do; yet he took the ball of a musket as if it did not faze him. She said nothing and waited for him in uncomfortable silence, unable to do little more than nibble on the sustenance Mi Lin had provided. The clamor of her heart inside her ribs belied the cavalier expression upon her oval features. If Isabella had noticed Royal's hungry stares enough to comment upon them already, then she could rest assured that they were not just a figment of her overactive imagination.

Royal emerged in dry clothes and bare feet, carrying his boots in one hand. His shirt was still unlaced, leaving his torso naked. Josephine kept her eyes averted, afraid of what he may see in them. Isabella rose and motioned for them both to follow her.

They were led down a short hallway. Instead of mounting the steps before them, Madame Kirkpatrick took them behind the stairs and slid back a panel hidden in shadow that looked like the rest of the wall. Quickly they were ushered in and the panel slid shut without a sound behind them.

Here lay a second hallway beneath the stair, with all the appearance of spare storage. At the other end, again hidden in the wall, was another sliding panel. A very plush and opulent set of quarters greeted them this time; candles had been lit and cast the room in their warm glow. The fireplace lay cold yet the chimney of the room had cleverly, Isabella told them with pride, been designed to funnel in seamlessly with the others high on the roof. Dark maroon velvet furniture and carpet filled the room; the walls were covered in a charcoal gray silk paper patterned with maroon flowers. Gold tassels adorned the poster of the enormous bed in the corner, the frame of which was deliciously polished mahogany. To the left of that were neatly packaged foodstuffs on shelves, beneath them sealed bottles and kegs bearing all types of labels.

"Everything you could want is here—the bell pull in the corner will draw fresh water. Please try to rest; you must be weary with your toils. I will be in to see you tomorrow; but now I must go or I will be missed."

She curtsied slightly and floated from the room, the last whiff of incense following her. The inner door slid shut. Josephine's skin tingled, over-sensitive, as she walked towards the mass of candles, closing her eyes and rubbing the back of her neck with both hands. The vibration of the thunder shook the inner walls despite their seclusion, making the room seem even closer. "Are you going to tell me what is going on, Royal?" she asked, simply but pointedly, her back to him.

Royal's eyes drank in the sight of her. He didn't move, mesmerized by the vision. He didn't want to think about Seymour. He didn't want to think about Blackbeard or Rembert or the whole bloody lot. He wanted to not think about anything—except he and Josephine in that bed.

But she was probably thinking of something entirely different, and she hadn't chosen to wear that tight, sensual dress, just like she probably hadn't hoped to be in a secret chamber in the center of a bordello with him. He knew Isabella was right. He had to tell her about Seymour. Though he had been so young, Royal still felt shame that he had done nothing and that he had nothing now because of it.

"Josephine, are you certain that no one could have seen you?"

Her hand fell a fraction before she paused. "I'm certain."

"It was only luck or fate that kept you from being discovered. I believe that my enemy's man saw me leave the tavern and chose to make his move. He's been trying off and on for some time and because of recent circumstances he has decided to move more quickly." Royal's eyes were hot, penetrating into the back of her skull. "I told you about what happened to my family. I've never told anyone about it, other than in vague terms, that hasn't known me many years." He sighed, and she could feel his torment. "Josephine, it was Carter Seymour, your fiancé, who was responsible. For all of it. By running into me, princess, you've inadvertently put yourself into worse danger."

Josephine's limbs felt leaden. She whirled her head around. His eyes told her that his words were the truth. The silence was nearly deafening. Slowly she turned to face him completely, the candlelight glowing across her, catching golden highlights. "Royal...Carter Seymour? He is the enemy you've spoken of?" The revulsion in her tone rang clearly to his senses. He felt his control slipping, yet part of him was still expecting Josephine Adelaide Beckham to dissolve from his presence.

"I'm sorry, Josephine," he coughed. His shoulder was throbbing again, and he leaned his weight heavily against the bedpost. "If he knows that you were with me even for a moment, he would think nothing of killing you. He ruined my family and stole our fortune. His obsession with you is fodder for gossip. He is nearly mad, and if he knew of our entanglement, he would go over the edge. I could handle Seymour on my own, Josephine—but you certainly have complicated things."

"Royal, you're pale," was all she said. It wasn't the reply he was expecting at all. She came to his side and urged him to lie down on the bed, her fingers naturally smoothing the dark hair back from his face before her hand fell back to her lap. Royal's eyes closed against the caress, as soft as the wings of a *mariposa*. He had to stop it. She would no doubt flee the moment she could.

Josephine was trying not to concentrate on her compounded hatred of Carter Seymour but it seemed almost safer than her ideas about the sea captain. Lord, he was handsome. And he was trying to protect her. It was a strange feeling, never really having known it; but no stranger, she supposed, than the fact that Royal already knew all about Seymour and his nightmarish ways, and that made her feel even closer to him. It was a dangerous, powerful feeling.

Impulsively she leaned forward and pressed her lips to his brow. His forehead was hot beneath her touch. When she leaned shyly away their eyes met and fused. "Why didn't you tell me?" she asked softly. "You really did not think that I would see this…rivalry for what it is? I mean— what he has done is horrible, inexcusable—but…it doesn't reflect on you. It was not your fault, Royal—"

He stared at her mouth, the movement of her lips fantastically alluring. His body was hot, his blood pumping hard with the multitude of thoughts dancing across his brain, the hunger for her gnawing at his belly. His good arm slid around the curve of her waist so she was resting in the crook, his eyes, heavy-lidded, not straying from her face. He pulled her forward easily, her delicate hands touching the hard muscles of his chest, the tips of her fingers spreading through the matting of hair where the laces hung open. It was crisp yet yielding, her hand unconsciously stroking it, exhilarated by the wondrous feel of it.

She may as well have been clawing ribbons of fire down his torso, her touch was so potent to him. His hold grew firmer and he lifted his other hand to her face, his pulse thumping at her aggressive behavior. His fingers snaked through the copper strands back to catch a tight hold on the back of her head. Josephine licked her lips as she looked into his carved face, the devilish glint in his eye causing her breath to catch. The feel of him may be improper, but to Josephine, nothing seemed so natural. He was in all probability the strongest man she had ever met, both mentally and physically. He seemed to swallow her with his size, and after years of always having to be strong and silent, it was an anomalous state of affairs to lean on someone else for a change, if only for a moment. She had never known a man's touch, and despite all logical reasoning, she did not know what to expect of it.

She ducked her head, her nose nuzzling into the bared skin of Royal's chest. She inhaled the masculine scent of him with shivers of delight as the hair tickled her skin. She rubbed her cheek back and forth, the light scratching noise tantalizing in her ear. His fingers were gently caressing her skull beneath her ear and along the nape of her neck. It was so easy to relax, almost too easy. Her limbs were hot and tingling, her insides feeling vaguely empty. Her toes curled at how good it felt to be wrapped in his embrace, how safe and secure. She sighed heavily, her own breath warm against her visage.

With a stifled groan, Royal pulled her up a bit further, his eyes smoky as they caught hers a fraction of a second before he brushed his lips across hers. Once, twice; and at her surprised little moan his desire exploded, his mouth sealing possessively over Josephine's, his tongue sweeping inside. He tasted the sweetness for a long minute, his lips and teeth catching hers, playfully encouraging her response. His hand kept her head down enough to where he did not have to strain his neck, his other hand rubbing her waist and back. She was so tiny, she only halfway covered him; but the heat she gave him was hotter than a thousand blankets.

Josephine had been completely unprepared. But even as she returned Royal's kiss as best as she knew how, she knew she had wanted him to do exactly that, the pleasurable sensations shaking through her body like the storm that raged above them. She clenched the edges of his shirt, boldly pressing herself tighter. He tasted so good, a bit like wine and something else she had never known. She was mumbling his name softly, unaware that he swallowed them up in his adoration.

Carefully he rolled her to lie on her back, his lips moving to her throat, his nostrils filled with her feminine scent and his hands unable to touch her enough. His kiss rained molten fire across her neck, his day's beard rough. Her eyes opened dazedly to his face, almost disbelieving as his dark head tossed up and his mouth returned with crushing force. Their tongues danced in slick, ancient harmony, the slant of their mouths harsh as ardor consumed them.

He made damn sure her breathing was as heavy as his own before he tore himself away, his manhood painful and his blood hot. Royal did resemble a wolf as Isabella had described him. Josephine's soul felt as if it had been raked over burning coals; he was looking down at her with arrogance and pride, his blue-green eyes noting her swollen lips with distinct pleasure. "Ah, Josephine, you can make a man forget everything," he chided, taking another slow, deep kiss without waiting for a reply.

When it broke the second time, Josephine had a moment to think— and she thought that no matter how innocent what they were doing might be, she knew full well what the end result of this path could easily become. She was curious, and her attraction for him was so strong it was nearly blinding her. She wanted more but neither could she fathom the complications. Royal was preoccupied with so many other things. She was afraid of getting too involved. "I'm frightened, Royal," she whispered, aware of her awkward babble but unable to stop it. "I'm more afraid than I can ever remember being. There was a time where I thought I had no fear, but no longer."

"I would never hurt you, not on purpose," he growled, confused and angry that she might be frightened of him. She pressed a finger to his lips to calm him.

"No, Royal, I am not afraid of you, never like that," she said, her passion replaced with a wash of frustration and self-doubt. "I'm just uncertain about the future, that's all. I don't know—" she sighed. "Well, there's a lot I don't know."

A tear came unbidden and slid down her cheek. To Royal it was like a knife to the stomach, making him feel every inch the monster. His jaw hardened and he leaned away from her, his body in agony, but even as he tried to cool his passion, his temper flared. "Tell me you haven't been asking me to do that all night," he challenged her, his eyes hot. "Tell me that if I kissed you now and didn't stop, you wouldn't want that."

She swallowed, confused by his anger and the knowledge that he was right. "I'm sorry, Royal," she said, for lack of other words.

That didn't improve his temper at all. Violently he backed away from the bed, his masculinity still prominent against the confines of his breeches. His fell mood blackened the room. Josephine gathered a pillow to her breast as she rolled to her side, watching him, her lips feeling tender. Now he truly did seem to embody the devil in the deep glow of the candle-light—powerful, alluring, yet deadly and unpredictable.

"I have already arranged for your protection here, for as long as it takes," he smote her, "but I will take my leave on the morrow. I do not know when or if I will return."

Josephine's eyes widened, her heart curiously constricting at his words. Something inside was pulling at her, making her want to beg him to take her with him though she knew not his destination. Yet neither would she allow such a weakness, for Josephine Adelaide Beckham had never condoned weaknesses, so she kept her pride and nodded regally. "Thank you for your kind assistance, Royal. I am very grateful for your help, and I wish you luck."

Royal's eyes seemed made of pure ice as he glared at her, his tenor deep and bitter when he spoke again. "Enjoy the cold, empty bed, with only your boredom to keep you company. If you will excuse me, princess, I think I need to pay a visit above stair. With even as sore and tired as I am, you've got me aching for a pair of welcoming arms."

Royal disappeared through the portal and left her alone, her nerves crackling with unspent energy. The rustle of her skirts and the bedclothes as she propped herself up echoed loudly in the room, which seemed overly vacant without Ashhurst's presence. Part of her expected him to come back, and when long minutes passed without his resurgence, the knowledge that he was indeed upstairs—and very likely with Madame

Kirkpatrick—made her stomach clench with jealousy.

She had no reason to be jealous. Josephine kept trying to remind herself of that fact. Royal Ashhurst did not belong to her, or she to him. Things had only become overheated because of outside influence—Royal wanted to hurt Seymour, and by keeping her he was doing just that. His attraction for her was simply misplaced revenge.

And as for her attraction to him...Josephine sighed, not caring for it at all. There was something about him that struck a chord in her. She couldn't place a finger on it—not a look, or a touch, or a scent—but there was definitely something there, and she could no longer deny it as she had since the moment she met him.

8

Royal slammed through the double doors that guarded the second floor of Kirkpatrick's, careless of the banging abuse the delicate French structures received from his hand. His teeth were tightly clenched, his jaw line prominent as his aquatic eyes scored across the ladies of the night who lounged in Isabella's waiting room, or the small enclave she called "the hook" for obvious reasons. When one approached him with a devious smile across her lips and eyes that roamed from his tousled hair down to his bare feet and back again, he should have smiled back. Instead, he emitted something akin to a snarl, and the welcome on her face fell into a look of contempt.

"Call Madame, quickly," the girl bade another, her Parisian accent accentuated by the slight sniff. "It ees a pirate!"

"Nay, sillee, ees Captain Ashhurst," another equally strong European voice chimed in, her sapphire eyes sparkling at him from behind a fan. "Yous remember, no?"

The girl's eyes widened. "Ah, yes, Captain," she recalled, her gaze casting downwards. "How could I be so foolish, hmm? Ees just…you look so deefferent, without your beard."

"Perhaps you need a reminder," Royal cut in sharply, his words as hard and cold as stone. "What was your name, sweetheart?"

"Call me Lillin, for that is my name now, Captain," she giggled. "But I believe when I stayed with you on my voyage to Ahmerica that I went by Jacqueline."

Jacqueline. Yes, he remembered her, though the last couple of years had done much to blur that portion of his life. His first—and for the longest time, only—job he had come across was transporting prostitutes and highly suspect liquor and opium to and from Europe. He had known Isabella Kirkpatrick as long as he could remember; for despite popular knowledge, he had been in Charleston for brief layovers while privateering, with nothing more than friendship between them despite the fact that he suspected she desired more. When she had asked him to collect her girls, she had also relayed in no uncertain terms that he was to take each of the virgins to bed in order to acclimate their bodies to the rigors that they were going to face. Royal had acquiesced, his conscience not as powerful then as the healthy urges of his body. When he thought about the women, and the people they would service, he had made it a point to give each of them as much pleasure as he knew how. Over time, they had taught him things, too.

When the tide of fortune had changed and the runs with ill-gotten booty became a thing of the past, Royal had ceased delivering girls for

Kirkpatrick as well. It was not something he regretted, but neither did he dwell on it. Jacqueline had been far from timid, demanding more and more of him during his voyage with her aboard, and it had been with a surprising dose of relief that he had washed his hands of her. Come to think of it, he hadn't crossed paths with her since then even though he had visited Isabella countless times.

Yet, ancient history had little to do with the way he was feeling now; all he cared about was that she had a pair of warm, willing arms, and he had a demon in his veins that needed exorcising. "I do not know your price, Lillin, but I will find a way to afford it," Royal choked, taking her hands and lifting them to his lips. "I have credit with Madame Kirkpatrick, I am certain."

She nodded and bade him to follow her, the reek of her fine perfume wafting behind her, clogging his nostrils though with his inner senses he could still smell the seductive scent of Josephine. Lillin's glossy dark hair tossed in generous waves across her hips as she unraveled it from atop her head, and as if his vision was slighted by opium it transformed to curling flames of red. Royal's brow creased, his skin burning as he squinted his eyes, beads of sweat gathering at the nape of his neck. A room opened before him, the door closing behind him without his being cognizant of it.

The prostitute was kissing his neck and chest, her hands moving swiftly across the hard contours of his muscles, her fingernails gently raking at the planes of his back. Royal stood as solid as a stone, his eyes faraway as he looked to the corner of the room, aware of Lillin's ministrations but unable to respond to them. His organ remained only semi-aroused, throbbing painfully nonetheless as he thought of another clandestine moment entirely. Of their own volition his hands reached up to Lillin's shoulders, his strong lean fingers grasping her firmly yet gently and pushing her back away from him.

"I'm sorry, I don't know what I was thinking," he apologized roughly, turning from her. "Your favors are marvelous, my dear, but unfortunately my mood is changing faster than the weather."

"I understand," she murmured, touching her lips. Her eyes raked over his face; tension and longing she recognized, just as she knew that these things were not for her. "I will leave you now. Take a moment if you need, but please do not linger too long." She left with nary a sound, her wistful hopes at once again feeling the expert lovemaking the dark captain offered crumbling.

The soft click of the door latch broke Royal from his reverie. He hung his head with a harsh, deep sigh.

"I'm tired, Isabella. I don't think I've slept in days."

"Ah, things are difficult, I know," she comforted. "Please take my chambers for tonight if you find the Burgundy Room a little too close. I will not return to them until late in the morning tomorrow. Will you be here then, love?"

"Nay. I'm scheduled to meet with Blackbeard, and from there I know not what will happen."

"Oh, Captain Ashhurst," Isabella chided, shaking her head. "You are forever fighting against impossible odds. Will the self-destructive vein in you ever run its course? I fear for your safety, Royal. Listen to me," she added, the urgency in her voice causing his bleak eyes to meet her own. "If Carter Seymour is as mad as you say, it is going to be difficult to keep your Josephine hidden. She seems rebellious and not prone to enjoying confinement, even as plush as her chambers are. And there is only so long she can stay here on my charity, even if I am doing it for you. She will have to earn her keep somehow."

"I will not allow her to be a courtesan," Royal growled, the deep pitch of his voice brooking no argument. "Have her wash clothes, clean rooms—her temperament could use it anyway—but she is to remain untouched by any of your clientele. She is to stay as long it takes. Any correspondence she sends I want you to intercept. I will not have a foolish note written to her dear friend Brad putting her in danger, and the girl, despite being blessed with common sense, is more ignorant of the spot she is in than I am. That she will be safe while I am gone, this I want you to promise me."

"And how long will that be?" Isabella asked softly, a small piece of her heart dying inside. "Blackbeard is a vicious bandit that even Seymour cannot compare to. Though I must confess I am curious as to the reasons for your engagement, I know that, try as I might, you will convey nothing." She smiled crookedly. "What if you do not return, Royal? And is it so very necessary that you go?"

"Do not fear for me, Isabella," Royal laughed, his rough voice humorless. "The world would not be amiss with the loss of a devil."

Isabella pursed her lips. "I think there are people who would feel the loss besides myself, Royal, though you may not see it as easily as I do. But luck and Godspeed to you, darling. I will await your return with crossed fingers and high hopes."

Royal's mind was twisted and torn as he relaxed his body, lying shirtless on the silken sheets of Isabella's bed a short time later. Even though he was certain he would be unable to sleep, the long stretch that he had been deprived of it had caught up with him, and he fell into a deep, dreamless slumber after turning over but once.

When the late morning sunshine at last coaxed him awake, Royal's mood wasn't the better for it; he had slept longer than anticipated and he had little time with which to bathe and dress again. There was certainly no time to stop below stair and pay a visit to Josephine Adelaide Beckham, and though try as he might to convince himself that neither did he wish to, he knew he was lying to himself.

The sky, washed by the evening storm, held up high in its blue transparency a blazing sun; and the kiss of the sun across the Lowcountry brought with it a suffocating amount of humidity. His shirt was already sticking to his shoulders, his damp hair refusing to dry even in the hot, whipping wind. The people wandering through the streets of Charleston had the same fearful look in their eye as they had the days previous; none met his gaze straight on as he made his way towards the docks.

The *Queen Anne's Revenge* swayed arrogantly atop the crests of the bottle green waves that pushed forward from the endless sight of the Atlantic Ocean, her flag flapping with belligerent pride. Royal felt his stomach muscles tighten with misgivings, but he continued on regardless towards the longboat tethered to Boyce's wharf. He kept his train of thought centered on what he would say to Blackbeard and what sort of reaction he could anticipate from the pirate. After some thought, Ashhurst had come up with nothing.

Scruffy men of varying ages and handicaps milled about, their crude laughter floating to Royal's ears. More than his life alone was at stake, and it was taking some time for him to adapt to the fact that for the first time in years, something he was doing was bound to have a profound impact on his life and the lives of others—indeed, on Charleston as a whole. It was as humbling as it was exhilarating, and as he looked about at his forlorn city, he knew he loved her deeply and would sacrifice whatever it took in order to keep her the pride of the colonies. The very sight of the scourges that crept through alley and lane brought about an instinctive rage, and he swore that after surviving numerous attacks of disease and natives, Charleston was not going to falter now.

A gaggle of men, numbering ten or so, paused as he approached. He recognized a few from the tavern but he had not spoken with any of them. He wondered if the mead-laden brain of the boatswain he had arranged the meeting with had been resolute. Kingsley was nowhere to be seen. Royal turned his gaze on each of them in turn and said lowly, "My name is Ashhurst. I've been sent to meet with your captain."

One of the men spit out a long stream of saliva and wiped the sweat from his brow. "Yeah, we've been waitin' on ye, ye mangy dog," he chortled, bringing peals of laughter from his counterparts. Royal said nothing. The man's petty insult slid off without regard. "Yer late."

"I was told noon, and that hour has yet to be struck," Royal argued, smiling all the while. "Yet I hope your captain has not been misinformed as to the time that was arranged by those beneath him and that he is not unpleased."

The men looked at the tall, bold stranger, soft-and well-spoken though he was, and thought better of any further harassment without leave from Blackbeard. Another unappetizing cascade of tobacco juice discharged onto the ground. "Well, c'mon, then. May as well git it over with. Chances are anyhows that I'll be lazin' the afternoon away rather than rowin' yer sorry hide back te shore." He laughed at his own little joke and allowed Royal to board the slim vessel first.

The mannerisms of the pirates were all too familiar, and Royal did not have to wait for rude urging before he picked up one of the oars to assist with the rowing. This simple move placed him a notch higher on the ladder of esteem, though the motion remained bereft of comment. His wound screamed its protest; Royal ignored it, hoping that it wouldn't begin bleeding afresh.

The air was slightly cooler over the water, and he leaned his head back to allow the wind to chill the sweat running in rivers down his neck. The odor of the craft was almost unbearable. The rotten smell of spilled ale that had turned in the hot southern sun, compounded with decayed sweat of the men, would have turned softer stomachs, yet Royal steeled his midriff and inhaled through clenched teeth. In the blink of an eye, he had stepped back in time ten years.

His nerves had all but abated by the time the longboat drew along-side the hull of the *Queen Anne's Revenge*. She was a beautiful ship, though battle-scarred now from her exploits as both victim and aggressor. The horrid Jolly Roger Blackbeard flew—a spade-wielding skeleton stabbing a heart, with blood dripping ominously—seemed to grin down from its posture on the mast, the grommets and hemp that held her straining tirelessly against the eastern Atlantic breeze. The ship was fearsome beneath Blackbeard's command—cannons, ready and able, lined her broadside and they all faced Charleston Harbor.

As Royal planted his feet firmly on the deck and looked west to the fair port city, his aquatic eyes shifted across several landmarks until falling on a nestled canopy of trees a bit to the left of St. Phillip's high reaches. He sighed despite himself as he wondered what Miss Josephine Adelaide Beckham was up to, and when he reminded himself that it was no concern of his, he tore his gaze away and forced himself to think more clearly on the issue that lay before him.

"If you would keep your blunderbuss to the side, I would appreciate it," Royal beseeched a grizzled old man who had been pointing the nose of his weapon at Ashhurst's head since he had stepped aboard. "I'm certain that if there is enough manpower here to blockade the port, you would also realize that one man alone, unarmed, is hardly worth wasting your time over."

"Cap'n gives the orders around here, not ye," the old salt replied and moved the gun barrel another few inches closer to Royal's head just to prove his point. "He says tae me, 'keep yer gun trained on any bugger that steps aboard til I tells ye not tae,' and that's what I'm a-gonna do."

Royal thought about telling the old man where he could stick his orders, but he refrained from further comment as he was led toward the stern and into the captain's cabin.

Blackbeard had certainly made himself at home in the opulent quarters he had stolen. Fine, rich linens were already stained beyond saving with various spillages of liquors and food. The books and charts that had once been neatly stacked, filed, and secured were piled in a lump on the floor, having been scoured for anything of value and then tossed aside. Empty plates and decanters lay strewn across the table, the last remnants of what they contained caking into a foul ring. The room had the same putrid scent of unwashed humanity; no matter how exposed he was to it, Royal was never able to get used to it. Perhaps it was the reminder of all that hard, lonely time at sea when he had had no choice but to put up with it; he didn't know.

And there, in the middle of it all, with one woman draped across his arm and another sitting on his knee, was Edward Teach—or Blackbeard. He was a giant of a man, even taller and broader through the shoulders than Royal. The pirate's deep, throaty laugh boomed in the room, making the cabin seem smaller than it was. Through two bushy, arching brows Royal could see Blackbeard's brown, glassine eyes, almost tiny in the roundness of his face; a cold, offhand flame burned there.

"Captain Blackbeard," he nodded, bowing low and touching his hand to his heart. "My name is Royal Ashhurst. Thank you for allowing me to come aboard."

There was a squeal from the doxy sitting on his lap as Blackbeard's meaty hand mauled her breast, squeezing it and pulling on it in a frightfully lewd fashion. Not a whit of concern shadowed his face as he pulled the woman's corset down, baring the softly rounded flesh and hardened tip to Royal's gaze. "Ain't she a sight, stranger?" the rumbling question came.

Royal wasn't certain how he should reply, but he averted his gaze back to the leader and nodded, though the sight was disgusting at best. "Captain, as I am certain you are well aware, I have been sent by Governor Johnson to hear the price you ask to end this blockade."

"Yet that is not yer only agenda," Blackbeard returned. Subconsciously, Royal felt the hair at the nape of his neck stand on end, though he did not turn his eyes away. "For I can see it in your face, ye miserable cur. There is more ye want from Blackbeard, is there not?" He reached forward for his goblet and drained the thing with one swallow, bellowing a sour plume of air after the fact. "I have not made it this far in me exploits without knowin' when something's afoot. Do ye smell a rat, Javad?"

A dark-skinned young man, perhaps twenty-two years of age, had entered the cabin behind Royal without a sound and was holding a cutlass inches from his neck. Royal cast a sidelong glance, and Javad smiled brightly, the gold of his capped teeth glinting in the rays of the sun. "Ayus don't rightly know, Cap'n, but ayus always itchin' for da taste of blood."

Blackbeard smiled approvingly, his rotten teeth shadowed by the hair that had given him his nickname. "Why don't ye have a seat, and perhaps I'll hear what ye have tae say. If me mood changes, I'll let ye know."

This brought another peal of laughter, and though Royal felt like telling the pirate what he could do with his moods, instead he shuffled his own acerbic self to the side and acquiesced. He pulled a cheroot from his pocket and casually asked the pirate for a match, his eyes boring into those of his adversary as he struck the flame and put it to the end of his cigarette. He was thankful when the sulphur burned his nostrils, safeguarding his sense of smell from the rancid stench of the cabin.

"To be honest with you, Captain Teach—"

"Me name's Blackbeard, Ashhurst, and ye'll do well to remember it." His voice brooked no argument, but his threat did little to unsettle Royal.

"I apologize. Blackbeard," Royal began anew, the hard planes of his face smoothing into distracted agreement as he leaned back in his chair. "I haven't come to circle the stick and try to win your favors with sweet lies. To be quite frank, if there wasn't something in it for me, I wouldn't be here. It is no secret in Charleston that I have no love for its upper crust. They have done nothing but scorn and ridicule my existence, but when it comes to handling the matter that you have placed upon their doorstep, suddenly the cowards claim that I am worthy of their attention. My story is complicated, but in any event, they offered me a small purse to enter the lion's den, so here I am."

"Did ye get the coin?" Blackbeard pressed.

"Not until I return with the information they seek."

Blackbeard made a long harrumph and shook his head. "That was yer first mistake, boy. Never let the bloody bastards take advantage of ye. That's what we're here for." He laughed, shifting the women on his lap. "I takes it yer a common man."

"I worked many years in privateering. Now I'm a very small shipper."

Blackbeard snorted. "Ye talk entirely too fancy not to come from a rich mamma's tit."

"My family was destroyed when I was but a child, though I read a lot." Royal's eyes glinted with something Blackbeard appeared to recognize, because the pirate did not press for any further information on his personal background.

"So you tried to clean up, rather than stay in privateering after the war," Blackbeard supplied, stroking his beard and watching his visitor carefully. "But no one'll have ye."

"If you must know, I am known more as the devil of Charleston than by my real name. Is there anything else you wish to inquire about my personal habits?" Royal kept his voice even.

The two men continued to study each other and Royal could still feel the presence of Javad's blade at his neck, though he did not lose eye contact with Blackbeard for even a moment.

"Did I sink one of yer ships?" Blackbeard asked some time later.

"Nay, but I saw my mainsail on your deck."

"Damn," Blackbeard returned with a snicker. "That woulda been the luck, eh?"

Royal only nodded, trying to think of a way to steer the conversation back in the direction he wanted. "You realize that this blockade is going to have the entire colony up in arms."

Blackbeard's horrid smile faded to something darker. "Hell with 'em. The Queen's left 'em, and they're not smart enough te catch me. They'll do what I say or this place will go up in flames."

"I was told to confirm that both Samuel Wragg and his son are unharmed. Proof of such good esteem on your part will ensure a rapid response from the delegation," Royal told him. "They are open to hearing your demands."

"Me crew is sick. Dropped anchor in Port Royal, Jamaica, for a month and the shabs were out screwin' anything they could. Over half of 'em caught Somethin'—they can't piss or have a hard time doin' it when they can. I need enough medical supplies to treat an' cure 'em; and whatever is in the treasure trove at the Exchange, well, I want that, too." Blackbeard leaned forward, dislodging the wenches, his lips curled defiantly. "An' ye'll have a look at the prisners, sooner or later. But I've taken a liking te ye, Ashhurst, and wouldn't mind having ye aboard for awhile. So how about pouring a dram and makin' yerself comfortable?"

Considering Javad was waiting patiently behind him for his leader's silent signal to slit his throat, Royal knew that there was little he could do.

It was clear that Blackbeard was looking for a drinking partner, and damn it all, he was going to be the lucky one. He resigned himself to his fate as he reached for a fresh bottle of mead on the table.

* * * * *

Josephine was nudged awake not long after Royal had left, the gentle hand on her forearm persisting until she opened her eyes. The hidden hope in them died as Isabella looked down at her grimly. "What's wrong?" Josephine asked, sitting up as she surmised that she dared not sleep any more. She never knew what she would wake to.

"Royal is gone." Isabella paused, watching the younger girl. She really was a beautiful anomaly, and with her graceful ferocity, she could fetch any price. Sultans would bargain for her and lords would surely keep her gowned and bejeweled in London's finest. Young and lost she may be, but the fear of the world would fade as she began to realize what a weapon her physical attributes were. A part of her wondered if a man like Royal knew what possessing a woman like Josephine entailed. "It is time to put you to work."

"What?" Josephine's mouth fell open. How dare he! He couldn't have possibly... "He doesn't have the right!" she exploded. "Thank you for your shelter, Madame, but I will be on my way—"

"Calm yourself," Isabella ordered, soft yet stern. "Neither he—nor I, for that matter—intend for you to service the men. You will, however, service the house. Because your stay has been extended, you will earn your keep rather than lounging the days away in this room. There are plenty of chores you are capable of, and indeed, some of them will probably do you good."

"I choose not to impose nor work," Josephine said then. "If I may borrow a cloak—which I assure you I shall return—I will be on my way. Enough time has passed where I believe I could successfully find aid through my friend. Indeed, if anyone was looking for me, they very likely have given up by now."

"Ah, but you have no choice, *cherie*," Isabella informed her sadly. "You have the freedom of the house, but no farther."

"You cannot keep me here!" Josephine flared, her green eyes flashing.

"There are guards near every door and, the windows, my dear, are locked tightly," Isabella informed her with a smile twitching at the corners of her mouth. Josephine hated her and her superiority—just as she hated the fact that she and Royal shared a past. "You are not leaving, but you will be vacating this room, and when you do, you will begin wearing this veil, and it shall cover your face at all times. Never take it off, not even when you sleep. There are several different colors to match your wardrobe, of course, in your new chambers, which aren't nearly so posh as the room you occupy presently—"

"And if I do not?" Josephine challenged. "You will excuse me if my words seem brusque, Madame, but I am nothing if not frank. You have neither right nor reason to keep me here, and I must say I am confused as to why you would even wish it. I sense that you are not fond of me, and though I may suspect the reasons for that, I do not wish to expound on them further. It is not because I am afraid of hard work—just as long as it is work of my own choosing."

"Please, do not refrain from telling me what you think of me, Miss Beckham," Isabella said coolly, her head tilted regally back. "You may think me no more than a common whore. You may think that I am jealous of you, and your purity." Isabella laughed softly. "I am comfortable with who I am, and the modest fortune I have amassed is more than enough to see me through any dire circumstance, including old age. It is also true, as you suspect, that I am in love with Royal." Isabella watched Josephine carefully, not missing the possessiveness and abhorrence in the younger girl's eyes, but instead of rising to meet it as her adversary expected, only sadness reflected in the face of the madame. "But it is a love that never was, nor will ever be. I am contented in calling him friend, and I cherish that relationship, perhaps even more so." Isabella's eyes did not stray from her unlikely charge. "The life of a madame is doomed to be a solitary one. My life is neither here nor there; it is but what you see. Yours, on the other hand, holds an uncertain future. You must conceal your identity, Josephine, to everyone, except Mi Lin and myself. She was beaten and raped as a child, poor girl. Came to me several years ago. Doesn't say more than a few words, and even then, only to me..."

"Please, let me go." Josephine's eyes were hollow with frustration. Lord, how her life had changed. Yet truly, she'd only slipped from one gilded cage into another.

"Don't you see?" Isabella pressed her fingers together and brought them to her forehead. "Royal has asked it of me. It is because he fears for you, Josephine. He has his reasons—do you doubt them?"

Josephine blinked. It was true—when she weighed the options, walking out the door alone into the chaotic world beyond without any sort of plan was daunting. She didn't even know if Brad was still in Charleston. And she did trust Royal implicitly. The difficulty was in accepting she had no other choice but trust him. "No."

"Then please, put this on and come with me," Madame Kirkpatrick asserted. "There is much to do before business picks up this afternoon."

Josephine did so, and as she followed in the footsteps of her benefactor, the realization that Royal apparently had concern about what happened to her began to sink in. That gave Josephine a strange spring to her step as she followed Isabella, doing her best not to wonder which prostitute it was that Royal had been with during the eventide. In fact, she tried not to think of it at all, for it made her stomach clench and turn at the knowledge that last night he had shared a bed with one of them, destroying any pleasure she felt at his care of her. She was almost thankful for the veil. It kept her flushed face hidden from the ladies of the world's oldest profession and her shock at what went on inside the walls of Charleston's most fashionable bordello.

9

Smoke billowed in acrid clouds to all corners of the ornate study in which Carter Seymour sat, his cigar in one hand and his glass of brandy in the other. The click of the solid oak door as his emissary left him alone sounded loudly in the stillness of the room. His eyes seemed dazed as they continued to stare at the portal, as if willing the mole to re-enter and tell him news of a different sort. Mindlessly he began to crush the cigar in his palm, a fraction of an inch at a time, from the butt to the glowing tip. When hot embers met the soft flesh of his hand, he barely winced as he compressed the smoldering cinders into nothingness.

So, Ashhurst was on his way to meet with Blackbeard, and his attempt to sidle the captain had failed. Yet, would such recourse affect him? Royal Ashhurst had as many enemies now as he ever had with his outright challenge to Lockwood and the others at the meeting the day previous. Seymour knew Ashhurst had to be feeling the pressure of this obligation. Seymour also knew that Governor Johnson had approached him for the job for lack of finding any other willing agents and that the governor's move had been a surprise to everyone present. One thing was clear, however—Ashhurst was entirely too close to the very situation Seymour wanted him the furthest from.

Royal Ashhurst had done nothing but complicate his life since his resurgence in Charleston. Seymour knew he should have killed him when he had had the chance. Things were not so easy now.

Though enough years had slipped through his memory to expunge Royal's father's face from it, Seymour hadn't forgotten the shadow he'd cast in their youth. Handsome, reckless, and ambitious to a fault, Benjamin Ashhurst had relentlessly pursued the shipping industry and knocked down any and all that had stood in his way. Younger than himself by three years, Benjamin was everything that Seymour wasn't. Though Seymour was born into a blueblood family without the stained heritage that Ashhurst had, Benjamin had a sparkle about him that drew people in the oddest sort of fashion. His relation to Lord Cooper helped, no doubt, despite being from the wrong side of the blanket, but his engaging smile and demeanor lured even those who sneered at his soiled family ties.

On the flipside, Ashhurst could be a downright cold-hearted bastard and fought as zealously as a wolverine when he thought any of his possessions were in danger of slipping from his tight rein of control. His son had apparently inherited the same characteristics—he also had years of revenge and scorn to motivate him, which made him dangerously unpredictable. In all truth, sleepless nights for Seymour had been few and far between where Royal Ashhurst was concerned over the years. The knowledge that he had destroyed a family and cast out into the street a lone young boy had done little to unsettle him. To Seymour, Royal was but an unfortunate casualty of war. It happened everywhere and at any time. Life was cruel, and people did what it took to survive. Sometimes it wasn't difficult. Most of the time it was.

Seymour hated Benjamin as much for his unlikely success as he did for the sheer fact that Benjamin had married the woman he loved, creating perfect domestic bliss that eventually led to their son. He had enjoyed watching Anne-Marie's agony at Benjamin's wake, for the pain that had turned her face to ash was no doubt akin to what he felt when she had married his business partner. Though those feelings for her had long ago subsided, he still recalled the brutal blow to his heart when he had heard of their stunning engagement and Benjamin Ashhurst's damned apologetic smile. "To the winner goes the spoils," he had said, and at that moment Seymour decided he was going to win the war. It took him almost ten years to do it, but he had.

Triumph had tasted cold and bittersweet the humid evening that Anne-Marie and her boy had stumbled upon his doorstep, hungry and wide-eyed. He had taken her to bed with the promise he would care for her child. Anne-Marie had cried the whole time, and to make her stop he had choked her. Unfortunately, when at last he had stopped choking her, it was too late; her body was frozen in a horrible, twisted shape, her gorgeous porcelain features a sickly purple-blue. He hovered over her body for near an hour before he moved, wrapping her in the sheet before he went to the door.

The wide-eyed boy sitting in the drawing room with his legs swinging back and forth turned to look as Seymour approached him, a haunting, aged look in the depths of his gaze. The shock of what he had done put Seymour in a trance-like state. He hated the boy. Hated the fact that he was a perfect symbol of both his parents. Benjamin's coloring, poise, and face were already prevalent in the youngster. He had his mother's damned sullen eyes, a very odd sort of blue that would not change as he matured.

The boy was crying. It was as if he already knew. Seymour drew his flintlock from the table and pointed it at him, his hand shaky on the trigger. Royal didn't move; he simply watched the strange man helplessly through his tears.

It was not so different a feeling from the one he got while hunting deer—the moment before the fatal blow was delivered, when the prey was peaceful, gentle, and still. The moment when it looked at him and told his subconscious that it did not deserve to die. It was a feeling that one had to overcome in order to enjoy the fruits of such sacrifice. Normally he could have done it—but this one time he could not. It wasn't the boy's age. It was something inexplicable that even a lifetime later Seymour still could not find words to describe.

"Get your sorry, miserable hide out of here," Seymour snarled, saliva dripping from his mouth to spot the floor next to his own fallen tears. The boy didn't move. Seymour brandished the flintlock high in the air before leveling it on Royal a second time. "Get the hell out of here, you worthless piece of shit!"

"No!" Royal protested, his voice bubbling and high-pitched. "Where is mum?"

"She left you." Seymour groaned, wild-eyed. "She's gone, boy. She wants nothing more to do with you."

"Where is mum?" Royal pressed, shaking his dark head from side to side slowly. "What did you do with her?"

"I said get out of here and don't come back!" Seymour screamed, half-running forward until he was close enough to deliver a whip of the pistol to the side of Royal's head. The boy punched at him, his little fists hurting more than Seymour expected despite the blood oozing down his tiny forehead. Seymour grabbed him with a roar and tossed him out of the plantation home onto the drive of rough river rocks, the sharp points digging into his tender, child flesh as he landed and rolled. His cries muffled into his torn sleeve, his head hung low as Seymour's booming voice met his ears.

"If I ever see you again I will kill you," the man promised him. "If you are wise, boy, you will get yourself as far from Charleston as possible." Then the door slammed, and for over twenty years he hadn't seen the boy again.

Yes, Seymour acknowledged, he had been far too weak at that moment. He could have prevented any chance of… and through the years he had wondered. Would justice return? Now his fears had materialized. If he killed Royal Ashhurst now, it would have to be done very carefully. People knew too much.

But Seymour didn't see how he had much of a choice. He had to find a way. The likelihood that Royal Ashhurst would have been chosen for the job of playing middleman to Blackbeard was about the same as being struck by lightning. The fact that Blackbeard had taken one of his own ships in the blockade enraged him as much as it surprised him, another blow from an unexpected quarter. Carter Seymour was fearful of the old, fell demons nipping at his heels, resurrected when he had at long last acquired the wealth and standing he'd sought. And the woman; the woman he had waited a lifetime for. Anne-Marie was a plain mouse compared to the erotic beauty of Josephine Adelaide Beckham.

Seymour turned in his chair, his chubby face covered in sweat from the midday heat despite the calming breeze ushered in through the open nine-over-nine windows. Josephine was missing, had somehow managed to worm her way into either the hands of death or secret safety. No one had seen her. Even Bradley Harding, the young man whom she often kept company with—much to Seymour's irritation—had avowed that he hadn't seen her. Seymour had toyed with the idea that Harding was lying, but a thorough search of his home had proven he wasn't.

Dark shadows had formed under Seymour's eyes, and though Seymour wanted to sleep, he did not dare, for the dreams that awaited him in the night grew more and more vicious as time went on. His temples ached when he woke, as if the torment carried on in the halls of his head were a physical thing. No matter how hard he tried to concentrate on other matters, Josephine's beautiful, bewitching face flashed before him, dancing with ghosts of the past.

He sensed that she wasn't dead. Seymour could feel the curves of her hot young flesh, thought of the boiling vixen blood in her veins as a lure tuned to his senses alone. He imagined her being held captive by some of Blackbeard's men. The idea of her being forced to spread her legs until the endless row of men tired of her was as enraging as it was titillating. Seymour knew that she needed the humility such an act would bring; she would be sorry then that she had left his side.

He withdrew his kerchief and wiped his face, restless as he stewed, wondering where Josephine could be. None of the old women Josephine catered to for errands had seen her; and now half of them had fled Charleston to find refuge up the Ashley and the Cooper at the plantations, their townhouses ransacked by pirates. Could she be finding shelter in an abandoned home? Seymour knew the blockade would inevitably end, the homeowners would return, and his dove would be flushed out. It was only a matter of time.

He left his house armed beneath his overcoat and ruffles. Careless of the late hour during such a strange time in the city, he ordered his driver to take him to Kirkpatrick's.

Seymour was near full arousal by the time the coach turned down Logan Street and drew to a halt in front of the bordello. Airy Spanish moss, torn from the limbs of the oaks surrounding the brick and stucco building during the recent storm, littered the ground and flowering shrubs in greenish-gray clumps. He left the carriage with the curt order to return in two hours and stepped over the depression in the ground still filled with rainwater onto the veranda, giving his name to the burly man at the door.

He was allowed entrance and climbed the ruby red carpeted staircase into the lounge, where three girls lay enticingly strewn across the sofas, wafting their fans in a pretty fashion to urge cool air across their warm skin. He could hear their laughter as he approached, but their smiles faded when their eyes turned to him.

"Mr. Seymour." An exotic African girl with coffee-colored skin closed her fan and moved upright. He had been with her twice; Cassandra was her name. He didn't like the way she responded to his direction in bed or the way she was looking at him now. She stood proudly, entirely too overconfident, in her delicately boned corset of deep lavender. "I believe Madame would like a word with you."

"Get her then," Seymour snapped, unconsciously rubbing at the bulge in his breeches as he looked to the other two, a pair of blondes cuddled together. They wore matching blue corsets with black lace trim and black silky stockings that covered their legs from creamy thigh to toe. Cassandra sensed the urgency of the situation and made a mental note to give Herbert at the door a piece of her mind.

She had seen Isabella twenty minutes prior with a veiled, faceless girl by the kitchen. Her feet were hushed as they carried her down the hallway, her tawny eyes searching out each open doorway until she found Isabella and the stranger clustered together in one of the small chambers at the end of the row. "Madame, I must speak with you," Cassandra breathed, darting a backwards glance over her shoulder.

"What's wrong?" Isabella asked, giving her apprentice her full attention.

Cassandra looked doubtful, her eyes flickering to Josephine. Isabella waved her hand. "It is all right, my dear, speak freely."

"Mr. Seymour is in the hook, Madame. Herbert let him in!" Cassandra blurted without attempting to conceal her agitation. "How can you allow him entrance, after what he did to Benzenia? He's a monster, Madame!"

"Hush, girl!" Isabella ordered, her voice tolerating no argument. "I make the decisions around here, Cassandra, and you know where you can go if you do not like it." Then her tone softened, and she gentled the harsh sting of her words both with the gentle pat of her hand and what she said next. "I do not like having him here, Cassandra, but he pays well, and as of now, the time is too precarious to shut him out. Let Paulette take him if she can. Her skin is as tough as leather—she seems to feel naught."

The prostitute nodded respectfully, though the rebellion in her eyes did not go unmissed. Isabella's palms were clammy as she watched Cassandra recede. She could feel the cold waves of apprehension coming from Josephine, and though she could not see the girl's face, Isabella knew full well the icy grip of panic the girl was caught in. She felt trapped in it herself.

"Do not worry, darling, he doesn't know you're here," Isabella reassured her. "He is a frequent patron, though I must attest his visits have recently become more commonplace and unwelcome." A babble of voices farther down the hall caught their notice; Isabella's eyes narrowed, then widened in shock. "Keep your place and your tongue, Josephine. He is coming this way."

Carter Seymour seemed to have aged another ten years in Josephine's estimation. She didn't move, didn't dare to even hardly breathe as the ogre of a man paced his way down the corridor, the folds of his face lustrous with sweat, his pale eyes beady and dour. "Isabella, I pay you well, better than you deserve for the uppity wenches you offer," Seymour ground out, the malicious hunger easily read on his face. "Paulette? I am tired of her."

His eyes roamed over the hooded figure standing as still as a stone alongside of the madame. She was a smaller girl, the generosity of her curves hidden from view by the draping robe she wore. "Who is this you are hiding?" Seymour asked, his eyes sweeping the girl up and down, searching for any hint of a clue that would reveal her to him. "What is her price?"

"She is not for sale," Isabella informed him, agitated. She really did want to give Seymour the boot. "She was horribly burned in an accident, and one sight of her face and body would make you recoil. You may have Paulette. The third door over, Carter. If you hadn't hurt Benzenia, you would have your choice," Isabella fenced, her voice strained with anger. She did not miss the way he was looking at Josephine curiously. She coughed to get his attention. "Go to your chambers, my dear," she ordered softly.

The figure nodded and swept away in a rustle of silk. Seymour's eyes caught the roundness of her bottom beneath the draping material and he smiled appreciatively.

"And I've told you before that I don't allow you to wander the halls," Isabella was saying. "Who else may be here is none of your concern. Do you want me to toss you out for good?"

"I'll be happy to take my money to Humboldt's House of Bawd," Seymour spat.

"Bah, her house is foul and catching," Kirkpatrick returned, "and you know it." She sighed. "I make the rules here, Carter, and you will abide them. Prove to me that I should retain you as a client. I already spoke to you about what happened with Benzenia. I don't ever want to hear about something similar again."

Seymour knew there were plenty of other places he could go, but it was also true that Isabella's house was by far not only the most fashionable but also the cleanest. Isabella had him by the short hairs and she knew it; otherwise, the bitch would never dare to threaten him.

"You always were an easy target for charity cases, Isabella," Seymour sneered, the searching passion in his eyes that stared after Josephine dying slightly at the smooth excuse she had provided him. "I don't know how you can afford to keep taking them in."

Seymour spun on his heel and turned toward the door where Paulette appeared, her face calm and her lips split into a forced smile. She closed her eyes as the elder man buried his face into the mounds of her breasts, his dense stomach pressing her back into the room. The door closed, a muffled groan from Seymour reverberating from the other side.

Madame Kirkpatrick found Josephine wide-eyed in her room, her fists balled together unconsciously as she paced the small area. "He will pay you no mind," Isabella reassured, admiring the rebellion in the younger girl. She had been the same, not twenty years ago. Yet, even as much as she respected her, a part of her would always envy Josephine. "But when you see him, you must remain mute, like Mi Lin, and steer clear. It is odd luck to have seen him so soon.

"I would banish him for good if it wasn't for the fact that Royal wishes otherwise. I care for my girls as if they were my own—they may as well be, for I am unable to bear children. There is nothing they could face that I have not myself, and this is why I fear for them." She sighed, a hard, distant look in her gaze made Josephine feel young and inexperienced. "It is fortunate that he did not recognize you, Josephine, for even the hounds of hell would not have compared to his reaction then. We must be more careful in the future, though I was surprised to see Seymour roaming about unfettered. This only confirms what I have already told you. Always check the halls; you are safe here, Josephine, as long as you are smart."

"I hope Paulette is all right," Josephine mused.

Isabella did not reply.

10

Royal awoke in the chair, his mouth feeling as if he had been chewing on cotton during the course of the night. He ached. Lord, did he ache, from the gunshot wound up to his neck and across his shoulders. He twisted his head around as he drew himself upright, his brain pounding as the spikes of daylight drilled into his eyes. At first he thought he was bound; yet it was only that his wrists had fallen between the slats of the chair as he had slept, and it took but a moment of cognizant thought, hard won, to remedy the situation.

Blackbeard lay on the bunk with the two women, snoring soundly. Javad still sat in the corner, watching him with one eye. "Youas bleedin'," he was informed when his gaze fell on the dark young man. "Ayus already got ye somethin' for it, but ayus didn't want te wake ye. Never know how one can be, nuhssir," he grinned.

The wiry boy was rather pleasant when he wasn't ready to kill, Royal surmised. "I need some water," he managed thickly.

"Youas need more 'n 'at, ayus say," he smirked, rising from his crouched position. "Come wit me."

He forced himself to move, though his body argued lucidly against it. It was with forcible expletives that he rose and took his first wobbly steps, though Royal felt better the moment he left the stuffy cabin and met the fresh sea breeze. Men were lounging on the deck, at ease in their posts. Javad crossed the planks of the deck to where a bucket of water sat. He turned and pointed to it. "It's fresh," he reassured.

Royal quickly assessed the sterility of it anyway before he dunked his head in, sighing at the feel of the water as it ran in cool falls down his torso. He looked offhandedly at the red stain on his shoulder and back to Javad. "Youas can't leave, but youas no prisoner," Javad cheerfully relayed, "but ayus got ye some clean wraps right here." He held out his palm and presented Royal with the dressing.

With a wordless nod of thanks, Royal stripped his shirt and tied it around his waist, the skin taut across the breadth of his shoulders and carved muscles of his arms. The sun's rays were a hot caress, turning the gold tan of his flesh to bronze as he, Javad, and Kingsley, who himself had rowed back to the ship an hour prior after spending the night in a dubious locale on the peninsula, played cards and dice on the deck awaiting Blackbeard's word. Provisions had already been restocked for the next voyage, and the three ate a moderate spread of biscuits and salted pork. Royal opted for fresh rainwater rather than *bumboo*, the nutmeg, sugar, water, and rum mixture the pirates favored. He had steeled himself for three years to stay away from the very poison that had nearly destroyed him once, and this duty had turned into a test of endurance worse than he had anticipated.

The sun moved, and Royal noted the passage of time with vexation. Rembert and the others were probably chomping at the bit, awaiting news of Wragg and his boy. He wasn't certain of how long Blackbeard was going to drag his feet, yet neither was there much he could do about it.

And every minute longer he was away from Josephine grated on him, for heaven knew he had ample time with which to think of her. He regretted his harsh words; the kiss he didn't regret at all. Her sweet lips left a lasting impression on him that, despite how he tried, he could not purge. He wanted to feel her in his arms and when it happened again, he wasn't about to let go so easily.

The slight reprieve he got from his thoughts was when Kingsley told him about the places he'd been—India, women-laden opium dens in the Orient, countless journeys between the West Indies and Europe. Threaded tales were woven with a mixture of emotions. Glory and gain were oftentimes followed by longing and sorrow. Royal's heart tugged at the thought of the vast seas and the high peaks of Nepal; but even that sense of yearning held only a limited amount of lure for him now.

Royal himself divulged to his old friend the amount of pressure he was under and now, with Blackbeard's siege, he couldn't help but wonder where his sloop *Navigator* was, if she was near to port or had seen the blockade from a distance and changed her course to a southerly direction. Captain Lawrence knew enough to dock at an inlet along the Edisto River in the event of any such catastrophe. He had searched for her masts above the floating waves while aboard the pirate vessel, but he had not seen her.

He mentioned in passing his scavenging to keep his business alive and avoid any undue infirmity caused by Carter Seymour's hand. Even Kingsley, pirate by trade, held aversion to Seymour's actions. At least when they were thieving ships they had the good grace and honor to do so firsthand and not in any sneaky sort of fashion.

"Carter Seymour...Seymour..." Kingsley's brow knit thoughtfully as he plied the rope in his hands to a smooth, even coil. "That sounds familiar, it does..."

"I cursed the name enough while aboard the *Dolphin*," Royal chuckled humorlessly. "The name is synonymous with Beelzebub to me."

"Nay, this is not a name from the past I be thinkin' of, Ash." Kingsley set the rope down, searching about for a fresh canister of linseed oil. Once found, he tossed a muslin square to his friend and together they began to rub down the sails, making certain each thread of the canvas was in good repair. Royal said nothing as they went about their work, yet his senses tingled; at last, curiosity propelled him to inquire further, though Royal felt no optimism.

"Seymour is a somewhat common surname," he prodded unceremoniously.

Kingsley smiled widely, the apples of his cheeks nearly hiding his eyes. "I follow ye, Ash. I'm tellin' ye, I've heard that name, but I can't think o' where—"

"Ashhurst! Where be ye, matey—" came a bellowing roar from the aft over the creak of boards and line. Blackbeard had emerged from his cabin, scratching at his face as he stumbled toward the popular pail that lay astern.

"I'm still here, captain, and awaiting the viewing of the prisoners," Royal said, giving the elder man a nod of respect though he found it hard to summon any. Blackbeard had a line of drool and something else crusted to his beard. Thankfully, it was rinsed in short order, and Royal counted himself fortunate he had made it to the water first.

Despite his insistence on completing his errand, Royal found himself launched in another day of debauchery; Blackbeard tried time and again to foist a whore upon his lap, and Royal coolly and continually pushed the girl from him. Blackbeard did take him by rowboat to see Stede Bonnet, and it was as Royal had originally suspected. The Gentleman Pirate was virtually a prisoner in his own cabin aboard the *Revenge*. Even a man who was supposed to be allied with Blackbeard in his schemes held no control.

Stede Bonnet was a man who came from a well-to-do family and turned to piracy, the word was, out of equal parts boredom and nagging wife. He seemed saddened as he watched the harbor through his small portal, the ruffles of his shirt beneath his red velvet coat growing stained as it ran across the dust of the desk in an endless fashion. Blackbeard's officious talk about the way the blockade was progressing only seemed to have an increasingly depressing effect on Bonnet, and when rounds of drinks were poured anew, he barely sipped at his, saying nothing. Royal's patience had worn thin as he pressured Blackbeard to the extent that he would—yet every time tempers began to rise, Javad would silently materialize from nowhere with his blade, and Ashhurst could only bite his tongue and feign serenity.

The stars shone brightly that night; Delphineus winked at him alongside the balsamic moon. His eyes strayed farther north to Ursa Minor, its permanence in the sky somehow a comfort as his foggy mind dreamed of another night altogether—heavy whispers of breath in his ear, gentle moans of desire. Flickering emerald eyes that stirred his essence into a boiling cauldron of craving. As Royal sat with one foot upon a crate, his hands guiding the forced bottle to his lips in an unending fashion, attempting to purge Josephine from his memory, he found the harder he tried to escape, the more he became mired in his want.

* * * * *

A succession of days followed Josephine's arrival at Madame Kirkpatrick's where she was charged with changing linens and washing clothes. Elegant French lingerie and a sordid compilation of costumes ranging from romantic to rancid with stockings and garters to match them all certainly gave her a pictorial education, along with the faint, yet ever present, moan of masculine ecstasy. Some of the girls Josephine would catch crying after their paramours left; others laughed, yet a wistful nothingness lingered in their aged eyes.

Isabella was polite enough to her, though distant. Nothing was ever said about Royal, or when the time would come for Josephine to leave. When the madame spoke to her, it was mostly about cleaning.

Josephine's hands were sore. Though used to taking care of domestic chores, a house with her father and herself was hardly comparable to a twenty-room bordello. Her hands were dry and every evening before bed she rubbed lard across them, the grease a soothing ointment to her cracked skin.

She had plenty of time to weigh her options. She knew she couldn't stay in hiding forever, and yet the strangeness of being on her own was still so overwhelming. She wondered about her father and the world outside. Josephine knew nothing of what was going on and it ate away at her, the seconds feeling as hours and the days like weeks. Sleeping was a difficult yet thankful reprieve; she ate little.

One thing she did have an endless supply of was time. During most of it she thought about Royal—his graceful yet carefree saunter, his sensual lips split in a ruggedly appealing smile, the strong length of his fingers, the first time he had touched her still memorable, his drive, his passion for life…and revenge.

Josephine wasn't obtuse. After Royal had told her of his association with Carter Seymour, every warning bell in her body had tolled, telling her that she was but one way Royal could gain leverage over his adversary. The raging furor in him was centered on destroying Seymour, and Josephine did not blame him. But neither did she perceive a heart such as his, soiled by a life of hardship and bitter resentment, being capable of love, and she did her best to try to keep wretched notions from her mind.

On the eve of the fourth day, she was coming around the corner of the second floor when she bumped into a man who had recently exited one of the rooms. She murmured an apology as she turned away, yet Josephine's feet felt weighed as stones, fear climbing as ivy up her spine when the man spoke.

"Josephine?"

It was but a whisper, though she knew his voice all the same. He turned around, his thoughtful gray eyes searching for her face through the veil. "I'm—I'm sorry, mademoiselle, I thought—"

"Brad?" Josephine cut in, her response automatic. "Brad, is it really you?"

11

The four o'clock hour was nearing the next afternoon when at last Blackbeard emerged from his lair, his black greasy hair hanging in limp clumps around his grizzled face. He ambled over to where Ashhurst sat, methodically casting dice, a hard look upon his countenance. Blackbeard's underlings were encumbered with swabbing the deck and telling tales to whittle the time. All of the men present turned their attention respectfully towards him when he spoke.

"Iffen ye want te see the prisners, ye best be comin' wit me," Blackbeard stated by way of greeting, scratching at his chest. "An then we'll be havin' a drink or two, Ashhurst."

Royal's jaw tightened. "As you wish it, so it shall be, Blackbeard," he replied, and then cast a look toward the port. "But I'm not so certain those in command in Charleston agree with me."

A flag had been raised in the harbor above the Court of Guard; black, emblazoned with an hourglass. It flailed in silent aggression against the powder blue sky. The stark symbolism was not lost on any of the mariners. Blackbeard's eyes narrowed, the rage in them unmistakable. Yet even he was growing weary of the blockade; three hundred pirates could only hold the colony for so long and Blackbeard knew it. "When did they raise it?" he demanded harshly. No one spoke.

"About an hour ago," Royal informed him at length.

"Why didn't any of ye worthless slugs wake me?" he roared. "Damn yer mangy hides! The only one outta the whole lot o' ye payin' any mind is the cur sent to parley. Ye oughtta feel lucky yer not feelin' me boot on yer backsides for this!" He stormed to the hatch covering the hold. Royal followed him silently, pleased things were at last progressing.

When the bolt slid back and the door to the brig swung open, the occupants inside shied away. Samuel Wragg and his son were huddled together on the floor in the straw, their faces pale and pinched from their imprisonment, though Royal doubted that it had been all that bad. There was no abominable reek of defecation, no sores on their wrists from biting chains or ropes. The child looked at him through wide eyes, pleading in an innocence that he had already begun to lose.

"So now ye see they're fit," Blackbeard growled. "I demand three thousand pounds of silver and medical supplies for me crew in exchange for their lives. If these demands are met peacefully without any resistance, quarter will be given and I will sail from these shores."

"Please, find a way to help my boy. If I live or die it matters not— just see to him, please!" Wragg begged, trying desperately to be brave even though his whole body shook. Royal admired the attempt. "But whatever you do, do not give in to his black demands!"

"Shut yer damn mouth," Blackbeard snarled. The pair recoiled visibly. "I wouldn't be against killin' ye just so I wouldn't have te listen to yer snivelin'."

"The exchange will have to be made halfway, in longboats," Royal confirmed, feeling pity for the boy, who shook with fear as he crouched behind his father. "I will inform the council of what it is you seek."

Upon deck once more, Royal's eyes strayed landwards. "I cannot speak for the council, or what their response may be," he began slowly, turning to face his adversary straight on. "But I will tell you this, my only hope is that this stand-off ends peacefully and as quickly as possible, for all parties involved."

"Quickly it may end, but peacefully?" Blackbeard laughed, something in his chortle tolling a hollow sound. He nodded his fearsome head in silent order. "For Charleston, perhaps, but maybe not so much for you. Noon the hour shall be for the exchange. I like ye, Ashhurst, I really do—ye've got yer secrets. I can relate tae that. But in order tae get me point across, something needs tae be sacrificed. I have a reputation tae uphold, ye know."

Royal felt the heat of his skin turn cold. His eyes were frosty chips of ice and the set of his jaw hard as a circle of crewmen began to advance on him. Kingsley's dark eyes were sympathetic even as he looked away, unable to intervene. Royal did not fight as his arms were seized, his gaze never leaving Blackbeard's, the flaring of his nostrils the only sign of the wrath that shook his body, even as he understood the pirate's reasons. "Ye'll live through it, I promise ye," Blackbeard laughed as the quartermaster and boatswain tethered him to the mizzenmast, his arms crossed before him on the other side of the pole. Javad stood silently by, a coiled mass of leather in his hands.

"Ye shoulda gotten more coin fer yer troubles, if ye get any at all," came Blackbeard's voice, foggy and unattached from Royal's world already. He centered himself, his legs firmly splayed apart and his weight pressing against the polished wood of the mast. "A small purse, ye say? Well, at least ye were good an' drunk last night, Ashhurst. Can't say I'm inhospitable…"

Royal barely made a sound as Blackbeard himself set the cat-o'-nine-tails to his back. The first stroke sang through the air as he continued to stare straight ahead across the thin strip of water to Charleston. The bite of the many-thonged leather came in an excruciating, multi-faceted sting of pain. A second stroke came; sweat dripped from his hair down his back. As the third and fourth administration was delivered, Royal felt the flesh splitting and the salt of his sweat commencing to burn.

All the while Royal kept his eyes on the high-reaches of the church steeples and his mind on a lost, temperamental slip of a girl named Josephine Adelaide Beckham. He pictured himself doing simple things with her—taking a picnic up the Wando cut or enjoying a sunset view west of the Ashley. He thought of her smile and her low, throaty laugh that was as gentle as the ripples of a babbling brook. He longed for her arms, wherein for him there was no pain.

After the twentieth lash Blackbeard ordered him cut loose and dumped ashore with a hastily scrawled note written in rudimentary English in the event he conveniently forgot the pirate's demands or was unable to relay them. Kingsley mustered the courage to ask if he could escort his old comrade but was denied the request. Royal was carried to the longboat and then to shore, his limbs weak and unresponsive as he fell further down a spiral of agony.

A small crowd on the wharfs paused in their movements as Royal was shoved out onto the dock. He collapsed onto the weathered planks, his eyes rolling back into his head. Delayed pain from his whipping intensified with every passing moment. The thud of a blade as it pierced a crumpled piece of parchment, embedding into the wood alongside of his head, vibrated in his ear. "Give the message te yer leaders, and take heed," an old salt warned them as the longboat rowed away. "Quarter will be given only to those who surrender!"

Royal strained for consciousness as the drone of voices sifted to his ears. He felt himself being lifted. By willpower alone he forced himself to move, fighting free to stand on his own feet. "Good God, man, take it easy," someone scolded. "We're trying to help you…"

"There's a note, but I can't decipher it—"

"What's happening? What did he do—?"

Saliva dripped from the corners of his mouth as Royal drove himself to focus on the crowd, a low-pitched groan rumbling deep in his chest. Several people took a step back from the strange and terrible picture, horrified by the bloodied, feral man. "Tell this to Governor Johnson— Blackbeard wants three thousand pounds of sterling and treatments for promiscuity," he coughed, his breath short and rasping. Every time his lungs expanded, the skin of his back burned anew. "Wragg and his son are alive and well." He took a shaky step forward and stumbled. Two burly men caught him. "Longboats, tomorrow at noon. Halfway between the *Queen Anne's Revenge* and the harbor. Tell the governor that Royal Ashhurst sent you."

One of the men in the pack blanched visibly. "The devil has sent his proclamation," he sneered. "Turned on ye in yer own fell plans, did he?"

"Aye, the spawn of hell itself has rent his own house asunder," put forth another.

"Avast, Leon!" came another voice, this one familiar. "Do as he says, or I'll whip ye meself."

Royal felt an arm around his waist and relied heavily on it to keep him upright as he began to walk forward. "Easy, Ash," Captain Lawrence ordered gruffly. "Yer hurt worse 'n ye think ye are."

"Take me to Isabella's," Royal ground out. The earth was close, closer than normal. Daylight dancing across the lush, rambling limbs of live oak, drenched in their filmy gowns of moss as they tossed carelessly in the wind, was a surreal sort of image. He had picked up speed and was nearly towing Everett.

"Ash, damn ye, yer hurt! Yer goin' the wrong way…we need tae get ye home…"

"I want to go to Kirkpatrick's," he mumbled.

"Shit, think about what's in yer pants when yer in a state tae use it," Lawrence snorted. "Nay, this time yer gonna listen tae me, Ash. Yer goin' home, an' I'm gonna see if I can git ye a doctor."

Lawrence managed to walk Royal up to the corner of Front Street and Tradd without too much effort, though heads turned and eyes widened. Everett recognized one startled sailor and he ordered the lad to fetch the governor's man, not trusting those on the docks to heed Royal's message.

It had only been but days since Royal had last seen his house and office. Though things were as he and Josephine had left them, to Royal it looked foreign. Desolate.

"I'm not safe here," Royal panted, his eyes crazed as they flit about the room. "Please, Everett, listen to me!"

"I ain't goin' nowhere just yet, son," Captain Lawrence sighed, his heart aching at the sight of him. "An ye know ain't nothin' getting past me. Now let me have a look at ye."

Blackbeard's brutality had left its vicious stain in a webbing of welts and incisions. The maimed skin of his back continued to steadily weep as Everett dabbed at the oozing blood, the lines around his mouth taut and his brow creased. Not half an hour passed between the time Captain Lawrence had Royal lying stomach-down on his bed, his haggard face resting on the soft feather pillow, and the moment Jonathan Rembert was at the door with a doctor in tow. Royal's bleary eyes sported erratically across them before they closed, accompanied by a soft groan, and did not open again.

"Never seen a man take so much an' still walk," Everett Lawrence said quietly, continuing to clean the wounds with care, though he allowed the doctor free rein. Together the two men worked in silent tandem. Rembert watched, pale-faced, as they patted dry the torn flesh of Royal's back. A jar of salve was produced, which they smeared on liberally over the excessively criss-crossed pattern of marks before covering him gently with another clean strip of cloth. Lawrence also re-dressed the gunshot. It was obvious to his experienced eye that it was not a new wound, and he shook his head to himself, wondering what exactly Royal had gotten to over the course of the last week. Messages from pirates and whatnot... It was certainly hazardous to his health, and while he prayed that he and Royal could have a good laugh over that, at the present it was iffy.

"He's in remarkably good physical condition," the doctor said, peering down through his eyepiece. "If the wounds do not infect, he will live."

"Governor Johnson is outraged over the price that Blackbeard demands," Rembert said, concern etching his brow. "The congress is being called together as we speak. The pirates, too, appear to be organizing on the docks. After such a supercilious action, we are reconsidering our plan. I wanted to personally see Captain Ashhurst," he said slowly, turning away from the beaten agent with a heavy heart. "This was completely uncalled for. Blackbeard is asking for a full assault on his armada. He should fly the red flag rather than the black!"

"Nay, an outright attack is foolish," Lawrence warned. "Ye ain't never known the life of piratin', an while I ain't wise in the acts of governin', I know what Blackbeard's about. He's sendin' ye a warnin'. Makin' an example. Do ye want the whole city tae look like this? Royal knew it. That's why he didn't fight. He ain't all black an' blue; an' I've seen Ash fight. Three or four men o' his size would easily look as bad as he before he was through."

The captain took a deep, steadying breath, his eyes looking out the window. "Damn ye, boy, ye give yer honor fer these blokes, an' not a damn one o' 'em ever done the same fer ye."

Rembert swallowed, staring at the unconscious man before him. He certainly seemed no devil. Sad as it was, he appeared all too human. "He's shed his blood for Charleston. That won't be in vain." He nodded solemnly. "When he is ready for visitors, without it taxing him too greatly, please notify me, Dr. Adams."

Everett caught up with Rembert at the foot of the stair. "Somethin's goin' on that I don't like," the captain relayed, observing the secretary to the governor carefully. "Royal wasn't unhurt before his whippin'. Someone shot 'im in the last day or two, though it caused but a scratch. Ye know anything about this, sir? An' Royal himself, he didn't wanna come here, to this house; said it weren't safe." Everett Lawrence drew himself up to his full height of five and a half feet, scratching at his beard. "I've been workin' with Ash fer the last six years, sir," he said gruffly, crossing a hand over his breast, years of wisdom beyond Rembert's own meeting him squarely in the eye. "Despite what may be said of him, there is truth and honor in him. He's never done me or anyone I know wrong, an' I know what wrong can look like in this world. If there is anyone who can help him, it would be ye."

Rembert paused for a long minute, not saying a word. He glanced up, as if he could see through the cypress boards to the captain, and then back to the old salt. A silent agreement passed between them. "I'll have guards here within the hour," he said, stepping out of the building and into the humid dusk.

12

Josephine's feet congealed to the carpet, her verdant expression scanning the hallway cursorily. Johns had been coming and going with more and more regularity, their rowdy laughter and the faint odor of alcohol incessant as the darkness deepened in the midnight hour. Brad was standing as still as a stone, his own warm gray-blue eyes incredulous as she urged him to follow her silently, still disbelieving that it really was Josephine Beckham he'd met in the antechamber of Kirkpatrick's.

Voices were heard coming up the staircase as Josephine took Brad's hand and dragged him to her room, the door sealing them off with a soft click just before they could be scrutinized by the passersby. Despite wanting to jump for joy at the familiar, reassuring face, Josephine lifted the veil and put a finger to her lips to advise his silence. When she spoke, it came in hushed tones, and though she flicked the latch, she did not doubt that if Isabella or Mi Lin wished to gain entrance they could do so.

"What are you doing here?" she asked. His eyes averted to the floor, where the toe of his boot had begun to make erratic circles. "What about your darling Rose? Brad, she would be so hurt if she knew you were here…"

"I think the real question is what are you doing here," he volleyed, an eyebrow askew despite the faint flush to his cheekbones. "And as for Rose, it is no secret that I love her implicitly, but she wants to wait for— for further intimacy until we are married. And while I've tried to—to—I mean, I'm no monk, and a man does have needs, Josephine." His pewter gaze flickered to her face; she looked different. Now she seemed somehow wiser than when he had seen her last. Then, she had been pale and drawn with stress from her pending marriage to Carter Seymour. She did not flinch at his improper language, and while Josephine Beckham had never been prudish, she certainly was no seasoned matron. "I'm sure you are well aware of that by now."

"Brad, you don't actually think that I—" Josephine blushed a deep red color, her eyes squeezing tightly shut as she shook her head, her scarlet tresses dangling in front of her in wayward strands. Her eyes were profound as she looked to him again, sighing, all too well aware herself of the needs he spoke of. "I certainly do know how this must look to you. But before I say another word, I must have your solemn oath that you will tell no one that you have seen me here. Please, Brad—everything depends upon it."

His jaw clenched, contemplating. He looked around the small room, as if assessing its cleanliness. He sighed heavily.

"You have my word, darling, you know that. And I must confess I am eager to hear your tale, considering I probably know more than you about the other half of it," he mused, the thin line of his mouth twisting into a rueful grin, a hand raking through the temples of his blonde hair in a troubled fashion. "You would not believe the maelstrom you've caused with your disappearance, Josephine, even amidst the crisis of Blackbeard's attack. Seymour has turned Charleston upside down looking for you. Nary a crepe myrtle nor hydrangea has been overlooked. Being his neighbor has had its moments this time—the house was positively pulsing with turbulence. And this whole week you've probably been right beneath his nose. I know he visits Kirkpatrick's often. Hell, the other day I was walking along the Orange Quarter and I saw his carriage turning up Logan."

Josephine didn't comment. Her skin chilled at Brad's confirmation of what she already suspected, and she bit her lower lip, her jaw set in a firm, resilient manner. "When I was walking the aisle towards him, I prayed for an escape. Then the cannon fire began and I knew it to be an answer to my prayers. I was running—to you, I think—when I was assaulted by pirates."

"Josephine," Brad sighed, worry striking lines into his forehead. She waved her hand.

"It is all right. There was no permanent damage done. A man came to my aid and helped me escape. He brought me here."

"Who? Perhaps I know him and can thank him for saving you. Even if he did bring you to Madame Isabella's."

Josephine swallowed. "You may very well know of him. Captain Royal Ashhurst."

Shock made Brad's jaw drop. "The devil? He saved you?"

"Brad, what do you know of him?" she asked seriously. Brad was still gawking, mouthing "devil" and "Charleston" over and over again. She sat on the edge of her small bed and propped her chin on her fist. "And not all that gossipy garbage, either. I remember little, but I know I've heard of him."

He exhaled heavily, rubbing the bridge of his nose. "The story, as I know it, was that his parents were as rich as King Midas and killed in some sort of peculiar accident. Everyone thought Royal was dead until he materialized out of thin air a couple of years ago. He challenged our dear Carter Seymour in front of God and everybody. Said that Seymour was the one who killed his parents and embezzled the fortune. Seymour blustered and wanted to challenge the rash Ashhurst to a dawn appointment in Philadelphia Alley but he said he did not feel that the drunken youngster would abide by any fair code, and would fight dishonorably. "

"And you believe that?" she asked. "You know as well as I do that

Seymour is a deviant, it is *he* who would do something unseemly."

Brad studied his childhood friend. "Josephine, Royal Ashhurst was thought dead for well over a score of years, and Seymour had been Benjamin's partner. It was normal practice for him to seize the company. You can't simply walk back and say 'it's mine' when you've been gone nearly a lifetime. Rumor has it he was deep in his cups, raving and spewing abhorrence like the devil himself. Unfortunately for him, the name stuck. If in fact what he said was true, he certainly should have gone about it in a genteel fashion. I've seen him around; moody and entirely uncultivated."

"That is not fair," Josephine defended, unaware of how her voice was rising. "He is more civilized than men who try to pass themselves off as such. Think about it, Brad," she pressed, her eyes pleading with deep emotion he doubted she was aware she was showing. "He may have been inebriated, but his words were the truth, and I think we should help him prove it."

Brad was stunned, his head slowly cocking to the side. "Josephine, what's happened to you? Do you have any idea what you're saying?" He reached forward and pulled her to her feet. "Come, darling, I'm getting you out of here…"

"No," she found herself protesting, biting her lip as Brad watched in disbelief. "I cannot leave. If I go with you, Seymour will find me."

"He's already searched my house for you. Literally." He pursed his lips, taking a deep breath to steady his frazzled nerves. "Josephine, you cannot stay here, in a whorehouse of all places! Why would you even consider it? If word gets out, you certainly would have very little reputation with which to find a suitor. Nothing but unsavory torment and sordid offers would find you. Be realistic. This is some rescue that Ashhurst has accomplished, I daresay. You definitely aren't any safer here than you would be with me. Your reasoning has become slighted." He looked at the soft, shimmering folds of her gown. "There is more going on than you're telling me, I suspect."

Josephine's mouth opened, then closed again tightly. "My only pursuit is to see justice done. Perhaps it is true that I have a personal agenda— to see Seymour chopped at the knees. There is nothing more to it than that."

If Brad questioned the truth of her words, he did not call her on it. Then he smiled and was the boy she'd grown up crabbing and fishing and skinning knees with. "If you won't come with me, darling, then tell me what I can do, though I have a feeling that I am going to sorely regret it."

* * * * *

Isabella Kirkpatrick heard the news about Royal when a midnight knock at her private chamber was followed by the strained face of Captain Everett Lawrence. He told her in a hurried voice all that he knew of the situation and Royal's condition, his hat twisting in his gnarled hands as he spoke. When he told her Royal had insisted on going to see her, Isabella's panic rose.

"Did he inquire after anyone else? Has he called for Josephine?" Isabella asked then, her pallor showing beneath her powder. Everett cocked one bushy brow. "A girl, whom has no doubt been searched for," Isabella relayed. "Carter Seymour's fiancée, in fact. She is hiding here."

"Yes, well—he's been callin' for a princess, off and on." Lawrence looked skeptical and yet afraid. What Isabella had just divulged told him much, though not everything. "He's delirious. It's understandable." He emitted a low whistle. "Seymour's fiancée? What the hell has that boy been doin'? Seems tae have a death wish, that's the bloody truth…"

"Is anyone with him? There is no doubt that Seymour would try to kill him again if given the chance," Isabella confided. If Royal Ashhurst could count no other friends, he could rely upon them; and he needed them now. Isabella crossed the soft carpet, clasping her fan tightly closed, her face pinched. She watched the grizzled old man as he turned to the fire, rubbing his legs. "The wind's changin'," he nodded, more to himself than to her. He watched the spiraling flames thoughtfully, rummaging around in his pocket for his tobacco. "The governor's aide has posted guards. He's observant, that Rembert. He's caught wind of somethin' afoul. When I told him somethin' else had happened tae Ash, he didn't look surprised." Lawrence lit a cheroot and blew a series of smoke rings high into the air. "The pirates have withdrawn from their sport and are organizing at White Point. From what I've been able to gather, Charleston is going to pay the ransom. There's talk that Colonel William Rhett may be trying to organize an attack, though not here in the port. Governor Johnson simply wants them gone before they set fire to Charleston. And strange as it is to think, Royal himself is somewhat of a hero, though he doesn't know it yet."

Isabella shook her head, though in her heart hope flared anew. "I wonder what is awaiting around the next bend, Everett," she contemplated, tapping her fingernails on the mantle. "Though he is weak and in pain now, it is not in vain. When he awakes, he will have Charleston's finest tripping over themselves in order to thank him for the great deed he has done. Bah! The bluebloods sicken me. They had nothing but hatred for him, and now they will revere him." She sighed, a strange light in her eyes. "Don't misunderstand me, Everett. I am happy for him. He deserves this chance to rectify his name in the eyes of others. Yet I cannot help but worry. Once Seymour discovers that Royal has Josephine in his charge, hell will break loose, and I fear the outcome."

"Perhaps yer worryin' too much, Isabella," Captain Lawrence countered. "No one has to know that this Josephine has been here nor of her involvement with Royal, which I don't even understand meself yet."

"Ah, if only that were true," Isabella replied, her eyes gentle. "I will say nothing more than the fact that fate and chance brought her to Royal. But the Lady is fickle. Just when Royal is to regain his honor, she threatens to take it again. Seymour is obsessed with Josephine, would rather see her dead than with another, let alone his most hated of enemies. If only it were to be on Josephine's head alone that she had taken refuge in my house, it would not be so bad. The scandal would subside. In this dark hour, no one would beget the girl ill will for happening across a sheltered door. Alas, I do not believe that Royal would ever let her go, even if she wished it. And she doesn't. She does not ask after him, but I can see it in her eyes."

"And for her tae be with Ash..." Lawrence chuckled humorlessly. "Is it for revenge, madame, or does he care for her?"

Her face was calm and poised. "You would have to ask Royal that question. But I certainly know he looks at her in ways I have never seen in another's direction. And this bodes nothing but more pain, for Seymour will learn of it. Mark my words, Everett."

He took a long, measured draw of his cheroot and held it awhile. "I best be gettin' back. Just thought ye might want tae know."

"You aren't going anywhere, Captain Lawrence, without me," Isabella informed him. "I would like to be by his side when he awakes."

Madame Kirkpatrick hurried up the stairs to fetch her shawl, her mind fraught with worry. It was with further mortification that she heard the hushed yet audible sounds of urgency coming from behind Josephine's door. Isabella's sapphire eyes narrowed as she paused, pressing her ear to the solid, smooth panel of wood, her palms clammy as she clenched her fingers together.

Both of the childhood friends jumped apart as Isabella flung the door wide, her face a mask of cool accusation. Josephine swallowed the frog that appeared in her throat, hating the flush of surprise that she knew the madame would interpret as guilt. Brad's brow tightened and he shoved his hands into his pockets. A tense second of silence blanketed them all.

"Well, now, that didn't take long, did it?" Madame Kirkpatrick breathed softly, yet her words were as stones, dropping one by one into a smooth, silent lagoon. "I take it you are leaving us, Miss Beckham?"

Hope flared in Brad's eyes as he sidled a glance at Josephine, but she knew he did not as of yet fully understand. She only looked at Isabella, reading many things in the elder woman's soul. She was extremely pale. Josephine paused as she identified that something was amiss, and terribly so. And while it burned Josephine no small sum to stay with this snake of a woman any longer than she had already, she had to take a chance on Royal. Fool though it made her, she had to try. "Nay, madame, if I may but encumber your hospitality but a while longer. Brad will say nothing; I trust him with my life. He is an old friend, and we recognized each other but by chance."

"I see," Kirkpatrick sniffed, her disbelief evident in the raising of one delicately painted brow. Her eyes shone with a mysterious light. "I trust you will have the good sense to be discreet where this establishment is concerned, Mr. Harding. I dare not have a visit from the magistrate or that pretty blonde I have seen you strolling down Ropemaker's Lane with may receive a word in the ear of your evening whereabouts." She watched Brad a long moment, making certain her words had adequately sunk in before she continued. "Now if you will excuse me, Miss Beckham, while you two have been keeping company I've learned a horrid bit of news. The price of the ransom has been relayed." She took a sharp, ragged breath, tears brimming her almond-shaped eyes. Absently she smoothed the folds of her gown at the waist, her voice strained as she spoke again. "Royal brought back the demands of Blackbeard after he was severely lashed with a cat-o'-nine-tails."

Josephine's heart plummeted to her knees and she sought Brad's arm to steady herself. Her skin chilled as she shook her head. "Nay, it cannot be true," hope directed her to argue, though she knew in her heart that Isabella told no lie.

"I will know more after I see him." Her frown did not go unmissed as she receded. Her next words floated, deceptively soft like the healing breezes of *chicora.* "If this tale is something you would care to trouble yourself to hear, Miss Beckham, you may visit me during the noon hour on the morrow."

13

Royal was in and out of consciousness throughout the course of the next three days, his dreams alternately sweet and terrifying. Exhausted and with his back ablaze, he barely recognized the fact that Rembert and Isabella had come and gone or that Captain Lawrence was glued to his side. Everett had tried and failed to administer the sleeping draught several times until at last he was able to coax the liquid down Royal's throat. The sizable dose of laudanum kept him from flailing, but it did not save him from his dreams.

His father's murder and his mother's replayed in agonizingly slow detail, mixing and shapeshifting weirdly into Blackbeard's sadistic laugh and Josephine's smile. Erotic images of past lovers twisted into gnashing, horned succubi. Carter Seymour's foul countenence and the stolen riches of the Ashhurst fortune jingled together as coins overflowed from Seymour's meaty hands.

But despite the past, the worst of them all was when Josephine kissed him, so soft and yet passionate, the taste of her a witch's brew that he could not get enough of, the affection of her emerald eyes digging tender hooks into his soul. She was mouthing secret words to him in an adoring dialect that he could not understand. He reached to pull her back to him, yet every time he tried, she was farther and farther away, until at last she was but a speck in the distance and then vanished. He could still feel her presence, but never again could he find her. He called and called for her, but the vapor did not reappear.

The sheets of his bed were drenched with sweat when at last he awoke, a cool wet cloth being administered to his fevered brow. He wiped the sleep from his bleary eyes and forced himself to focus. Everett was peering down at him, a hint of a grin half-hidden by white whiskers.

"It's about time ye woke. Ye've been sleepin' long enough."

"God, I feel terrible," Royal coughed, managing to sit up despite argument to the contrary. Though his arm felt weak, he reached behind him to gently probe at his wounds. Lawrence and the doctor had done a good job of changing his dressing. Even though he was still bound by bandages, he could feel the raised, shell-like contusions beneath. The skin between the wounds stretched to compensate with every movement and breath he took. Lawrence cleared his throat and cocked an eye in warning.

"Ye should—yer lickin' was one o' the worse I've ever seen, but ye'll be all right. Yer healin' better 'n expected."

"Blackbeard—what's happened—"

"It's all right, son," Captain Lawrence comforted, waving at him to get him to lay down again. "It's over now. The curs turned tail an' ran after they got what they came fer."

Royal ignored the order and raked a hand through his tousled dark hair, fighting back the odd feeling of vertigo. "How long have I been out?"

"Long enough. A couple o' days, I reckon. I knew ye wouldn't sit still otherwise, so I had tae drug ye. I think I may've used a little much, though. Yer tolerance is way down, anyway."

Royal's head snapped back, the glassy haze over his cerulean eyes clearing, only to be replaced with a smoky burn. He hadn't noticed they weren't alone; Kingsley was standing in the corner, his hulking frame blocking out the sunlight of the window to such a degree Royal couldn't believe he hadn't detected the man's presence. His eyes narrowed as they fell on the burly black man, a flash of him turning away coming to his mind's eye.

"What are you doing here?" he asked sharply.

"Ash, ye got tae know—" he swallowed, fidgeting with the kerchief in his hands. "I dinna want tae see ye go through what ye did. There was nothin' I could do to stop it. I did some thinkin' after that, an' while I know ye can't promise me nothin', I want tae come an' work for ye, iffen ye'll have me. I couldn't do the sweet trade no more. Ye always was a good friend tae me, Ash, an' ye dinna deserve what Cap'n Blackbeard gave ye."

Royal's train of thought sported erratically through his head. "Isabella...does she know?"

"I'm of a mind that there's not too many folk in Charleston who don't," Lawrence replied, his eyes deep and thoughtful. "She's been here to see you several times."

"Alone?"

"Yes." Lawrence did not miss the tightness of his friend's face. "Iffen yer wonderin' about what's been goin' on since ye went out, Ash...well, yer not gonna believe it. Yer a bit o' a hero."

Royal laughed outright, though it was an empty sound. "It would take more than being beat like a dog with mange to clear this name," he ground bitterly, not appreciating Lawrence's jest at all. He ignored the old captain's statement entirely as he moved to relieve himself in the bucket and then lay back on the bed and closed his eyes once more. He was tired still, and it felt good to lie down.

"The winds are changin'," Lawrence murmured. "I told Isabella so."

The Devil of Charleston

* * * * *

Jonathan Rembert walked in his usual auspicious manner towards Carter Seymour's townhouse on Meeting Street, just off of Dock Street, his mind slowly turning over what the hardy old sea captain Everett Lawrence had planted in him several days before. The seed had germinated beneath the roil of Blackbeard's siege of the colony and now he had a moment with which to nurse it further. The exchange with Blackbeard had been made as Royal had negotiated. After a brief summit, everyone had agreed that Blackbeard was beyond mad and would very likely torch the city if they didn't get rid of him. With a heavy heart and a gleam in his eye promising retribution, Johnson had ordered the ransom paid.

The *Queen Anne's Revenge* and the *Revenge*, along with the two other ships that made up their criminal fleet, raised their mainsails to catch the wind nearly a week after they had arrived, their hulls urged along by the rushing waters of the evening Atlantic tide. Even as they became specks in the distant waves, with Charleston bathed in a golden sunset behind them, South Carolina was plotting her own revenge. Honor decreed now that they return the favor.

While the groundwork was being laid for the pursuit of Blackbeard and his clan, Rembert had found a little niche of his own. There certainly was something poignant about Ashhurst's tale, or what he had heard of it, so he had decided to do a little more research into the matter, for the secretary was nothing if not thorough, and this was appearing to be a divine mystery indeed.

He had gone to the vault at the city's annals building and ferreted several hours away before he had found what he was looking for—records and bills of sale that dated from the mid-1680s to the early 1690s. The parchments were old, crumbling and speckled with mildew, the ink slightly blurred in places from the dampness of the tomb-like structure. Another hour was spent poring over each page individually until at last he came across the codicil to Benjamin Ashhurst's will, dated the 26th of November 1689. It stated that Royal David Ashhurst would inherit the family assets at any age, though the ownership would be held in trust and good faith by Carter Seymour until the heir reached the age of twenty-one.

In another stack, not nearly as decayed as the first, lay the minutes to a brief court hearing that had been held in February of 1715. Royal's petition for his seventy-five percent share of Seymour Transport had been thrown out for "lack of evidence to support Royal Ashhurst's claim," seeing as he had been presumed dead for so long, and therefore, the riches of the Ashhurst estate were Seymour's outright. Further through the transcripts, heavily worded with a slew of baroque language, the dialogue translated to Ashhurst being unruly in the court and ending up in the provost dungeon beneath the Court of Guard for nearly two months, and thus being expelled from any further legal action on his part.

His curious and systematic mind had painstakingly scrutinized every written word of the codicil, following the gently slanted script until at last it ended at the bottom of the page in Benjamin Ashhurst's bold signature. He compared it with other signatures he had found in the stack. They all matched. Nothing seemed amiss, yet for some reason the content of the appendix did not sit right with him. It was then that he noticed the answer was looking at him plainly in the face. There on the page was an obvious statement that at any age Ashhurst was expected to inherit. There had been no provisions drawn up by either party as to how long Seymour was to hold the business in trust, but John knew as most anyone did that only a death would void the codicil.

John wondered if Ashhurst had ever even seen the will; it did not appear to have been moved since the records were deposited after Benjamin's death. He searched more recent files for any indication of what had transpired for the merchant company from 1693 through 1698, but the ledgers were either missing or incomplete.

So he decided he would pay a short visit to Seymour and see if he could discern for himself what Carter's take on the situation was. Recent files looked neat and by the book in black and white, and he could understand Seymour's claims; but surely an agreement could have been made to both parties' satisfaction. A strong pulse of ethics was what nitpicked at Rembert's conscience as he cut through Mulatto Alley to reach the refined house on Meeting Street. There had been a blatant stonewalling somewhere along the line that was too much of a discrepancy to ignore. He gave his card to the edgy servant who greeted him at the privacy door.

Nearly fifteen minutes passed before the same servant returned and bade him to follow across the piazza and into a dimly lit foyer, the scent of candlewax and freshly cut wisteria and crepe myrtle blossoms the only reprieve to the dark severity of the single house. When he entered Seymour's study, even John's usually tranquil composure felt ill at ease.

The room groaned beneath the weight of onerous silence. Smoke hung in slow moving circles. Seymour looked at him almost blankly, a vacuous expression in his beady eyes. He had lost weight, and though he was still corpulent enough for two men, the skin seemed to hang in sallow sags from his face, as if the globules of flesh were more than his skeleton could bear. Dark crescent half-moons ringed the sunken orbs of his eyes. His skin was translucently pale, almost tinted a bluish-gray color. "Good eventide, Mr. Rembert," Seymour gurgled before coughing harshly.

Jonathan pursed his lips as Seymour turned his garish head and spit a wad of phlegm into a sweetgrass wastebasket that was overflowing with crumpled papers and cigar tips. "What brings you about at this late hour?"

Rembert cleared his throat, clenching his teeth to force his stomach to settle. "Just a few questions, Mr. Seymour, and nothing more."

"Well, then, please have a seat," Seymour extended gracefully, filling a glass with a hefty dollop of brandy for himself, and he poured a noticeably smaller amount into a second glass for his visitor. Seymour swallowed half of his and was pouring his next round before John could even bat an eye. Seymour seemed apprehensive, his eyes refusing to meet those of his visitor, his gaze flitting in an erratic fashion everywhere but John's own. "Come, what are your questions? It could hardly be so pertinent as to call at ten bells, but I'm willing to indulge you, secretary."

"Mr. Seymour, what do you recall of the events that transpired beginning with the death of your former partner Benjamin Ashhurst?" Rembert said plainly, his soft-spoken words still delivering a hammering blow and sharp needles of discontent to Seymour's spine. Seymour's hand was shaky as he set the glass of brandy to the side, his eyes flickering darkly.

"It was a dire time, though the years have done much to help abate my memory of it," Seymour replied, his voice almost a whine in the quietness of the room. "Benjamin and I were both fearless, and being at the top of the pecking order for ones so young was a heady thing indeed. We were like brothers, adolescent and daring. Charleston herself was an infant then. His passing was unfortunate, untimely, and heartrending. It was years ago, Rembert, but it pains me still." He paused in his histrionic prose, his fingers tapping lightly on the desktop, his eyes at last rising to meet Rembert's own. "May I ask as to why you are inquiring, John?"

"Perhaps a better question would be about this abhorrence you embrace for Benjamin's only son," Rembert stated just as smoothly, his finely-tuned instincts and observant eye picking up Seymour's slight change in tone and the way he blinked rapidly, consistently fiddling with whatever mundane object his hands came across along the top of the desk. "I know all about what has been said, and what the popular belief is. But I would like to hear it straight from the horse's mouth, so to speak. You're right, Mr. Seymour. Charleston was young. Many people including myself were not here. Many others have died or returned to England or the Antilles and Barbados. The years have a way of erasing the past, or covering it."

"Is there any particular reason you are dragging this up from the sepulcher?" Seymour snapped. "Royal is nothing like his father was. He is a demon hell-bent on stealing what is mine because of the unfortunate winds of long ago. He could have come to work for me if he had not been such a disgrace when he returned to Charleston. I would have welcomed him as if he had been my own son and shared the business with him if he had been fit. Instead, his bitterness had eaten him alive, and somehow he became convinced that it was my fault his family had come to ruin. His mother quickly wasted away in her sorrow. I tried to provide emotional support for her but she became a recluse. I doubt she realized what her actions would mean for her son, but women are inferior-minded and never do understand such matters. I never heard of either of them again until he returned a few years back."

"It is true that Royal Ashhurst was a mess—a drunkard and a rogue—when he returned to Charleston, and your reluctance to welcome him more than understandable," John began, knowing full well he was treading on thin ice as it was but still feeling the urge to push the matter further. "But I believe somehow a great injustice has been done—and while I'm not here to accuse you, Mr. Seymour, I am telling you that legally this matter may reopen. If you know anything at all about the deaths of Benjamin and Anne-Marie Ashhurst that you have never told, you may consider telling me now."

"Are you doubting my word, Mr. Rembert?" Seymour said slowly, his heart fluttering and his palms growing clammy the more the obnoxiously persistent secretary continued to probe him, his stomach turning to water at the blatant threat to his eminence. "Ah, I see Captain Ashhurst has taken this opportunity with which to try and wheedle you and the governor. This matter has gone before a judge once already, Jonathan, if you didn't already know."

Rembert's nerves were strained, though he willed his tongue to remain silent. He sensed Seymour's smokescreen. The words seemed to come easily enough, but to Jonathan it was as if they had been rehearsed countless times over and were not an immediate response. Seymour had gotten too used to the skeletons in his closet; Rembert could smell those old bones as if they were a courtesan's perfume. "I see," was all he said.

"There is nothing that I haven't told and retold a thousand times," Seymour breathed steadily, looking Rembert straight in the eye. "One thing I will tell you is that I have a business arrangement in North Carolina that I'm leaving for early on the morrow. I wouldn't want you to think I'm running away. So, if you will excuse me—" he held out his hands ceremoniously but did not rise. "I must retire now."

Rembert nodded and made his way towards the door as Seymour's low voice reached him. "You had best be careful of what you say, and to whom, Mr. Rembert," the merchant advised. "I am no peon to a secretary, even one who works for our esteemed governor. Whatever sort of quest you envision yourself to be on, Jonathan, you would be wise to rethink it."

"Are you threatening me, Mr. Seymour?" he asked, not turning around.

"Just a bit of advice, John, and nothing more."

As Rembert walked down Elliott Street towards the warehouse district, the stickiness of the night left his shirt and face damp with sweat even though he felt his blood run cold from the meeting. Palmetto bugs chirruped from the shadows and darted across the sand and cobblestone. He knew full well what Carter Seymour's standing in Charleston was, just as he knew of Royal Ashhurst's reputation. It was true that his investigation would certainly need to be done carefully and in a divergent way. But investigate he would, even though Rembert had the feeling that things were going to get a lot worse before they got better.

14

Royal woke alone, his small domicile noiseless save for the rustling breeze that touched and lifted scattered papers on the writing table. It mingled with nature's serenade, the floating chirrup of jays and red-breasted finches calling from their perches in the live oak limbs high above Tradd Street. The constant babble of voices that had pervaded his waking moments over the last span of days had diffused into easy tranquility. The light of the late afternoon sun glowing gold and crimson across the foot of his bed brought with it a sense of peacefulness that to Royal had been a long time in coming.

He felt a resurgence of energy through his body as he forced himself to get out of bed and ready his tub. He opened the trapdoor in the corner of the ceiling, being careful to keep from stretching his lesions apart as he moved; from there a pull drew fresh water from a cistern atop the roof. His mouth felt dry and he was somewhat lightheaded, belying his use of the laudanum. Several times he had to pause and steady himself to keep from falling over.

He took his time bathing and shaving, doing his best to dispel the misery of his wounds and restore some measure of humanity. When at last he emerged, patting dry the raw skin of his shoulders and rubbing the hard planes of his chest, arms, and legs, he dressed meticulously in his finest clothes, his critical eye discordant even to himself as he stared at the image in the looking-glass.

His clothes were in good repair, but old and out of fashion, the cut and color of the garments simple and stark. The whiteness of his ruffled shirt and cuffs beneath the black, lightweight, and sleeveless five-button vest lent some measure of light; but from the edge of it the black continued down in snug-fitting breeches to the tips of his battered leather boots. He wondered as he looked down at them when he had last oiled them, and found he couldn't recall.

And his face. Every time he examined himself of late, Royal noticed new lines around his eyes and in his forehead, the march of time going on in its unending way, mortality a taste upon his tongue. He looked the very devil he was called. He had shaved his cheeks and throat, leaving the beard across just his chin and upper lip, liking the change even though he contemplated the subconscious reasoning for it. He could hear Isabella sighing already, and he wondered if perhaps she was right. There were several other ways he could have shaved, certainly other clothes he could have worn; he could visualize the madame telling him how now was not the time to flaunt convention, et cetera, et cetera, but it did not matter to

Royal. He would keep his pride and let the whole colony of Carolina rot if needs were so. If he wasn't accepted now then he never would be, yet neither would he ever pretend to be something he wasn't.

He went downstairs to where two young men were sitting with their feet upon his desk, idling time away as they smoked cheroots and played at dice, betting each other mundane things that would never come to pass outside of the small room. At last they noticed their company. With mumbled words of apology and scraping sounds of the chair legs across the floor, they righted themselves and came to attention, the same familiar flash of mistrust shining in their wide, youthful eyes. Royal's own were but slits upon them, walled and hidden from view by his heavy lids.

"You are free to leave," Royal said by way of greeting. One of the guards opened his mouth to speak, only to close it again without transmitting a word. "I realize you have been sent here by Rembert's orders, but your presence here is hardly worth taking note of, considering that I was able to come upon you without using a whit of stealth in the process."

The second man was braver than the first and found his tongue. "I— I'm sorry, Captain Ashhurst...the outside perimeter of the building is secure—" he floundered for further speech, but only came up with disjointed sentences and a very red face. Royal growled low in his chest, his direction brooking no argument as he pointed to the door.

In short order the guards had vacated his premises, and Royal sat down in his chair. He finished what remained of their nooning meal before reaching alongside with a heavy hand to the drawer that held his bills. Usually it was overflowing and he oftentimes found it hard to open, quite unlike the receivables drawer, which was lucky if it held but a scrap— but he had not misplaced the pile there. He rummaged a little further back and his hand still came up empty.

His jaw tightened and a rippling swell of panic started in his stomach as he began to hunt for his books in earnest. The month-end ledgers were neatly stacked, but the roll of parchment that held his current debits and credits—and the scheduled ports of call for his fleet as outlined by his own small, bold penmanship—was still missing. He searched through every drawer, his movements growing faster with each passing minute as the wave of rage submerged him.

Jonathan Rembert entered Ashhurst's office as the late spring sun dipped below the horizon, a mountain of purple billowing clouds in the distance bestowing the ancient god with a silent ovation as he took his nightly rest and allowed the moon her reign of the heavens. Damp, sultry heat was thick in the air. The winds had picked up out of the southeast steadily over the course of the last hour; this coupled with the flashes of lightning echoing out across the distant savannah presaged the coming of another storm.

The secretary's face was grave as his eyes fell on Royal. "It's good to see you up and about, captain, though I believe the doctor's instructions were to make certain you were bedridden for the next two days longer at least—"

"Where the hell are my ledgers?" Royal lashed, his eyes blazing a fiendish light. "What sort of squalid torment has been fed for me to swallow with relish now, *monsieur?*"

"Hold up, Captain Ashhurst," John interjected, setting down a parcel, wrapped neatly in brown paper, that he carried in his arms. "I apologize for any undue confusion and concern. I must confess I am surprised to see you when you were sleeping so soundly but a few hours ago. I have the notes of which you speak—"

"You have no right to interfere," Royal scathed, his eyes narrowing as Rembert looked at him and blinked as if there was nothing at all wrong with what he had done.

"Creditors were knocking down your door, ready to take you off to the provost for delinquency. As you can see, I had little choice but to step up and take care of some of your liabilities for you," he stated, pragmatic.

"But, as I said, it's good to see you moving about," Jonathan commented as he withdrew a sizable bottle of sherry and two tumblers amid the rustle of brown paper. "I brought you this, both as a sort of get well present and for the benefit of your guests, which will presumably be more frequent in light of what has transpired."

Royal's gaze didn't flinch, but he murmured a word of grudging thanks even as he forced himself to pass on the round, the urge to take it swift and strong. "Frankly, I don't have as much faith as you do, Mr. Rembert. What did I do? I was Blackbeard's lever to the silver, his spectacle to the crowd. I did nothing to endear my black soul to the local populace, that's for certain. In fact, I'm awaiting one of my creditors, one who will very likely foreclose on *Stormchaser*—that is, unless the deed has already been done in my absence from conscious thought."

"Your payments, Captain Ashhurst, are up-to-date," Rembert revealed. At first Royal wasn't certain he'd heard the man correctly. "Your friend Captain Lawrence and I took the liberties of seizing the reins during your infirmary. Kingsley, the gentle soul who had to be pulled from your side, has done his best to help where he can. He and Everett are still dockside. You've missed quite a bit while you were recovering abovestair in between those four walls. *Navigator* and *Courtesan* are both back in port, though the latter is certainly the worse for wear. I apologize for stepping into your affairs, captain, but the timing made the decision for me, and I know what I would have wished were the roles reversed.

"I'm not certain if you heard," John went on to say, "but Carter Seymour has left the vicinity."

"Thank you, sir," Royal waved gruffly, feeling contrite, though Rembert's last comment intrigued him. "As I'm sure you've seen there isn't much in the way of assets to protect anyway."

"That is something that may change, and sooner than you perceive." He took a long drink of the alcohol, releasing a small sigh of contentment as he did so. "The governor has spoken highly of your honorable sacrifice in a public way. He wants you to assist Colonel Rhett in pursuing Blackbeard's flotilla. It was he who put up the money for your creditors, Captain Ashhurst, as payment for your service. While it wasn't the full five hundred pounds, circumstances did make the contract somewhat null. I hope you understand, captain."

"I suppose I should feel grateful for your assistance," Royal replied, his awkwardness at the situation mediating any thought that Johnson was trying to worm his way out of the deal for a lesser amount, for it was certain that things had not turned out as planned. Yet the surging wash of relief Royal felt that *Stormchaser* was secured but awhile longer made the compensation acceptable to him. "Though I must profess, Mr. Rembert, I am curious as to why you would go to such lengths to assist me, when I have done nothing for you other than what was necessary with this dilemma."

John swished his drink in the glass until a small amber whirlpool gleamed in golden swirls, its tenuous funnel stretching downward. "Captain Ashhurst, I sense you are a man who does not trust easily, and no doubt for good reason. I will not sugarcoat the fact that the governor's announcement of your gallantry and his support of you has brought a slew of reactions, most of them negative. But I have begun to know you and feel that perhaps there may be something I can do to help you in regaining what is yours." He paused, scratching at his chin as he looked at Royal matter-of-factly, wisdom and insatiable curiosity burning in his dark brown eyes. "The truth has a way of coming out in the end, captain. I don't believe my conscience would allow me to sleep at night if I stood idly by when there may be a part I could play in correcting a grave injustice, even if it isn't in the best interest of certain upstanding citizens of the community. Law and justice know no bounds, and men of wealth, I have come to know, are of the same mold as men of no means at all." Rembert polished off his drink with a flourish, not missing the surprise on the captain's face.

"I don't think I will be able to accept the governor's proposition," Royal said then, thinking what an odd feeling it was to have someone of

Rembert's standing as friend; and the solidity of such a friendship that was already to be tested. Royal's jaw was tight as he looked at Rembert, his lips a thin line.

"If it is because of your injuries, captain, it will be some time before Rhett is prepared to depart." Jonathan laced his fingers and peered at Royal. "But somehow that doesn't strike me as being something that would stop you."

"Nay, you are correct." Royal leaned back in his chair, wincing and coming back forward an inch before slowly adjusting his weight in a more comfortable way. His eyes were heavy-lidded as he watched his company, his air of nonchalance exactly that. "Pursuit of proving what really happened with my family by the hands of the head of Seymour Transport is as important to me now as ever before. Yet, I would gladly put it to the side but awhile longer in order to give my services to South Carolina in any way she may need. However, another situation has presented itself, one that I cannot tarry from."

"Which is?" Rembert prodded. Royal's eyes emanated from his dark face, iridescent against the tan of his skin.

"I intend on marrying Josephine Adelaide Beckham," he said. "And I dare not leave her side, for she will have need of my protection when Seymour returns to Charleston."

Jonathan's eyes bulged noticeably, and he sputtered as he sought to control his shock. "Seymour's missing fiancée? There's been plenty of talk about the girl, that's for certain. Her father went into mourning this very day, presuming her dead." Rembert shook his head, still disbelieving. "Captain Ashhurst, do you realize the consequences of this? It may not be legal. From what I understand, Seymour has already paid for her hand—"

"As you can see, the grave does not come as easily as everyone seems to believe," Royal replied, his tone cold. "And it will be legal. I'm certain you could help me with that, were you to be so inclined. I found her running through the streets, for God's sake, and gave her shelter. Then I was attacked—by Seymour, I'm sure of it—and took her somewhere else that shall remain undisclosed. Seymour would never marry her after the truth is told that she was with me, in any event. Besides, think of what her position was to him—she was chattel, no better than a slave."

Royal came to his feet and strode to the corner where the spider sat munching on his latest catch. He watched the action a long minute. "She is still untouched by my hand, John, though I am ill-equipped to resist her any longer."

Rembert's stomach churned as he thought of the Pandora's box Ashhurst had so neatly opened and placed before him. "You are going to push Charleston over the edge if you intend on following through with this ambition," Jonathan advised, shaking his head. "The scandal will consume you both, Captain Ashhurst. Think about it, for her sake…or does that not matter to you?"

"It is not for revenge that I am taking Josephine as my wife," Royal growled. "She will not oppose the match, Jonathan—and that is all I have to say on the matter."

"Your mind is set, then." There was a moment of strained silence before Rembert continued, his nerves on pins and needles. "You could lose any ground you've gained in regards to your reputation, Royal, though in all honesty it does not change my mind about helping you." Rembert ran a hand across his lips, exhaling slowly. "Seymour's *raison d'être* is slipping. I paid him a visit when I first began to investigate your claims, sir; he was pensive when I approached the subject. If—" he paused, blinking as he tried further to clarify to himself what Royal had been telling him. "When you take Josephine Beckham to wife, you had best be prepared to expect the fallout—especially from that quarter."

Royal's eyes shone with something akin to hunting instinct; deep, black desire flickered in foreshadow. "That, Mr. Rembert, is something I am counting on."

15

Rumbles of thunder charged the skies and rain had begun to descend to the dry, thirsty earth, its caress in the beginning much more gentle than the last time he had followed the trail to Kirkpatrick's on Logan Street. His heart had not lost its uncertainty. If anything, it had increased tenfold, yet his worries now were of an altogether different sort. His footsteps quickened as he passed Orange, and then Legare; at last he took a right and crossed over Broad Street, the warm and alluring glow of candles from the cathouse beckoning rich and impoverished men alike to its arched door.

Herbert allowed him to pass, and he went straight to Isabella's private quarters. She was burning a pungent roll of incense that he could smell as soon as he turned the hall. She loved the stuff, and he always searched for different, exotic scents for her when he was overseas. It was a small measure of friendship that she adored, though it was some time now since he had been abroad. He still remembered this scent—a rosy, musky combination that had come from the Netherlands.

Isabella was radiant in her mauve and cobalt gown, the bodice dangerously low and encrusted with hundreds of sparkling sequins. Her eyes searched his wisely as she extended her arms in welcome, the relief evident across her ivory countenance. "Royal, you should be resting," she scolded. "And you've shaved, I see."

"Nay, madame," he replied, releasing her. "I've done naught but rest these past days away while the shadows stride ever on. How have things been for you?"

"For me, Ash? Or for Josephine?"

Royal's heart gave a small squeeze as he looked at the poignancy in her sky blue eyes. "I care for you deeply, Isabella. You must know that."

"But you will never love me." Her words were solid and brave, though her voice wavered but a smidgen. "That is something I know as well and shall learn to bear. But because of the way I feel about you, Royal, I must warn you about these feelings you have for Josephine. It is not out of selfish intent that I say this, but of caring for you. I do not want to see you hurt."

"I have thought of her." He swallowed as her eyes cast down. He had known her long enough to know when something wasn't right. "Isabella, what are you trying to tell me?" he asked, feeling a jab in his side of unexpected anxiety though he tried to shrug it off. "That you believe I am nothing but milquetoast from the magic of her charms? I am not as easily led as you believe. Has something happened?"

Isabella pursed her lips a long moment. "This place has had two superfluous visitors in your absence, Royal. Carter Seymour for one; Josephine was with me, though disguised. He did not recognize her, and he has come and gone several times without further incident. He does not look himself—he has a strange light in his eyes, even for Seymour."

"And the other? You said there were two," Royal pressed softly, his jawline tight.

"Yes. The eventide Everett told me you were hurt—" she paused, her breath shaky. "I was coming down the hall to collect my wrap when I heard voices outside of Josephine's door. I came in, quite unannounced, and found her there with Brad Harding. He's a young, dashing fellow, quite popular I am told. They seemed to conspiring some sort of plot, though I know not what."

"Is she still here?" he asked, feeling the warm tingle of his blood in his veins turn to icy rivers.

"Yes, though I offered her the door if she chose. That I cannot lie about," Isabella confessed gently. "She came to me once in my chambers and I informed her more fully of your condition, and that you didn't want to see her, that you had told me to keep her away. She has said little to me since then, though she has worked hard. Never have I seen the silver shine so brightly. I did not want her to go running to you and put you and herself in further danger; and, I suspected, you needed time to collect your thoughts. Truth be told, I couldn't help but wonder about her, after seeing her with Mr. Harding."

Royal said nothing as he looked at Isabella, understanding full well what she was implying. "How many times has he been here?"

"Twice, though the second time was very brief, just this morning." Isabella's eyes were soft upon him. Her sympathy did little to placate him. "She is abovestair, very likely reading in her room as she has done every night at this hour."

Without a word Royal turned and strode from Kirkpatrick's span of lush velvet and sweet smoke. "Royal, you don't know which door veils her," Isabella called to his back. He didn't reply, knowing deep in his subconscious that he would be able to follow the enthralling scent of her anywhere, even if it was to his own demise.

Royal climbed the stairs, his breathing heavy in his own ears. His lined brow creased down into a pretentious scowl as he thought of what Isabella had said, raw anger churning in his gut. Though he could provide no viable reason for it, it ate at his insides anyway, and by the time he came to Josephine's door, the high spirits he had felt during the daylight hours at the prospect of seeing her again had shifted into an invidious flame. He approached noiselessly; the door was ajar.

Josephine sat on the edge of her bed, a weak hand lifting to her brow to try and relieve the headache pounding at her temples. She had been working diligently and the strain had begun to show. It wasn't so much that she wanted to keep Isabella happy; rather, it was more important for her to keep her mind off of other things. What Brad had told her made her want to explode with frustration and longing; and still, *still* there was nothing she could do about it. The search for her had all but abated; her father believed her dead, and Seymour was causing no end of worry.

And Royal.

Josephine felt her chest tighten, her jaw click as she mused, for he was always in the back of her mind if not in front. She had tried to stay detached; Lord knew she had. She had not broken down before Isabella when the sordid details of his whipping had been retold. Josephine had not asked about him, telling herself she wasn't affected by it. Deep down she knew she was only lying to herself, for she was only relying on Isabella's body language instead to tell her what she needed to know.

"Good evening, princess," came a voice behind her.

She whirled at the sound, her cheeks flushing with heat as her eyes fell on Royal's self-assured stance in the archway of the door. His arms were crossed casually across his chest. One of his long legs stretched out in front of the other, the dark presence of him running from his hair to the tips of his boots. His eyes smoldered like a bed of coals as he watched her intently. She had no idea how long he'd been standing there.

"Royal," she breathed softly, his name tantalizing on her lips. She wanted to run to him. Instead, she clasped her hands before her, though she was unable to keep the smile from her face. "It's good to see you."

"Did you miss me, lass?" he asked, his expression giving away nothing. Nary a muscle twitched. Josephine was speechless as they locked gazes. She felt desire blazing through her veins at the sight of him, the time they had spent apart seeming to be both an instant and an eternity.

"Royal—I heard—" she paused, something in the sound of his voice ringing discordant.

"What did you hear?" he pressed, moving from the doorway, closing and locking it behind him, the sound strident in the quiet room. Slowly he began to circle her, the unbidden wash of pleasure and desire at seeing her again coupling with the blistering irritation of her extemporized visitor. It forced his pulse to throb hotly.

"That you had been chosen to negotiate with Blackbeard and his pirates. That's why you left," she said, "and that you had been flogged with a cat-o'-nine." Her last words tasted foul as she said them. Her eyes cast downwards, lest she betray the depths of her emotions. A thousand words lingered on her tongue.

"What's wrong? Has it been so very bad for you, Josephine?" he asked her, his hand reaching to her chin, his palm warm.

She sniffed as she dared a look at him, her breath catching in her chest as her eyes scanned his rugged face, its strength and definition. Her cheek tingled from his touch, the coarse feel of his thumb caressing her skin rousing a heat low in her belly. "Do you really think it's been easy, Royal?"

"I can think of worse fates than cleaning rooms," he snapped, releasing her abruptly and turning away.

Josephine felt as if she'd been slapped. His coldness snuffed out the warm rush to her limbs, made her feel selfconscious. "I meant being away from you," she blurted.

Royal stopped his pacing, his mouth hard and his eyes glittering. "Ah, but in not a week's separation you certainly found some comfort," he ground out. "I know Brad has been here to see you. Did he hold you and caress your troubles away, Josephine? Press a friendly kiss to your cheek? Were you cold and reserved, holding your hands as you are now, or were you hot and ready for him?"

"That's none of your business," Josephine challenged him, his mulish tendencies abrasive to her taut nerves when she felt ridiculous enough already. At her reply the heat in his eyes intensified, and he took another step towards her. Butterflies and a strange quickening coursed through her from her toes to her solar plexus. "Brad is a very dear friend of mine and we often exchange pleasantries. I've told you of him before. We met here by chance…"

"Is he your lover?" Royal pressed harshly.

Josephine shook her head slowly, her eyes squinting in dismay. She turned and walked towards the window, her eyes searching the heavens for some sign of direction, for the Lord knew she had lost sight of hers. Nothing was as it should be. "What does it matter to you? You certainly find your own comforts in these very halls, Captain Ashhurst."

He growled lowly behind her, the sound loud in the tiny room, beckoning her to look back. Turmoil washed across her spine, its trail electric as she stared at him. His lips were tightly compressed into a hard line.

"Come here, Josephine."

"Why?" she wanted to know, unable to stop staring. Her eyes moved to his forehead, where a new line had etched its way in and then back to the blue depths in the pools of his. The image of him lying in bloody tatters on the bed as Isabella had described him flashed to her. Her knees felt shaky, her throat constricted. The sight of him blurred.

"Josephine, come here," Royal worded the command again, softer this time, pleased when her feet shuffled her closer to him. Her head was down. He sighed, unfolding his arms to touch a finger beneath her chin, his movements guiding her head up to face him. Her cheeks were wet with tears, her intelligent, encompassing gaze ringed with red. His cocky, heated air sapped what was left of her strength. It vanished with one quick heartbeat.

"Oh, Royal," was all she could emit before she was bubbling over like a fountain in the rain; and once she started, she couldn't stop. She cried harder when he pulled her into his arms, the feel of him reassuring and safe despite his anger. She had missed him, terribly so, and she mumbled something to that effect into the solid wall of his body. Her hands were smoothing over his chest, her fingertips resting on his collar-bone as she sniffled.

"Put your arms around me, princess," he muttered.

"I don't want to hurt you, you've been hurt so badly already," she choked. "I was worried about you, Royal. I wanted to see you, but Isabella told me you didn't want me to come...."

"She did, did she?" Royal soothed, resting his cheek on the top of her head, inhaling deeply. The fiery, silken strands of her hair exuded an alluring scent that seemed to be natural to her. No matter where she was or what she was doing, he'd noticed, she always smelled the same—like a bed of jasmine at full moon.

"I—I don't think she did it to be nasty," Josephine blubbered. Royal Ashhurst was an inexplicable bequest, the likes of which she had never known, and now she feared losing him. It was also far too painfully clear that she knew now what the loss would mean to her. She had met many men in her life, but none of them had even come close to making her feel the way Royal did with one warm glance.

He was rocking her side to side, telling her it was going to be all right, though everything else was all wrong. She sniffed again.

"I want you to know I was thinking of you while Blackbeard was doing his handiwork," he said then, his voice rough and tentative. "The picture of you I had in my head I held close to me. It helped get me through it."

In all truth, he wondered if he'd thought of little else. Josephine's sobs began to subside and she cautioned a look to his face that was but inches apart from her own. Rough, dark hair thickly shadowed his chin and upper lip, the lines around his eyes white compared to the tan of his forehead and temples. She could not resist the urge to lift her fingers to stroke his goatee, her gentle sigh of gratification echoing chords of wistful longing. "I didn't feel the pain at first, princess," he added quickly as another crocodile tear rose in her eye. He kissed it away tenderly.

Royal's hands rubbed across her shoulders, his thumbs touching together briefly as he gingerly circled her neck and then cupped her face in his palms. His eyes were heavy-lidded as he leaned down and captured her mouth with his own in an instantly deep, searching kiss, his body shaking with the taste of her. Her lips welcomed him, fed his starving soul as she melted beneath him. Royal groaned as he continued to hold her face, kissing her with a passion he couldn't deny and feared would never come again if he released her.

Josephine's fingers snaked through the dark hair curling across the nape of his neck, the strong grooves of his shoulders meeting her touch. The heat radiating from his body sparked fires on the pads of her fingers, continuing on through her limbs and torching her from head to toe. His tongue fenced hers, his teeth nipping her lower lip, tugging free her inhibitions. Josephine whimpered as she held onto Royal, his arms wrapping snugly around her and keeping her tight to him as he lifted his head, his eyes obscure and intensely hot. For a long minute he said nothing.

She was looking at him so innocently, yet desire he read there too, a desire that matched his own. Royal's gaze raked her face; her skin was smooth, with only the barest hint of a wrinkle, reminding him of her age. Would she still look at him that way in not ten years when he began to gray? Royal didn't know. But even as he stared at her, every part of his rational mind telling him to leave her be, that he would only lose her as he had everything else that had meant something to him, he knew he couldn't allow himself not to take that chance.

"Josephine, what sort of life do you wish for yourself?" he asked quietly, his gaze searching her tear-stained face for any hint of deception even though instinct told him there would be none. "A grand home? Servants to see to your every whim? A closet full of gowns and jewels for every occasion? There are men, good men, without a dark past, who can give you these things, and aren't nearly fifteen years your senior."

Every second that ticked slowly by was a lifetime. Royal prepared himself for her answer, his jaw tightly locked.

"A life with you in it, Captain Ashhurst," she smiled shyly, her reddened eyes turning suddenly warm, a stray hand awkwardly wiping away the streaks on her face. "You are so handsome, Royal, but more than that, you are a good man," she whispered, her lids drowsy.

His eyes blinked and smoldered as he slowly turned his head to the side and back, licking his lips and exhaling heavily through his nose. "It's all in your mind," he countered brusquely.

"Nay, it is not," she argued. "And no one shall ever convince me of otherwise—"

Royal gathered her as tightly in his arms as he could without crushing her and, with a feral rumble in his chest, caught her mouth, his lips greedy yet tender as he claimed her for his own. Their breathing was instantly hot and rapid as they fused, their tongues dancing where they would, each of them unable to get enough of the other, their murmured urgings blending into a bellow of need.

Josephine's hands rested low on his waist and across his good shoulder, stroking the length of his arm with a gentle caress. Royal groaned as he lifted her up, his hands reaching down to grasp her bottom as he pressed the core of her against him, her skirts ruffling up to her bosom and away. "*Mi bonita mariposa,*" he whispered, the lyrical rhythm of the exotic vernacular he spoke lulling her, captivating her. "*Tu'eres mi alma, mi corazon. Tu'eres el amor de mi vida....*"

God, he could feel the intense, throbbing heat of her against his manhood through his breeches. Josephine cried out and arched her back at the strange, aching feeling of his iron-hard arousal, her arms bound around the strong column of his neck. "Royal, please," she begged as his lips ran a fiery path across her throat, the feel of his teeth as he nipped the curve of her shoulder sending shivers down her spine. She knew not any other words; she only knew she didn't want him to ever stop, for there was so much more, though Josephine did not fully understand what nor how to ask. Her fingers clenched the hair of his head tightly, and she began to wriggle spontaneously from the pleasurable sensations he aroused.

Royal thought he was going to lose control when she did that. "Tell me you want me, princess," he urged thickly as he began to carry her. "I need to hear you say it."

He leaned forward and in a dizzying, decadent moment the bed was beneath her and Royal was above her, lying between her legs with his weight supported on one arm. "I need you, Royal," she said, the emerald jewels of her eyes opening towards him and taking his breath away. His jaw clenched as he fought against the pains of his body, his erection the worst of them all. She kissed him boldly. Royal moved his hands across her, feeling the soft swell of her breasts, the curve of her waist in a dreamlike state. His hands seemed almost magic to her. His mouth was ruthless on hers, taking what he wanted, yet his hands were mastering her in a firm, reverent manner.

"You realize that you will belong to me, and me alone, Josephine," Royal grated, allowing her one last out before he could not stop. Hell, the agony he was in would last him days if he didn't have her, but he would find a way. "Because I will never allow you to be with another."

Josephine reached behind her and began to unhook the top closures of her gown, her eyes glazed with passion and her lips swollen from his kisses. "Nor I, Royal," she whispered, a warning twinkle of her own not going unseen. "I will have no trespass from you."

His lips twitched at her jealous command as he bade her to cease in her movements. Josephine flushed, shy and embarrassed. Royal smiled arrogantly as he leaned back and unbuttoned his vest, chuckling at her uncertainty even as much as he appreciated it. He was going to enjoy teaching her everything he knew about the art of making love.

"I don't want you to rob me the pleasure of doing it for you, princess," he reassured, "for there is no task that I would enjoy doing more."

He drew his shirt off his shoulders, his eyes holding hers, shielding the unbearable sight of his back from her. He came forward again, kissing the corners of her mouth, catching her lower lip playfully between his teeth. Josephine's skin seemed to melt beneath his touch as he worked at the hook and eye closures, teasing the sensitive flesh of her lower back with the roughness of his palms. "Aye, you've been made in the image of Isis, Josephine," Royal whispered into her ear, gnawing on her lobe, the bridge of his nose nuzzling the back of her neck. "Would you descend into the underworld for your Osiris, little one?"

Shadows of passion clouded her eyes as she clutched onto him, the erotic sensation of her gown slipping free of her flushed body and rustling to the floor loud in her ears. Her limbs and hands moved chaotically, racing across his arms to the curling hair of his chest. The softness of it tantalized her nipples as he guided her chemise off to join the gown on the floor. Royal's entire frame felt engulfed in flames as her naked body rubbed against him, her searching lips finding the hollow of his throat, her small teeth nibbling tentatively at his shoulder.

"Lie back, princess," he implored her, his voice hoarse. The apples of her cheeks were bright red as she stretched out, her legs on either side of him. Royal's azure eyes drank in the sight of her; the candlelight glowed across her soft skin in amber droplets, her hair crackling with fire. Her generous breasts curved into rosy peaks, her hardened nipples begging for his mouth. From these mounds, her flesh moved further down, flat across her stomach, to be lost in the gently curling auburn hair covering the apex of her thighs. Royal's eyes drew to slits as he stared keenly at the soft folds of her womanhood, the hunger in him palatable. He cast a look upwards. Shyness he read in her face, yet her unmasked passion made the green chips of her eyes smolder as he'd never seen in another. He licked his lips, the desire it seemed he'd ached an eternity to taste so sweetly dripping from his tongue.

"Don't be afraid, princess," he reassured, his hands roaming up her legs from ankles to hip. "There may be pain, but I will be as good to you as a man can be." He ran a series of scorching kisses down her torso, spending an agonizingly slow amount of time with her breasts, licking the crest of each until Josephine was arching her back, her soft moans a blissful music vibrating through the small room. And then his head was laving circles across her stomach before dipping down even lower.

Josephine squirmed at the white-hot stabs of pleasure Royal generated as his tongue drove into her. She bucked against his face, the steel bands of his arms keeping her pressed to the bed, centered for his scorching onslaught. He tasted the sweet honey in gentle laps and strokes, murmuring piquant words of her beauty and her response to him. Josephine was nearly mad with pressure building in her lower abdomen, and she cried out his name in a hasty, repetitious blend, enraptured as her body splintered apart in racking waves of delight.

Royal's head rested on her breast as she adhered to him, tears sneaking out of the corners of her eyes as the intensity of what happened rippled through her limbs, her skin electrified. He fumbled with his breeches, at last getting them unlaced. His thick, heavy member was iron hard, pearlescent at the tip. "Relax, princess," he instructed hotly in her ear, his breath irregular. She had barely caught sight of his masculinity; so strange in appearance it was—but it seemed very large. She wondered how he would fit.

"Royal—" she began when he cut her off with the commanding onslaught of his mouth, his arms bracing on either side of her, the head of him gently probing the outer folds of her femininity. She could taste herself upon his mouth as he slid his tongue between her lips in a languid fashion, her moan of contentment and her body's unconscious relaxation beneath his own welcoming him. With one powerful, well-placed thrust he buried himself into the damp heat of her, her legs snapping instinctively around his waist. Royal clenched his teeth and howled, his head thrown back and his eyes glazed as he stared unseeing at the ceiling, his whole body quivering with elicit sensations. God, she was so wet, her tight little sheath squeezing him, resisting his incursion.

All the sweet, dreamy pleasures she had been enjoying suddenly vanished as Royal took her, the length of him so deep inside Josephine swore she could feel him in her stomach. Tears rooted in confusion changed to those of pain. The most secret part of her throbbed uncomfortably. He began to move, his groans of ecstasy ringing in the air, mingling with the scent of their twisted bodies. "God, you feel good," he murmured, his mouth running a trail of blazing kisses across her face and throat, his teeth biting softly on her chin, her jaw, the lobe of her ear, and the curve of her neck as he slid in and out of her, his pace hastening with the pulse of his beating heart. Josephine's eyes were tightly closed, yet her tears managed to manifest themselves on her cheeks anyway, rolling down to dampen Royal's shoulder. She tried to wriggle away, but he held her tightly, mumbling hot words into her ear, his ragged breath telling her to relax, to open herself for him.

She obeyed, and the tip of him seemed to penetrate even further. Josephine cried out as he pushed into her, doing his best to keep himself steady even as the white-hot rush of graphic pleasure liquefied his insides. "You are so lovely, princess...I swear it won't always be this way for you...." He kissed her brow, the bridge of her nose, her lips in an ever-rotating fashion, until at last he felt the eruption of his desire stir deep in his loins. Royal bucked against her softness three times, harder than he intended; but he was loathe to stop himself, the frenzied pitch of his need coiling like a snake around his body and soul.

His body went limp and he fell to his side next to her, his solid arm curling around her waist and tugging her close to him. Royal nuzzled his nose into her hair, drawing in her delightful scent until his lungs could no longer expand, and then he exhaled slowly, a satisfied twitch to his lips. "My sweet, giving little princess," he soothed, bestowing an extended series of fond kisses to her brow, his hand stroking along her side from the curve of her breast down to her waist and back again. "It will be all right, I assure you. It will get easier with time, and eventually you will feel the pleasure that I do."

"Royal, I'm sore," she complained, her eyes misty as they turned to look at him.

"It will pass, Josephine," he mumbled, taking a slow kiss. "It will pass. *Tu'eres lo mas hermoso que conosco.* You will be fine, little one. You are strong enough."

She emitted a muted sigh before snuggling back into the crook of his embrace, the warm afterglow of their passions leaving her skin flushed. He smiled reluctantly to himself, brushing back a wayward lock of her hair from where it lay against her cheek. She whimpered in protest when he moved to finish undressing, stretching out like a sleepy kitten until he returned and hauled her up to his chest in a tight embrace.

Royal lay awake long after Josephine's soft breathing had evened in deep slumber, trying to make sense of his disjointed thoughts and reason. A part of him wanted to push her away, to give her a gentle kiss and bid her good luck as he had every other woman in his life, but the other whispered voices of his heart told him something else entirely different—that she was the one he couldn't afford to let go. There was something about her that made him ache to pull her closer even as the wall around his soul tried to keep her out, his long-dead heart stirring in ways he had tried to turn away from in vain.

16

Torrential rains that began as a seemingly harmless early summer squall continued to pound the Lowcountry with increasing velocity as time wore on, the wind shear lifting debris, Spanish moss, and dead branches from the ground and bending the tops of the trees in a crazed fashion. The wind itself stirred from a low moan into an earsplitting shriek and lightning spangled its portentous glow like paranormal fingers stretched downward from the skies. The glory that was Charleston in the daylight hours had morphed into a twisted, ghostlike splendor that was more sinister than inspiring. The peninsula had flooded from the bay to the market and now the sea was creeping its way farther to the north and west; high tide was still several hours away, and if the downpour did not relent, nearly every building south of the powder magazine was doomed to have their foundations steeped with water.

Despite the fact that the calendar had at last rolled through May it was still early in the year for tropical tempests, though a spring hurricane had not been unheard of in the nearly fifty years Carolina had been inhabited by European colonists. Windows shook from the winds and were hastily boarded with their storm shutters. Dinners and private parties were put on hold as the elements reigned supreme. Carter Seymour had left notice at his office shortly before the onslaught of the weather that he would be traveling north to meet with an important client and would not return for the better part of two weeks.

Despite the lack of socializations, word nonetheless crept across the grapevine that something wasn't quite right with Carter Seymour. Blackbeard's blockade had certainly rattled everyone, but it wasn't clear whether it was that or the estrangement with his young fiancée at the start of the whole piratical affair that had left him debilitated. What was apparent was that he had turned a cold shoulder to everyone around him, had been seen mumbling strange phrases to himself as he rode his horse absentmindedly about town, and his appearance had gone from posh sophistication to unkempt disorder. His displeasure with the talk bandied about in regards to Royal Ashhurst was hardly concealable, and while many of the Charleston society weren't impressed with the quixotic tale of the sea captain's brush with death in the name of their beloved city, an equal number of people were, and that was enough to send a wildfire of gossip dancing from gate to gate, from the docks on up through Mazyck's Pasture.

Yet, communications with the rest of the world were nonexistent while the slow-moving tropical storm lashed the Carolina coast—and for the occupants of Kirkpatrick's on Logan Street, the time of enforced seclusion did not come amiss as they fed upon their desires for one another. Royal initiated Josephine to a thousand hallowed pleasures, unable to feel her enough, to show her in action what he was unable to say with words.

Josephine was held spellbound by the sensations he aroused in her. The long-dormant passion sparked into an inferno she could not extinguish. The look in his eyes as he nestled himself inside her hurtled her to the brink of madness, the thunder and shake of her body beneath his hand an apocalyptic revelation. Her heart was constricted with chaotic emotions as she clung to him, her response growing evermore wild as she grew accustomed to the swelled length of him. The scent of him in her nostrils, upon her skin, intoxicated her. Josephine cherished those hours, and when Royal wrapped his arms around her and held her so tightly she could not breathe, she wished that Providence would not tear him from her again.

But the moment changed, as moments are wont to do, when the weather finally cleared. The sunlight split through the miasma, diluted at first across the saturated ground, gaining intensity slowly throughout the morning hours until the maelstrom of the previous days would have seemed to be but a dream if it wasn't for the jumble of flora littering the thoroughfares. Josephine, snuggled deep in the circle of Royal's embrace, watched a shaft of light start as a crack beneath the shutters. His soft breathing tousled her hair as he slept, and the beams grew ever brighter as she idly stroked the skin of his forearm, being careful not to rouse him. Warm feelings of comfort and rectitude faded away as worry inundated her naked body; she turned ever so slightly and Royal's hold tightened around her waist, conscious of her even in his slumber.

Josephine sighed, the rush of tears spilling unheeded down her cheeks as she rested her brow against his chest. The beauty of their clandestine affair echoed sentiments that she did not want to fathom, so frightening and incredible they were. She wondered what she would do when he was gone, for Josephine held no illusions that he would stay.

He had said very little over the last two days other than to reassure her of one-dimensional things that would not matter much in future times. Instinct told her what her rational mind did not want to comprehend; Royal was a man driven by his fury, and though his passion for her was true, it was that and nothing more, secondary to the pursuit of his name and pilfered inheritance. When it was time for him to go, she would let him, Josephine silently avowed, and would never speak of the love she had for him; Royal had enough burdens of his own, and she would spare him what she could.

"Why the tears, princess?" she heard him murmur above her.

Josephine hastily blinked her eyes. Lord, she had left a puddle on his chest without even knowing it. She said nothing, pretending she was asleep, an endeavor that didn't work at all.

"Answer me, Josephine," he ordered. His lids were only half open, the blue-green intensity of his eyes smoky and dynamic as he slid his hand along her jaw and made her face him, his thumb catching the last remnants of her concern. He had never met a woman who seemed to cry over nothing at all, and the ambiguity he felt in such tender situations was certainly not something he was adept at handling. It made him gruff and short, his voice sounding more severe than he intended.

"I don't want you to go," she blurted. "You may not wish to hear it, Royal, but it is the truth."

"Who says I'm going anywhere, princess?" he pressed, sighing heavily at the emotions in her eyes. "Of course, I do go here and there from time to time, and I may not always tell you what I could, but I answer to no one, Josephine. I never have, nor will I ever."

"That's not what I'm asking," she protested, though she could tell he did not believe her. Lord, he really was difficult. Josephine moved away, pulling the sheet with her to cover her nakedness; she stuffed away the hurt feelings she felt pointlessly when he did not reach for her. "I just wonder where I'll be a month from now, for I have never needed any-one," she betrayed, hating her frustration. "And I'm afraid that now I'm needing you."

"You made it the last twenty years of your life just fine without me," he reminded her coolly.

"Oh, I'm certain I will be aright," she sniffed proudly. "I know it matters naught that I miss you."

"It's all in your mind," Royal told her, and not for the first time, the defenses inside him chipping asunder with every tear as he scrambled to gather them in vain. "Why would you miss this grouchy old bastard?"

"Because I—" Josephine caught herself, biting her lip. To her ire, he laughed, once again lounging against the pillows carelessly, his hand rub-bing at the goatee she was so entranced with. Lord, she had been com-menting on it for days. Royal winked at her fiendishly.

"Because why?" he pressed. Josephine only scowled. "Come, tell me why, princess."

"Nay," she said, feeling the rosy flush creep up her neck.

"Because you love me?" Royal asked candidly, his face a careless mask. Josephine's lip pursed and her chin jutted out irritably. "Aye, you do, lass, I can tell."

"You can't tell," she muttered, her cheeks hot. "I—I am fond of you, Royal, though you are acting like a varlet to the highest degree—"

"Fond?" He pushed himself forward, his arms catching her and pulling her back to lie against him. She kicked weakly, to no avail. Royal's chest rumbled with amusement as he began to kiss her, his mouth greedy and hot as he conjured her response. "The way you are fond of your Brad, princess?" he laughed against her lips. His hands caressed her and drew her to sit across his lap, her legs around his waist. Josephine's drowsy lids flickered open to see his good-natured teasing, his kisses continuing slow and steady for the better part of an hour before he made love to her as if she were porcelain in his hands.

Yet, he did not linger overlong; rising and drawing on his breeches, he gave her an odd but gentle look, leaning down to press a last kiss to her lips. "Things will be hard for you soon, princess. Do you think you are strong enough for it? Contempt as you have never seen the likes of will show its feral head."

"You insult me gravely, Captain Ashhurst, if you believe otherwise," she stated smugly.

"Well then, princess," he said, watching her, "you had best pick out a wedding dress."

* * * * *

Royal David Ashhurst married Josephine Adelaide Beckham on June 6, 1718, beneath the cover of darkness at the Independent Church on Meeting Street. The ceremony was witnessed by Isabella, Everett and his wife Jean, and Kingsley. Josephine missed Brad, but as their union was, as of yet, the kernel of a secret, it could not be helped, and as she looked across the room at the man who was to be her husband, she knew that she was wanting for nothing else.

Soft candlelight filled the still chambers, the gently flickering glow casting a warm circle around the couple as the rector read their vows. Josephine wore a simple pale blue gown, with full sleeves and a modest yet enticing scooped bodice. Her face was freed of the veil and her eyes sparkled brighter than a thousand diamonds as she looked up at Royal, her trembling lips parting into a wide smile.

The sea captain was so handsome to her, his proud stance accentuated by the austere black of his dress, his presence so unlike that of any other. He drew her with his eyes, the strong profile of his mouth that she could still feel upon her own. She could scarcely breathe as his gaze smoldered over her, her limbs quaking at the unshielded desire he betrayed without conscience. Royal was going to be her husband; and Josephine was proud of him, for he was a noble man above all things and held an honest heart.

Her hair had been left loose, the tumbling mass of fire engulfing her back to her waist. Even as the man of God read the passages, and they repeated and said what was necessary in turn, Royal was threading his hands through it, pulling her closer until she was tight in his embrace. She looked dreamily up at him, her wayward thoughts disrupted when she noticed his brow had furrowed.

"Josephine, do you take this man to be your husband?" the priest repeated.

Josephine's gaze covered Royal's face as she fought for her voice; the slight squint to his eyes as he awaited her response, the white creases around them belying his seniority. And his eyes themselves were so beautiful and strange, the light in them a blissful revelation.

"I love you, Royal," she said.

The corners of his mouth twitched the barest inch; his arms locked tightly around her waist. Her hands could feel the thud of his heart in his breast as he pressed a kiss to her brow before brushing his lips to her tears and then her mouth, a salty taste upon them. Tenderly he swept away any misgivings she may have held to the side.

The pastor stood idly for a long moment as the couple embraced. The kiss did not relent as time passed, and after several minutes, he decried to no one in particular, "I now pronounce you man and wife…and as for the other business, well, it seems to have already been taken care of…"

Royal at last lifted his head with a sigh, his heart pounding at the unabashed emotion he saw upon her face. As he slid his mother's ring onto her finger, he knew he could no longer ignore her love, could no longer pretend that it didn't exist; and as he stared down at the tiny form of his lady, Royal wondered how on earth he would be able to keep her love, for he did not see himself as deserving of it. He smiled awkwardly at the fit of the ring, lifting her hand to his lips. "You realize that you have encumbered yourself with this ill-tempered swindler indefinitely, princess."

"Why you seek to push me from you I'll not understand, nor entertain the reasoning behind, Captain Ashhurst," she retorted, her eyes hot as she stood on tiptoe to press a bold kiss to his lips, his shoulders strong and warm beneath her hands. "Yet I assure you, this is a burden I accept graciously. I care not what may be said of you. I care not that you do not have a grand and gracious home. But you will one day, captain, and I shall help you."

Royal's eyes were burning oddly as he drew his wife into the iron bands of his embrace, her protestations of smothering the only thing that loosened his hold even a degree. "You deserve better than me, Josephine

Adelaide Ashhurst," Royal murmured, "but even the devil himself could not wrench you from my clutches now."

"Aye, are you saying you love me, captain?" she asked, breathless at the way her married name sounded and the marked possessiveness in his words.

His face was a mask of composure, yet Josephine did not feel disappointed as he cupped her face in his calloused hands, the pulse at her throat catching his eye. He ignored the fact that they were in a room full of onlookers as he grinned his alluring smile, his eyes sparkling with promise. "I'm saying that tonight I'm going to make love to you, wife," he said, laughing at the blossoming red color her oval face had become. "And every night thereafter until I am a doddering old man."

17

Blackbeard sat upon a log next to a roaring bonfire that men, with bottles in their hands and their arms outstretched in the air, danced around. Liquor and hearty laughter spilled through the night as the pirates celebrated their latest conquest; but there was no sign of the merriment his crew shared mirrored in the face of Blackbeard.

The fire crackled, popped, and waved in the night, the smoke of it doing little to abate the insects that swarmed from the underbrush. Blackbeard stroked his namesake in a casual way as he looked at Carter Seymour through his bushy brows, his lips smacking on the damp leaf of the cigar wrap that was held precariously at best from the tips of his searching whiskers. "Ye know I had tae take yer ship, Seymour," he growled matter-of-factly when he had had enough of Seymour's ramblings about the *Destiny*. "Iffen ye don't want there to be any suspicion about yer involvement wit me, then ye should see the value of yer loss, so tae speak."

Seymour rubbed his face repeatedly, damning the hell-hole swamps that were as bad, if not worse, in Beaufort Inlet than in Charleston. "She was on her way out, damn it! She had been delayed. And she bore the Transport logo on her flag."

"Yer all pissed off over nothin'," Blackbeard thundered, hammering down his earthen bottle. It shattered into a handful of large chunks, the remainder of the rum spraying over the ground and his boots. "Yer insured, ain't ye? Now why don't ye tell me what's really on yer mind, Seymour. And thanks again fer yer help with the Wragg situation; here's yer hundred pound share. That oughtta be some comfort."

And with that Blackbeard shook with a peal of laughter, the heavy pouch of coin landing with a jingling thump at Seymour's feet. Seymour gave it an irritated kick to the side, hating Blackbeard as much for his mirth as for the position the pirate had put him in.

"Did you have to make Royal Ashhurst into a bloody martyr?" Seymour asked, his voice shrill amongst the rabble. He ran his hands back through his thin, sweat-soaked hair and down across the buttons of his fine, stained garments before toying with his dirty lace cuffs. "Though the weather has turned for the worse, don't think that Charleston society will stop because of it. You should've saved me the trouble and just killed him like I asked."

"Yer man was the one who afouled the attempt in the first place, not me," Blackbeard parried, searching aimlessly behind the log for a re-placement jug of rum. "Ah, me dearie," he sighed to himself as he located a full one among the empties. "So he's a sufferer for the bluebloods' cause. Ye'll survive this momentary rally to his side, just like he will his floggin'."

Blackbeard chuckled lowly as he remembered how Royal had stood proudly and made nary a sound as he endowed one of the worst lashings he had ever given, second only in memory to what he had given the old thief of a quartermaster. Blackbeard did not know what it was that had sparked such a heated vendetta between Carter Seymour and Royal Ashhurst, and neither did he particularly care; but Blackbeard was no fool, and he could sense that the strength and drive of a man like Ashhurst ran fathoms deep. It was part of what had stayed his hand from delivering a fatal punishment. That, and he preferred intimidation to any real blood-shed—killing was a waste of time and valuable manpower, not to mention the fact that he owed Seymour nothing. Politics of the genteel sort in Charleston was not something that he concerned himself with now, nor would he ever. If Carter Seymour liked to fancy himself on the rebel side of the law, he'd best be prepared to suffer the consequences. Greed may hold a hangman's noose, and while Blackbeard did his best to avoid such maladies, if another wished to pursue such a path, then so be it. He didn't understand the rich and he didn't pretend to; all he had to do was think of Stede Bonnet, and Blackbeard would shake his head.

Bonnet had decided to break course with Blackbeard, his love for the city of Charleston tugging at his conscience. He had left that very afternoon, and though his route had remained undisclosed, Blackbeard had the sneaking suspicion that he was on his way to beg for a pardon from North Carolina's Governor Eden—with the spoils of his conquest stowed aboard his ship in a locked chest. Blackbeard had let him go without fanfare—the man was a weak leader and, in Blackbeard's estimation, needed to return to Barbados posthaste and leave the marauding to those who did it properly. Though it meant the loss of a good ship, Blackbeard still had two others besides his beautiful and fearsome *Queen Anne's Revenge*, and he did not perceive that he would miss Bonnet overmuch. He chuckled to himself as he thought of how he had already snuck upon and stripped the *Revenge* of its plunder and marooned the crew; Bonnet was in for a rude awakening when he returned from Bath, that was for certain.

Seymour was unable to muster even a slice of Blackbeard's relaxed air, thinking of the offhand meeting he had held with the pirate he had met by chance in St. Augustine, Florida, a year prior. What began as a risqué and exciting idea had quickly spun out of control as messages came and went over the months, petitioning him to assist with their raid of Charleston with the hollow promise of protection for his merchants.

When at last Blackbeard had come to port, Seymour met him under cover of darkness on a small barrier island, swept up in a plot of kidnapping that had seemed surreal until the Jolly Roger was seen; and by then it was too late, far too late to worm his way out of it. He hadn't been thinking clearly, that night most of all, reeling from the fact that Josephine had vanished into thin air, and still she had not returned—but he fully expected that to change upon his return to Charleston.

Seymour had felt something strange in the air that day, and it had not abated, beginning with the moment Josephine Beckham left him at the altar. Indeed, it had only compounded with time. Now it was nearly palatable.

The haughty, careless pleasures he had enjoyed without recourse for twenty-six years, the house of society that he ruled as if he were a lord of the *ton*, had been built on a shaky foundation—its legacy now crumbling like matchsticks beneath a gale before his eyes. The devil himself seemed to be ever behind him, his cryptic invitations to indulge himself awhile longer a mocking curse to his soul. He had passed the coin of avarice to the ferryman's grasp long ago, and now the destination of that journey was nearing.

"It is no use, no use," Seymour muttered. Royal Ashhurst had become the guide to his hellish dreams the past nights, taking him on a tour of perdition and the crimes he had committed, his voice echoing like a thousand cries of the damned. He was unable to eat even though his belly growled loudly; the taste of the fine rum Blackbeard had commandeered in Barbados bitter upon his tongue. "Royal Ashhurst troubles me, Captain; he must be eliminated, though I know not how."

"What's no use is yer sniffin' around these boots," Blackbeard snarled, his eyes moving across the marshland grasses to a group of women around their own small fire, the curves of their flesh beckoning him in the golden light. "Consider our arrangement finished, Seymour, iffen ye like." Blackbeard laughed uproariously, slapping his knees as he stood and stumbled his way towards the women amid the crackling sounds of the night. "Yer place is in Charleston, Seymour, not here," came the sinister baritone to Seymour's ears, and Seymour thought it wise to heed the dismissal, for a thin young black man with a wide, toothy grin was looking at him with marked interest from beneath a copse of beechwood. As he receded to where his schooner *Sundown Too* was moored on the inlet, Seymour fumed with the knowledge that he had lost far more than he could have ever hoped to gain in dealing with Blackbeard.

* * * * *

Michael Beckham jumped at the sturdy knock to his door, his gaze flitting to the window and then back, his clammy hands lacing together. His nails nervously picked at the cuticles of the opposing hand as he peered through the peephole to the other side. Though his door held a wreath belying his mourning status, Beckham crept on eggshells every waking moment as he awaited Carter Seymour's return. Beckham did not like the look in Seymour's eye when he informed him that if his daughter were not produced by the time he returned from his pressing engagement, Beckham would find himself, mildly put, in a heap of strife.

Beckham had already spent the money Seymour had paid for Josephine, and it was this more than fatherly concern that ate away at him, for Michael found it hardly likely that Josephine would be discovered alive at this late of a date. Nearly the entire denomination he had received had gone to creditors, not assets, and there was no way he would be able to repay Seymour in any timely fashion, if at all.

Beckham's eyes narrowed as they fell upon the tall dark shape of a man with his back to the door, his face turned outward onto Church Street. He had a proud stance—his head held high, his shoulders squared. His hands were clasped behind his back, his fingers as silent and patient as their owner. In the gloom of the watery lamp it was hard to decipher more. An assassin? Beckham scratched at his face, unaware in his paranoia that he left four red streaks alongside his temple. "Who goes there?" he wheezed.

"My name is Royal Ashhurst," came the reply as the stranger turned, the eyes on his brutally carved, goateed face seeming to penetrate through the viewer and right into his own. "May I come in...Mr. Beckham, I presume?"

Michael's gaze ferreted throughout the small room, the panic in him thickening the air. What would the devil want with him? "Go hither," Beckham managed, watching the caller. The weak order seemed to have gone unheard. "Be gone, man—this is a house of mourning..."

"If you will allow me to come in, we could talk about that," Ashhurst said mysteriously. A thin, layered mist gathered around his boots as the humidity deepened. "There is something you need to know, Mr. Beckham, and perhaps something you could help me with in return."

"I have naught to say," he whimpered and was to leave it at that, backing away, when the captain's voice came a third time.

"Mr. Beckham, we can do this the easy way or the hard way. In either event, I am coming through that door in the next few seconds."

Beckham gulped, his pale skin as white as caps of the Atlantic waves, the tick of the lonely clock upon the bare mantle loud in his ears. He squinted and blinked several times, flicking the latch and admitting his guest.

"Thank you, sir, for your hospitality," Royal said, scrutinizing Josephine's father, bewilderment blatant upon his countenance. When she had told him they were nothing alike, she had failed to mention complete opposites was more likely of a story; Michael exuded the air of a whipped dog, and he scurried mindlessly before Royal now. "And I apologize for what may seem the utmost discourtesy at this time for you, but I am here to inform you that your bereavement is unnecessary. Your daughter, Josephine, is not dead, but alive, and altogether well."

A slight stain of color worked its way unto Beckham's pallor. His eyes shot towards the door before back to the dark stranger who seemed to swallow the room; Michael knew not whether to weep in relief or despair. "How is this, Ashhurst?"

"She has been with me, in my protection," he said evenly, "and now she is my wife."

18

The sweet-tempered winds of June swept through the alleys and passageways of Charleston, bringing with it to every nook and cranny word of Royal and Josephine's marriage. Distress over the young girl's whereabouts had quickly changed into stunning controversy as the scandal broke loose, setting the town on its ear and causing no end of speculative talk. Stares and harsh giggles of contempt from the local populace upon the rare occasion she did venture out made a bitter blend amongst the backdrop of dancing hawthorn and dogwood, yet Josephine did her best to take no notice of it. She kept a glowing smile on her face as a shield against their ruthless barbs.

Josephine had decided at last on going to her father's to see if she could come to some sort of compromise with him, and Royal had insisted adamantly that he accompany her. He expected Seymour to return to Charleston any day now, and he did not savor the idea of his wife walking alone and unprotected with the upheaval that their astounding marriage had caused. Josephine leaned back on her heels with her slim arms across her chest as she looked up into the face of her diligent husband, knowing that his presence would be but fuel to the fire where Michael Beckham was concerned. One look at Royal Ashhurst would have her father roiling in a pool of angst, and with his brief, practical note stating that never again would he acknowledge he had a daughter, she did not want Royal causing a commotion and making things entirely worse.

He had taken great exception to her disownment, more than Josephine would have expected. At first she had protested going to her father at all. She certainly felt estranged from Michael, almost sad because of the sheer lack of feelings she held for him—but he was the only family she knew of. She had nothing of value there now save the odd childhood keepsake and her clothes, though she wondered what sort of condition they might be in, or if they were even still there. She had the clothes Royal had acquired for her, and Isabella had generously given up a dress or two from storage that was as modest as the closets of Kirkpatrick's could boast, and while they were still a bit on the daring side, they would do for the present until she could sew new garments.

She and Royal had held their first heated argument over the whole affair. He refused to allow her to wear the ones he had procured in public, saying that the worn-out castoffs were not fit for her. The other gowns he had refused because he did not care for the way she was exposed. Josephine had grown more and more exasperated with each passing minute, finally telling him that she would go about in breeches and a frock if it would suit him better, but the bottom line was that she was not going to stay cooped up inside his house.

"Royal, you're worrying about trivial things," Josephine argued. "I do not care what may clothe me, be it of homespun cotton or something far more luxurious."

"I will not have people gossiping about my wife," he growled, "saying that I do not take care of her the way that a man should. It is true you steal the breath of every man you meet as it is, princess, and whilst I am loathe to gown you in that which shall entice them even further, I will not have you running about in shabby rags."

"The gowns Isabella gave me are far from shabby, Royal," she protested. "Take your choice of which is more to your liking, for until I make a new wardrobe, that is what I shall wear. That is, if you believe speaking with my father will do any good. It is very likely my belongings have been burnt in effigy with each minute we waste arguing."

He sighed heavily, his cheek flexing, knowing full well that he could not bring himself to tell her he had stolen the other dresses and that he would only be acting selfishly if he did not allow her to collect what she would from her father's home. "Fine, madam, if that is how you wish it," he acquiesced, his voice belying that it was anything but fine with him. "Change, and quickly then, for I have much to do this afternoon..."

"You cannot go with, Royal," Josephine informed him. "I will not have any further conflict than what is already standing."

"The hell I'm not," he bristled, looking down at the tiny figure of his bride, whom apparently thought she was going to be able to order him around at whim. She was serious, he could tell, as he looked into the depths of her eyes and then to her adorable lips. They were set into a measured, determined pout that made him think of kissing and not much else. "Josephine, the danger has not alleviated. If anything, it has only increased tenfold."

"Bah, you are worried overmuch, Captain Ashhurst," Josephine said, rising on tiptoe to press a kiss to the corner of his mouth. "I shall take Kingsley with me, if you can spare him for an hour after tea. He will make certain I'm safe. Now as you said yourself, you have an engagement of a pressing sort, and I am not of a mind to keep you from your duties. So if you will excuse me..."

"Not so fast," Royal growled, drawing her back to him, his arms tight around her as he demanded a more thorough display of affection, which Josephine happily provided, her eyes dewy and a soft grin to her features as she broke away a long minute later. She had nearly slipped from the room when Royal stopped her.

"Josephine," he said impatiently, "you've still forgotten something."

"What, pray tell?" she blinked innocently. Royal's gaze was warm as he fixed his eyes upon his wife, her lips still puffy from his kisses.

"You didn't tell me you love me," he grinned.

Her eyes closed slightly as she blushed. "I love you, Royal," she said, still shy with her sentiment, and darted down the staircase amid the soft shuffle of feet.

It wasn't until he was already halfway to the docks that he realized his little minx had found a way to circumvent his authority without even knowing it, and he made a mental note to punish her with severe kisses for it later.

Royal spent most of the day at the shipyard, the slight reprieve he'd felt of the monetary pressures only amplified with one assessing glance at the *Courtesan*. She was in miserable shape, her masts cracked and her hull springing little fountains doomed to split wide to damning rivers. Severe damage had left the sails sieve-like beneath the soft sea winds. The crew had removed her cargo and dispersed in as many directions as the perfumes and cloth, swearing never again would they sail aboard such a deathtrap.

The cost to his livelihood was insurmountable. Royal stood stone-faced as he realized he would have little choice but to assist Colonel Rhett—granting the offer was still upon the table—for there was no other way he would be able to secure the immediate funds he needed. *Courtesan* had been scheduled for a pickup in Barbados by early August, before the tropics grew dangerous—yet nothing loomed before his first ship but a long overdue decommissioning.

Daylight was fading as Royal at last tore himself from the porous craft and acquiesced there was no other option before him other than to pursue the pirates, aiding Colonel Rhett's cause for as long as it may take. His heart was heavy as he walked home; and when he sat himself in his office, Josephine's laughter bubbling down from abovestair, he knew somehow he would muster the fortitude. He would have to. He would not allow his wife to be on the streets, for after having been there himself, there were few people he would wish such a fate upon—and he would certainly rather die there himself than allow his young, spirited bride to see one iota more than what she had experienced already. He wondered how her visit to her father's had gone; and while he was curious of what she would tell him, and what Kingsley's excuse for not returning was, a comprehensive diatribe was something he would welcome later rather than sooner.

With a sigh he began to flit through the stack of mail that had been growing upon his desk, his eyebrow cocking slightly at the fine invitation amongst the invoices. Clinton Montgomery, a dabbler in rice planting and a man who owned a profitable sugar plantation in Barbados, it appeared, was holding a gala for his daughter's coming-out party, and he of all people had been invited. Royal was halfway to penning his declination of the offer when he decided he would allow Josephine to make the decision as to whether or not they should attend, for though his understanding of marital behaviors was limited, he suspected that this sort of thing fell under feminine rule.

At the bottom he came across a simple packet of parchment, folded in thirds and sealed with black wax, the imprint upon it illegible. There was no return address. He turned it over several times before his finger slid beneath the fold and broke the seal. A wash of nerves shook every bone in his body.

His seawater eyes scanned the contents once, twice, three times. There were four pages in all, and as he read them over, a core of vigor shot across his spine to the tips of his limbs. His amusement came of a sudden in a capricious ricochet that lifted to the rafters and beyond; yet when Josephine came down to see from what his mirth stemmed, Royal only trapped her with laughing kisses and refused to say any more. Kingsley saw an opening and wisely darted out the door with a brief nod. "Ah, princess," Royal groaned good-naturedly, swinging her around in his arms before he set her away from him, berating his outlaw friend the furthest thing from his mind. "You are a very naughty sort of wife. Is it part of your evil, wicked plan for me to suffer so when we are apart?"

"Suffer, hah," Josephine snorted, her eyes sparkling. "I doubt you've ever pined for me a moment, Captain Ashhurst—"

"Tell me you love me," he instructed. Lord, he couldn't get enough of hearing her say it, even though every time since their wedding he'd forced it from her sweet lips. The fact that he had never told her of his own feelings mattered not to Royal; though he could see a longing in her eyes, and suspected she would welcome his love, emotions were something he had always alienated himself from—and now he found it a hard road to tread back upon. When he thought the words, he felt insecure, even to himself.

"We already did this once today, Royal," she sniffed, her mock-disdain enflaming his passions. "You are well aware of the way I feel, captain."

"Remind me," he ordered. When her chin jutted out and her eyes glistened with an unsaid challenging retort, he grinned at her mysteriously and informed her that she would be sold overseas to a sultan named Habeeb unless she placated him.

"I love you," she murmured, though she tilted her head mutinously, her delicate eyebrows askew. "And out of respect for that, captain, you will cease ordering me around from now on."

"I received an invitation from Clinton Montgomery, a man of esteem in town. It appears we have been invited to his daughter's coming-out party," he relayed with a wicked gleam to his eyes, not unlike that of a child who is concocting some sort of odious scheme with which to properly horrify his onlookers. "I am leaving the decision to you as to whether or not to attend, though be forewarned, the reasons behind the invitation may be less than straightforward."

"It will probably be a foppishly frilly event that would bore me, and you, to tears," she grinned, his energy flowing through the inches between them to ignite her own. "Yet it appears that by marrying me you've been held in higher regard than you were previously. Perhaps it would be a good opportunity to show Charleston that you aren't a gloomy specter in the dark."

"Modest little wife, aren't you?" Royal scathed gently, his handsome smile fading. More like it would be an opportunity to gawk and have a spectacle, he thought. Then his eyes at last took note of the unmistakable signs of worry that marked her own. "How did it go at your father's?"

"Not well." Josephine pursed her lips. "I managed to scavenge a few of my things, but not my relationship with him. He said not a word to me, could not even look at me. I'm worried about him, Royal, though my affections for him are not what they should be. Our marriage is causing him to suffer. It looked as if he were preparing to sell his modest furnishings, which makes me suspect that he owes Seymour a great deal of money and that he shall be hard pressed to find a way to return it. I remember how angry I was with him that day just before we went to St. Phillip's," she mused. "And though I know that I am unable to live my life at his fancy, I cannot help but pity him. I think he's always done another's bidding. I'm not certain his lot in life has come simply by his choices alone."

"There is naught you can do about another's life, only about your own," he murmured, cradling her head upon his shoulder as he stooped to accommodate her. "Are you regretting marrying me, princess? Is that what you are saying?"

"Captain Ashhurst, you are unbalanced and fishing for compliments."

"I already know that you want me," he scoffed smoothly. "In fact, I recall you making sweet little moans just last eventide that stated something to that effect..."

"Stop it," she blushed. "When is this extravaganza at the Montgomery's? I don't have anything proper to wear..."

Royal had begun nibbling the side of her neck, his hands boldly reaching to her bottom and pulling her hips forward to grind against him. His kisses burned her skin as they slowly worked towards the corner of her mouth, the weak, absentminded pleasures he evoked in her making any sort of reason fade into garbled chaos.

And then he laughed, a rich strain to his tenor that Josephine had not heard before somehow a comfort. The constant darkness that seemed to bleed from the sea captain's disenchanted spirit even when he smiled for once seemed to scatter beneath the light in his eyes. "You will have it by the time of the gala, come hell or high water, and be the most stunning sight any of them have ever seen," he avowed. "Lord knows I will have my hands full keeping the vampires at bay, for they will be waiting to feed upon you while I am encumbered with the drudgery of managing your ex-fiancé."

Butterflies flitted through her stomach at the thought of seeing Carter Seymour anew. Though there had been times Josephine swore he could recognize her beneath the shroud, no situation had ever gone awry whilst she hid at Kirkpatrick's bordello. But now things had changed. Even though Josephine had thought many times of how eventually she would meet him once more, the thought of giving him his just desserts all over again in such an ostentatious manner was as unsettling as it was promising. But she had to be more reserved, more dignified. Even if Charleston was a roiling, bustling seaport, it had an aristocratic air, and Josephine knew how delicate the line of propriety really was.

She wanted the best for her husband, and herself, and she had the sense to realize that any sort of rash behavior was bound to do more harm than good. Fate had given them plenty of that. "Royal, promise me that if it appears a scene is brewing on the horizon you will have the good common sense to control your temper or vacate the premises. I suspect that the Montgomerys and their guests will not be impressed by any sort of cross masculine temperament."

"Oh, ye of little faith," Royal smiled, which reassured her not all.

* * * * *

Feathery streams of cloud lingered in the amethyst and rose painted sky, with but a golden glimmer atop the insurmountable plumes as Seymour stepped onto the docks. He took leave of the *Sundown Too* and cast a wary eye to the dotted whale oil lamps as they were being lit farther up Front Street. Their warm welcome reflected across the soft hues of the buildings in the row, the graceful sweep of oak and palm amid the soft wails of the gulls an ointment to his fevered brain. He rubbed at his sore eyes, his body tense with the anticipation of uncovering what had transpired in his absence.

Sleep was beckoning him; he'd shared but a few fretful hours with her during the sail, and he was loathe for her company again. Nay, he would not find rest until he had taken care of the unfinished business he had with Josephine Adelaide Beckham. One night with his length slammed inside of Josephine would go a long way towards alleviating the stress he carried cramped between his shoulders.

First, he would punish her. And perhaps after he had found his release he would beat her again, for Josephine needed to be shown the error of her ways and feel a sliver of the humiliation she had so foolishly bestowed upon him.

The streets were quiet as he wound his way towards the Beckham residence, his feet crunching on the shell and soil lane. Heavy scents of blooming flowers were borne on salty breezes that tenderly lifted his shaggy hair and calmed his tenuous senses. The divided land of the *Grand Modell* slipped away as he continued on, until the door he sought loomed darkly before him. A lone candle shone in the window.

Seymour knocked harshly, the rap of his knuckles loud in the serenity of the night. He heard the shuffle and ill-placed movements of the clerk before the door was swung open to admit his entrance.

The room was bleak and empty, with only but the most necessary of amenities. Seymour learned everything he needed to know with one look into Michael Beckham's whimpering eyes. It was not unlike a sight he'd seen in his slaves. Pure, unadulterated desperation.

"Where the hell is she?" Seymour roared, his hand lashing out and twisting a fistful of Beckham's coat. He shoved Michael to the side, his eyes wild as they looked down at Josephine's father. "Has she departed?"

Beckham sniveled and wiped at the fearful tears that slid down his cheeks. He knew to speak no other than the truth; and what did it matter, for everyone knew. Seymour was a jumble as Michael had never seen him. Greasy clumps of hair hung loose, his clothes malodorous and soiled.

"Nay, she has not, Mr. Seymour," Michael coughed. "I shall repay you every piece of eight, I swear it—"

"Where is she, if she is not dead, Michael?" Seymour demanded, feeding on the other man's fear and weakness. "Where is your daughter?"

"I have no daughter any longer," Michael wheezed. "I have disowned her, Mr. Seymour…"

"Why, you ignorant fool?" Seymour raved, the veins in his neck bulging, the pulse through them hot. He kicked one of the crates between them to the side, the sound of splintering wood echoing through the chamber. "Damn you, what has she done?"

"She has married, Seymour," Michael cried as Seymour towered over him, a silhouette against the pale light of the sputtering candle.

"Who?" Seymour's eyes seemed to shine in their fell nature as time suspended. "Who shall die this night?"

Beckham felt his stomach turn to water as Seymour's hand strayed to the flintlock and then the gleaming dagger at his sullied belt. Beckham felt a warm wetness down the leg of his own breeches, and he wept with horror and shame. "Captain Ashhurst," Beckham sobbed. "He has taken her as his wife."

Seymour's heart stopped beating for the briefest of seconds, his skin turning cold as he glowered over the clerk. His vision tunneled, his gut twisted. "Nay, it cannot be," he breathed.

"Yes, it is true," Beckham moaned, the shadows on the wall preternatural as they melded before him, the blows upon his body and the cries he emitted because of them secondary to Seymour's own muffled sobs. "I tried to have it annulled, Seymour, yet Ashhurst has testified to the consummation—"

Beckham never had the chance to finish his sentence. Seymour fell upon him, the crazed path of his arm as he slashed downward black and severe against the bare wall where none bore witness save the heavens.

Minutes later Seymour stumbled his way blindly towards his single house, the thin light of the moon urging the darkness to follow. Quietly deceptive sounds of an alley cat on the prowl rustled hedge and shrub, the sprinkling of dying blossoms to the earth a whisper upon night's breath that was swallowed whole by Seymour's tormented soul.

Josephine…his dear, beautiful Josephine—he could see the slight tilt to her regal head as she cast a look over her shoulder, the slim length of her arm and the way her hand was shaped as it cradled a teacup. He had searched for her, hired bloodhounds to follow her scent that by ill-fated chance had been washed away during the storm. He had been shamed before the eyes of Charleston aristocracy because of her, and still he would have accepted her, given her everything.

Now, Seymour mused in agonized cycles, the pained thoughts of her in the embrace of Royal Ashhurst making him reel, the steps and then the looming foyer of his mansion an unholy sort of prison, she would need to be destroyed. He said not a word to his butler as he barged through the door and went straight to his chambers, peeling off the blood-stained clothes and hiding the articles beneath his bed. The reek of his body odor transferred instantly to his new garments, but Seymour paid no heed. Bathing was too much of an effort; he had too much to do. He would find out everything about Josephine Beckham and Royal Ashhurst. He would make her pay for her dissent. Josephine could rot in hell in the arms of her devil lover.

19

Curling wrought iron gates were opened wide in welcome as Charleston's upper crust celebrated in true fashion the coming-out of one Regina Montgomery. It was not nearly so lavish as what many had attended in London or otherwise, but all remarked it was pleasant to see some sort of genteel activity taking place in such a barbarous and civility-barren land. The last coming-out party was for the dowdy Samantha Claybourne almost two years ago who had been a less than charming sight to see. It was a breath of fresh air to all after the tension surrounding Blackbeard's storming of the harbor, and it wasn't long before the Montgomery girl's coming-out had turned into a colony-wide excuse to let off a little steam. Relaxed old Clinton Montgomery was simply happy that he hadn't suffered too badly from the pirates and that his hospitality was destined to be the talk of the town for months.

"Are you certain you wish to do this?" Royal asked, noting the pallor of his wife's skin as they walked toward the eminent threshold. "We can still go back, princess."

"I will not allow the asinine privileged of Charleston to get the best of me, and I am going to prove it to them all tonight, Captain Ashhurst. Quite frankly, I am proud of you and our marriage. If they do not like it, then they can all go to hell."

"I hope you control your tongue better than that," he said mildly, touched by her vehemence on his behalf even as he shook his head. The bawdy little lass had actually told him to watch *his* mouth. She had been spending entirely too much time with Kingsley.

Josephine took a deep breath and squared her shoulders, looking everywhere but the ground as Royal led her up the staircase to the main door, open like the rest to catch a bit of the cooling breeze. The drone of voices echoed from the back courtyard, crowded as it was with the larger than expected number of guests. She smoothed a wayward hand across the softness of her deep blue silk gown, still reeling from the richness of it since he had presented her with it that morning.

Regina Montgomery was dazzled by all the attention. A willow of a girl with glossy brown hair and a ready smile, she greeted each of her attendants with a regal nod. Her youthful, dreamy eyes strayed to Royal in the twilight, her shoulders straightening as she extended her hand boldly. Her father stood unfaltering nearby, his peculiar gaze encompassing and probing all who met his offspring.

"Captain Ashhurst, I'm so glad you could make it," she supplied, altogether ignoring the woman upon his arm, and Josephine snapped her mouth shut before a snide retort could find its way out. Though perhaps only four years Regina's senior, Josephine felt far older and seasoned when she looked into the younger girl's eyes. She was also feeling strangely moody lately. Josephine had to remind herself of that.

Neither did she miss the twinge of surprise in her husband's face, for Josephine suspected such a greeting had never come his way, and it was this more than anything else that kept her silent. "I've heard the terrible story of what that filthy pirate did to you, and I have to say I speak on behalf of everyone here when I say that we are immensely grateful to you and the way you managed to bring about a peaceful resolve to the whole affair."

Royal highly doubted that everyone would be as grateful as the bubbly Regina Montgomery was, but he bowed unassumingly nonetheless and murmured a word of thanks for her kindness. "I see you have weathered the storm quite well, so to speak," the girl pressed further. "Word has it he had delivered quite a harsh punishment—"

"Regina," came her father's stern voice.

"It is quite all right, Mr. Montgomery," Royal supplied. "I am still in some pain, but I am also on the mend and certainly shall survive Blackbeard's achievement." His eyes gleamed as he watched Clinton Montgomery look from him to his wife with barely concealed astonishment even as he knew this was bound to cause a thrill among onlookers. "If I may introduce my wife, Josephine."

"I have had the pleasure of seeing you before, Mrs. Ashhurst," Mr. Montgomery said. "If I recall correctly, it was during a sunny morning at St. Phillip's."

Josephine saw Royal's cheek flex involuntarily, and though her own insides gave a subconscious squeeze, she kept her head tilted up and a smile upon her face. "Why, yes, Mr. Montgomery, that was a beautiful sunny morning indeed—and made all the more beautiful by the fact that the same day I was fortunate enough to meet my husband. He makes me exceedingly happy, and I don't quite know what I would do without him." *There, put that in your pipe and smoke it*, Josephine thought.

"Then it is a fortunate turn of circumstances, indeed, that has brought us all together this eventide," Montgomery acquiesced. His own eyes held a measure of respect for the slip of a girl who stood so boldly before him. It was clear that she was standing in open defiance of her public shame and of any confutation that may be aimed her way because of it. And he could full well understand the arrogance written in Ashhurst's eyes. He had to admit, the man had gained a trump in the deep-rooted war with Carter Seymour. Clinton Montgomery was, after all, every bit the ruthless sort of businessman who could respect the same trait in others.

"Please, enjoy yourselves. There is dancing in the garden, and at the striking of eleven bells, captain, I would be honored if you would join us in the parlor for brandy and cigars."

The couple nodded and Regina Montgomery reluctantly stood back to allow them entrance. Josephine's lips curled at the corners as they walked away, still feeling the girl's impious glances at Royal's back even though she could not see them. "And the ladies will be in the garden for a showing of new dresses by Miss Twyla," Regina piped in so cheerily Josephine felt her mood soften slightly.

Time seemed to stand still, like everything else, as Josephine followed Royal into the courtyard. The orange glow from the sconces that regally stood guard at the breezeway cast a warm hue across the elegantly curved moldings of the double house. The highlights of her copper hair were set ablaze, the skin of her shoulders a succulent peach. She stood proudly, her eyes not fleeing from any dismay nor lingering upon those who beamed with interested reverence. She may have committed a crime of scandal, but Josephine had not regretted it then nor did she regret it now.

She only prayed that Royal didn't, either.

Royal watched the men of the crowd survey his wife, and though he found most of their looks objectionable, it was for entirely different reasons than scandal. Subconsciously his hand strayed to hers. Half of the eyes fell away immediately. "Vampires, all," he murmured to himself, though the corner of his mouth twitched.

Soft strains of violins drifted across the yard, blending with the merry socialization of the colonists and the mumble of slipping fabrics. A disseminating moon grinned enigmatically at them from between the robes of the cosmos; it was all too easy to imagine that the world was little more than this condensed space, that the only tribulation one could face would be the heat that infringed with the coming dawn.

"Ah, I spy someone I would like for you to meet," Royal said, leading her to where a dark-haired man stood in deep conversation with a graying merchant. "Josephine, if I might introduce you to John Rembert, secretary to the governor. He is an upright soul and a good comrade to have on your side."

The gentleman, for he was of obvious stature even before the formalities were exchanged, was quite handsome in what Josephine could only describe as an intellectual sort of way. He held dark russet eyes that burned with a delightfully curious intelligence, although this, too, was mediated by a calming, stalwart charisma that radiated from him without a word. Josephine could tell instantaneously that John Rembert was honest, and she warmed to his no-nonsense disposition straight away.

Rembert could see full well why Ashhurst had done what he had. John had been curious as to what type of woman could have motivated such passions, and after meeting her, he could better understand. "Very pleased to meet you, Mrs. Ashhurst," Rembert greeted, taking her hand and bowing to touch his forehead to it. "You look stunning this even-tide."

"Why, thank you," she replied politely, and responded in kind. "With all this merry-making, it seems hard to believe that not even a month ago we were all but prisoners enslaved to Blackbeard."

"You are correct about that, madame," Jonathan replied with a nod. "But a busy month indeed all the same and all around the table, I'd haz-ard guessing."

They made small talk for some time, and while at ease, Josephine kept getting the feeling Royal's mind was somewhere else, that he was waiting for the hour to pass so he could speak privately with the secre-tary. What he could possibly have to say that he couldn't in the presence of herself she didn't know, but it made her mood sour once again.

She was no simple-headed wench! Sudden frustrations stung at her eyes but Josephine kept a calm mask on and held them at bay. Men had their silly ways, but she wanted to be more to Royal than just the sensual woman in his bed and on his arm, the skewer with which to lance Carter Seymour. She wanted him to respect her as a friend and an ally, too. He had seemed to respond to that instinctively at first; but now with more time and heated nights between them, Josephine thought of how the very hottest flames burned quickly. Wood that burned brightly extinguished itself rapidly to smoldering ashes that just as quickly grew cold.

But she loved Royal more and more every day, feared it as much as she embraced it for the erudition it offered. Her interests in investing had waned or were focused in another direction. Josephine wanted to sup-port her husband, and a curiosity of sailing had now evolved into a pas-sion though she had yet to step foot aboard a craft. She wanted to help him with the tedious work of his affairs so he could focus on other things.

As Royal talked with Rembert, Josephine remained mostly silent, offering a friendly nod every now and again in response to those who had deemed her worthy of the attention. She found it hard to relax and, after awhile, gave up trying.

The tolling of eleven o'clock shook her out of her trance-like rumi-nation. It was then that Josephine realized subconsciously she had been awaiting Carter Seymour's arrival and in Royal's presence that did not seem too terrible. Her nerves tingled, propelling the occasional series of bumps to rise upon the skin of her forearms despite the energy that swathed the party-goers. The music paused and the pleasantries between man and woman momentarily concluded as the sexes separated, and Royal inevitably left Josephine to her own devices. Just as she was prepared to set herself quietly in a corner of the garden and watch the people, thus curtailing her boredom and her fears, a friendly beacon of light shone upon the bleak horizon in the form of one Bradley Harding.

Not every male had adjourned to the study—some by lack of invite, others because they preferred to take a sampling of the feminine virtues that had attended the party in droves. Brad had just made his appearance for the evening, in company with his fiancée Rose and her mother, Lady Orchid.

The threesome was handsomely dressed from head to toe; Brad in a dark maroon silk waistcoat and breeches, and his fiancée in a pale yellow conservatively cut evening dress. Lady Orchid kept her silver-streaked hair primly secured in a severe bun. She wore a crisp, gray ensemble that served to make her look older than she was but was elegant just the same.

Josephine's broad smile beamed at the troupe across the grounds, and with a mischievous grin, Brad lifted his hand in greeting as he made his way toward her. He could sense the appreciation in her even from a distance, and his heart went out to her even though he knew that Josephine was well and able to handle herself better than most anyone would anticipate.

Lady Orchid, who went by that and answered to nothing else, bestowed a derisive look upon him as they approached Josephine. She was a proper sort of lady, direct from London, and even though her bloodlines were far from blue, she was as talented at putting on airs as any aristocrat should be.

Rose, on the other hand, met her with a warm smile. At first jealous of Josephine's relationship with her fiancé, it had taken time to put the girl at ease. But once accomplished, she had become a dear, casual friend. Rose was sweet-tempered and, in Josephine's memory, had never had anything ill to say about anyone. She was a bit of a mouse in her mother's shadow, Josephine surmised—but better that than to be a domineering old witch. She thought then of meeting Brad on the stairwell at Kirkpatrick's, and though she felt like giving him a kick right then and there all over again, it was not her concern.

"Josephine, you came," Brad said excitedly, his pale eyes shining in the dark. "I bet that will put all those imperial dogmatists on their ear. Good for you."

"Yes, Miss Beckham, quite the surprise," sniffed Lady Orchid, her eyes narrowing even as she touched the arm of her charge as if to ward off any evil spell that Josephine may cast. "That an invitation was extended, that is. Apparently Regina Montgomery needs a little instruction as to who is fitting company and who is not."

Rose's cheeks tainted a rosy hue and she bit her lower lip, her eyes averting to the side. "Mother, Miss Beckham is now Mrs. Ashhurst," the timid little thing ventured. "She married the captain a few weeks ago."

Josephine felt like cheering. With Rose and Brad's own wedding approaching, it was clear the girl was at last finding a footing of her own. Before Lady Orchid had a chance to cut her daughter to the quick, Josephine spoke. "And I'm certain you are looking forward to your own married condition," she smiled warmly. "The beginning of September, if I recall correctly?"

Rose beamed. Lady Orchid frowned. Brad kept a calm smile but his eyes twinkled at Josephine. He was as anxious as anyone, as he had put it once, "to rescue his little flower from wilting" under her mother's rule.

"I'm very sorry I missed your nuptials," Brad said softly. "I bet you were a sight to see. Congratulations, darling, and you have my best wishes. Married life agrees with you. Isn't it fantastic the way the right pairing can make all the difference in the world?"

Lady Orchid opened her mouth, and then it snapped shut to a thin line. Disapproval marked heavy lines in her aging skin. Josephine didn't think she could count even one laugh line.

"Ladies, and the gentlemen remaining, if I could have your attention, please," Regina Montgomery's voice rang a lilting alarm. "If we could all gather round and give Miss Twyla our utmost attention. She is going to be sharing with us the latest fashions direct from Whitehall, and as a special treat for our gentlemen attendants, the latest rages sweeping St. James."

If this was civility, Josephine thought, her eyes straying to the house, then she didn't want it. Not at all.

"Have you had the misfortune to cross paths with Seymour yet?" Brad whispered in her ear. Josephine didn't turn to look at him, but her skin chilled just the same. "I saw the light on in his study yesterday, so I gather he has returned from North Carolina."

"Nay, though I suppose he has received an invite here," she murmured. "Do you think he is aware of my marriage?"

"I wonder if Seymour is aware of much of anything," Brad replied. "I have been watching him out of concern for you, Josephine, and I fear that his grip on sanity has slipped. He looked downright despicable, as if he hadn't bathed in weeks. And he paces. Endlessly. Something worries him, and more than just you, I'd surmise."

"I wonder what his genteel friends would say about that," she smiled, though it did not reach her eyes. "And thank you, Brad, for keeping your eyes peeled. Something is going on that has not been disclosed to me, but it is something significant, I'm certain. Royal has been very tight-lipped and preoccupied as well."

"Well, I am going to continue keeping my eye on him, at least until his curious behavior has mediated," Brad soothed, patting her hand as the lovely Miss Twyla came by toting a bundle of fabric. Josephine politely fawned over it before the seamstress moved on. The descriptions of the material and design were lost on her but she kept up appearances anyway. "You may extend an invitation to your husband to pass by my stoop at any time he may need."

"I'm certain he will wish to take advantage of the situation," Josephine said, though she wondered if there would ever be a time she could mention it.

20

Royal had pondered all evening as to how much he should relay to John in regards to the secret correspondence he had received. Even though he did trust the secretary—for without him, Royal knew he certainly wouldn't be in the standing he was presently—Royal had sworn vengeance, and vengeance he would call his own. He did not think that Rembert would look too highly upon his mannerisms in the pursuit of it, but he would not be swayed and had said nothing of his ideas to anyone except Kingsley, who was busy guarding the fort on Tradd. He had come last night as soon as the *Sundown Too* was seen in the harbor.

"Your wife is very plucky," Jonathan commented as they crossed the grounds, leaving the open breezes and flowered air to the feminine sector as they headed for a smoke-sated drawing room that was bound to play havoc with his nose. "She seems unbothered by what cannot be the warmest of welcomes."

"Josephine is a fighter, stronger than any woman I've ever known," Royal replied without hesitation. "She has taken what has been given with more aplomb one would expect a courtly woman to be capable of."

"I understand Seymour is back in Charleston," Rembert mentioned. "Got back late yesterday from what I hear. From what I could construe, he was preoccupied to say the least and I also understand he could very well make his appearance tonight. In fact, I'm almost surprised I haven't seen him. I didn't think that Carter Seymour would ever miss the chance to be in the middle of a social circle."

"I wonder if perchance he has heard of my marriage yet," Royal smiled, unshaken. "Whilst I am not keen on having any sort of skirmish with him here, I would not find the opportunity to insert the hooks a little deeper into his flesh amiss. Seymour is walking a very thin line, John, and a very stunted one as well. I wonder how long it shall take before he is pushed to the end of it."

If Rembert questioned his meaning he said nothing; he was hailed by an officer of the court just before entering the house and he bade Royal to continue on without him.

Royal's spine tingled as he entered the Montgomery drawing room. The dark wood and green wallpaper were crowded closely with thirty bobbing heads; a myriad of wigs and canes stood catching evening's glow through the nine-over-nine panes. His face was a smooth, calculated mask as he looked every man who took his notice in the eye. Several backed away, disdain upon their countenances; minutes passed amongst whispers, until at last someone spoke to him.

"Captain Ashhurst, good to see you about," said Josiah Sandall, his eyes twinkling as he extended his hand. "And congratulations, I hear, are in order."

"Thank you, Mr. Sandall," Royal nodded, a slight twitch of a smile catching the corner of his mouth. Sandall had remained a true supporter at every turn and he would not forget that. "I realize my marriage announcement has been a shock, but we are quite happy."

"Quite happy? I daresay, the devil is always happiest when luring the innocent," came the retort from the man to Sandall's right, a slave runner named Russell Reid. He stood two heads shorter than Royal but he still managed to look down at him over the bridge of his nose, his hands clasped together amid a pile of lace ruffles behind his back. "You do realize, captain, that your bride has been a public disgrace from the moment she began screaming like a shrew at her farce of a wedding to Seymour. Then she disappears, was kept hidden from her family and public knowledge by you—and you betray not a word of it to anyone!" He smiled prudishly, a sneer in his voice. "Now her father has disowned her and because of you, Captain Ashhurst. If you were wise, you would consider leaving Charleston immediately. I doubt anyone here would believe a word you have to say."

"Your ties show all too well, Reid," Royal replied, keeping his voice even though he raged to strike the pompous ass down for what he said about Josephine, the thought of the pure pleasure it would bring him a zest upon his lips; yet he stayed his hand. He smiled unexpectedly. "Though I wonder how quickly you will seek to sever those ties."

"Mr. Reid is correct," charged Lockwood, poised with a cigar butt inches from his lips, the loose smoke wavering from the mass humdrum. "I don't know why we should entertain a phrase. You've certainly lived up to your reputation, Ashhurst."

"That is twice you have asked me to expect your apology, Lockwood," Royal said. "I'll not have a third."

"What's this all about?" queried a round-faced merchant, smoothing out his waistcoat as he stood, having overheard the fracas and ready to contribute his twopence. "Captain Ashhurst made a chivalrous sacrifice for our city, counsel, one that I'm of a mind I would find hard to give; and so, Geoffrey, would you. And at least the man did the right thing by her." He stuck out his hand, and Royal shook it readily. "You chaps can't say it wasn't just a bit obscene the way Seymour raved about her. She's young enough to be his granddaughter, and I have a sweet little one of my own," he added with a snort and a swill of brandy. "My name is Leonard Jones-Vendrame, son, and I tip my hat off to you."

"There is much more to this story than I think merits repeating at the present time," Royal volunteered, indifferent to the disparagement aimed his way. "But regardless, the deed has been done, and I would think that those of esteem here in South Carolina would have something better to discuss than my personal affairs."

"There is a war brewing," said another merchant, his eyes already turning bleary from a vigorous consumption of spirits. "Anyone who may know anything about Blackbeard or Bonnet would do well to speak of it or find themselves incriminated along with them when the time comes."

"If you think that I went through every manner of hell on behalf of you and yours for nothing, sir, then you are gravely mistaken," Royal scoffed dryly, the criss-crossed wounds of his back intrinsically itching. "And I learned quite a bit of useful information that has been relegated to those of proper authority. Believe me, sir, if anyone of this colony does have ties to the pirates, you can rest assured their necks will stretch upon the gallows as is fit."

And that was how the conversations continued. Lord, he didn't know how he would survive this night, thinking that he would almost rather be back among the rats and stench of the privateer ships than among all this crass falsehood that seemed to pervade the upper-class. Royal felt his irritation getting the better of him, but he breathed deeply to forestall his short temper from boiling over. After all, he had made a promise.

From across the room Jonathan Rembert watched Royal through disguised lashes. He could sense a change in the sea captain, had not missed his veiled allusions over the course of the night. The angry, harsh lines to his face had smoothed, the glow in his aquamarine eyes less suspect and more—Rembert couldn't put a name to it. Knowing and wise, perhaps. Like he was playing the world for a fool, and the universe did not have the grace and decency to realize it yet.

Rembert had noticed, too, that the reception he himself was receiving had apparently been mediated for his unlikely support of the resident evil of the colony. Mr. Bartholomew Hort, who had always been a little pretentious but certainly respectful, had refused to look him in the eye as he greeted the secretary with cool indifference. And Russell Reid, who was deep in Carter Seymour's pockets or vice versa, was shooting pointed looks in his direction. John never failed to marvel at the speed with which news traveled; but he was of a mind that Seymour very likely would say nothing of Rembert's investigation, unless it was in some offhand attempt to squelch it—and Seymour, despite his threats, knew better than to try to tamper with him, or should.

Nerves caused a line of hair across the back of John's neck to stand up as he thought of the slow-burning fuse he'd ignited. He knew that Seymour would not receive the notice of his pending litigation until tomorrow but the anticipation of what would soon follow had begun to stir in his gut. John Rembert was not a man who shied at the first signs of a battle, nor did fear overtake him in the heat of it—and that was why he had the job that he did. But this situation was explosive, unpredictable—and very likely could set off a chain reaction that reached far deeper than anyone could have guessed.

Seymour was guilty of the crimes Ashhurst accused him of. This was something Rembert was convinced of now. The most baffling part about it to John was the sloppy, blatant way Seymour had pulled strings to oust Ashhurst from Charleston society. Rembert couldn't understand why Seymour would have been confident that his ruse would lie undiscovered, considering the nature of the deception. Was his ego so great that he felt invincible? Or was it the years that had passed in between that had made him so lax? Rembert was of the notion that power was a fragile, fickle thing and not to be assumed. The greatest of kings and lords had fallen over the simplest of matters, and Seymour was not nearly so celebrated as any of these.

The judge that had banned Royal from any further investigations or access—well, John had discovered that he had died not even four months ago, and with him any possibility of revealing what he may have known.

Carter Seymour's level of respect from the colonists was waning. His embarrassing scene with Josephine Beckham and now her very public marriage to Captain Ashhurst had put all sorts of curious eyes upon him, and he didn't look good, not at all. Rembert figured his business assignment in North Carolina could very well have been an excuse to escape his shame. Doing business of a sudden now in North Carolina was idiocy by his measuring stick, for control of pirate activity was far more lenient there than in Charleston.

Yet now he had returned and had stayed closeted in his house on Meeting Street, though his spies had been quite active from what Rembert's own peeks had told him. Sweaty and malnourished, sullied and untidy Seymour had swayed up the steps to the single house before locking the darkness out, or in. Rembert almost felt sorry for Carter Seymour—the slow demise of a soul was an unpleasant thing to behold, whether it be justified Providence or not.

* * * * *

"The smoke in here is beyond reproach and I can't tolerate it any longer," John commented wryly. Royal agreed, finding it an excellent excuse to vacate the mind-numbing and tiresome talk that was only bound to be rehashed at the council meeting on the morrow. The clock tolled in a lengthy fashion as the hands snuck to midnight, and the rowdiness from outside had increased tenfold with every quarter hour that passed. A few groups of men still stood in stodgy deliberation, and though Royal had tried to escape discreetly, he had found himself waylaid and was simply thankful that John was there to add some measure of intelligence to the conversation.

Royal sighed heavily when they reached the courtyard. He had every intention of locating his wife, but he found his strategy foiled by the elderly Mr. Amerson, a wealthy planter from Barbados. The aging Mr. Jack Amerson had been studying new forms of rice planting in his spare time and was ready to debate the subject with just about anyone who would listen, swearing high and low that if the colonies wanted to utilize their natural surroundings, then rice planting was the future for Charleston and her plantations. Royal didn't argue with him, and in fact found his ideas to be sound and promising; but he was not a cultivator and neither did he have interests of that sort.

He leaned back against the rough stuccoed brick wall that enclosed the social event, careless of the draping resurrection fern and passion flower that crushed beneath the weight of him as he tried to concentrate on what was being said. Yet time and again the azure intensity of his gaze flitted back to Josephine across the lawn as she laughed up into the face of her debonair dancing partner. Surprised that she was dancing at all, let alone having a good time of it, Royal watched with cagey concern.

Soon he was staring outright and still she took no notice of him, enamored as she was apparently by whatever anecdote the flaxen-haired lad was feeding her. The boy was obviously enraptured by her radiant smile, and Royal's annoyance was spurred further as the young man grew bolder. His hand casually slipped from her shoulder to the small of her back, and though it was but the faintest of actions, Royal could see the gentle motion to his wrist, a barefaced indication he was caressing her.

"So what you've discovered from your man Kingsley is that Blackbeard has plans on mooring off the North Carolina coast?" Mr. Amerson was saying, attempting to draw him back into the conversation. "Captain Ashhurst?"

"Excuse me," was all Royal said, leaving the man abruptly with no answer to his question and a bewildered look upon his face.

Josephine wondered if the smile on her lips looked as false as it felt. The chap James had insisted on two dances in a row, and even though the ring that adorned her finger shone as brightly as the stars, he seemed to have taken no notice. Her thumb absently toyed with the wrap of leather on the underside that kept it in place on her hand. She had begun to suspect that he was deep in his cups by the way he kept lurching forward, almost using her as a post with which to steady himself rather than a dance partner. When she dropped the obvious hint by mentioning her husband would be awaiting the next dance, he had only kept a firm hand upon hers and told her how beautiful he thought she was, his eyes moving persistently to the swell of her breasts.

Now his hand was at her back. Couples were twirling around them, and Josephine clenched her teeth against the sensation of being trapped in the crowd.

"Miss Ashhurst, you are like a droplet of dew upon a single blade of grass to a parched wanderer," James gurgled.

"Oh, I'm of a mind that I'm not," Josephine bantered lightly, groaning internally. *No, he couldn't actually be rubbing my back, could he?*

"Miss Ashhurst, you instill a man with a thousand poetries," he blabbed. "Your beauty rivals that of Diana and any other ancient deity."

"Please, sir, you exceed yourself," Josephine ground out, growing agitated.

"May I call upon you on the morrow?"

"No, you may not," came the low, sharp order from behind. "And you would do well to keep yourself away from my wife for the rest of the evening before I decide to take exception to the way you are fondling her with such familiarity."

James paled as he turned and looked up at the dark, towering devil who stood as calm and patient as a coiled snake behind him. He was already outstretching his hand, drawing James's former dance partner into an embrace that stretched the reaches of propriety. "I—I apologize— oh, the dev—I mean, captain, I didn't know she—"

"Obviously," was all Royal said, and he was sweeping Josephine away across the soft grass, his strength and the assured way he led her making the movements feel as if their feet were light as feathers.

She smiled genuinely, a softer action than what her jaw had become sore doing, her eyelids drooping ever so slightly as she relaxed, the feeling of security she felt in Royal's presence adding new spark to the will inside her even though her senses were somnolent. She had wondered if they were to be separated all evening. She was also becoming aware that people were staring and whispering, and several of the other couples had stopped in their own steps to watch.

"Royal, you're holding me a little close," Josephine whispered, not certain if he was even aware of what was deemed appropriate even though she was thrilled at the feel of it, her body becoming fluid with a mind's eye flash of him above her. "People are staring, and they really don't need more to talk about."

"There seems to be some confusion amongst the crowd," he remarked coldly, and for the first time Josephine looked up into his eyes and saw an incensed flame shining brightly. "I seek to remedy that."

Rakishly he drew her even closer. She was nearly touching his chest. Josephine felt the color stain her cheeks and throat. "Royal, please!" she insisted, her voice a hiss in his ear.

He didn't look away from her upturned eyes, but he acquiesced after another long moment, the smile on his lips cruel and callous. "Is that better, Mrs. Ashhurst?" he asked.

"Yes," Josephine managed, the masculine scent of him alluring in her nostrils, the heat of him drawing her spirit irresistibly. Desire was copious on her tongue even as she forced herself to remain focused that there was a throng of people around them and that he was angry with her about something.

She could feel his hands on her, stroking her, rubbing her. Josephine could imagine the pressure of his shoulder muscles as her nails raked them. She tenderly touched the wounds he'd finally allowed her to see. She could feel the pulse of their bodies as they danced the ancient art of passion and tasted the cavern of his masterful mouth.

Then the dance ended, and Josephine blinked several times to clear the fog banked behind her lids. Royal was watching her intently, anger's red glow emitting from the shards of his eyes.

"We're leaving," he ordered lowly. "Now."

"Just a moment, captain," she replied softly. "We have to say our proper *adieus* lest we risk being uncouth—"

"Hell with it," he said, lacing his fingers tightly with hers and pulling her towards the ivy-woven exit with determination. "I will make your apologies tomorrow night at the council meeting."

"You will do no such thing," Josephine argued, her temper stirring as he dragged her along as if she were no more than a temperamental child who had begun to cause a ruckus. "A little decorum, please!"

Royal ignored her.

The darkness of the evening closed in around them as they wound their way through the sandy streets back to Tradd, the flexing of Royal's jaw and the quick pace with which he took his strides the only indications that something was wrong. She made a motion to say something and then decided not to, for Royal was in the oddest sort of moods.

Josephine felt her irritation at his churlish behavior heighten, but when she dug her heels into the ground in order to be contrary, Royal kept right on walking, yanking her back to his side with a snap. Josephine's forehead grew creased with confusion as they entered the office and made their way up the stairs. She had to pick up her feet lest she trip on the steps.

"Royal, what on earth—"

Royal slammed and locked the door to the chamber. Sounds of the night and Ashhurst's presence were all that filled it as he struck a match in the gloom and methodically lit a series of candles on the mantle. With the flick of a wrist, the last wisps of sulfurous smoke evaporated.

"Josephine, look at me," Royal commanded, and instinct responded, her willful thought process just a second too late. He was working fast at the buttons of his vest, the laces of his shirt. His skin glowed by the soft lumens of the candles as he yanked his clothes off with a jerk and threw them to the corner of the room in a twisted ball. His eyes were hot upon her, his arms falling to loose arches at his sides though his shoulders hunched back.

"Smile at me like you smiled at him," he ordered, advancing slowly. Breath rasped in his chest at the frenzied want of her—the way her tiny little body was draped so temptingly in silk and the defiant part to her mouth. Both stirred a savage bestiality in him. "Come, now, princess— let me see it."

"Royal, you're talking nonsense," she bit out, the damp heat between her legs jumping to a pulsing throb as he loomed over her. She gasped with a start when he lashed out a hand to clasp her jaw and tilt her head up, his grip tight but not bruising.

"You find enjoyment in teasing men and mastering them with your charms, don't you?" he scathed, his other hand running a careless knuckle across her nipples. They sprang to life against the bodice of her gown, fire trickling down to her stomach from his touch. At her soft moan the flame in his eyes deepened and his mouth dropped open slowly. "But you like that you cannot master me and, in fact, that the very opposite is the truth."

"Royal, you needn't be jealous," she whispered, hating the desire that burned her from the inside out despite his unpredictable aggression. He just watched her through drugged eyes as his hand began to apply gentle pressure to the curves that ached for just a little more.

"Why? You must be partial to it, for you incite it," he snarled, and then his mouth was upon hers, his tongue lancing her lips apart. Both hands moved to take pleasure in a tight grip on her bottom, then her waist, until he was working at the intricate laces of her ball gown. His kiss was powerfully stirring, his passion thawing her cool reticence as his tongue traced along her lips, spearing into the far recesses of her mouth. Her mouth parted to accept him with a soft cry, the instantaneous weakness in her knees pressing her body to him with unspoken wanton wishes. "Are you thinking fanciful thoughts of me now, princess, when I am but an impassioned monster before you?"

Her rebellious skin was heating beyond conscious comfort. "I cannot resist you, Captain Ashhurst, no matter how I may try," she complained before his kiss deepened until all she could feel and see was him.

When her gown fought against him, Royal did the only thing an enterprising husband could do—he ripped the damn thing from her body. Though Josephine's cry of protest over the abuse to her finery met his ears, he was inspired by the ignoble and carnal desires that washed him with mendacious sweetness and in response he laughed low and rich.

"I shall replace it with a dozen others, princess," he soothed her, nipping at the lobe of her ear as he worked her out of her shift until she was naked in his arms, the gentle swell of her buttocks in his hands. "Yet if I could have my way, you would remain naked as you are in my bed for a lifetime."

Royal moved to sit on the edge of the bed, guiding his wife to her knees before him, the tightness of his jaw and his hands upon her neck sending a pulse of superiority through him. He felt like a powerful, underworld pagan god as Josephine's lips enclosed his swollen member, her wicked tongue lashing fire across the length of him. Her eager hands stroked his thighs, her enthusiastic replies to the pressure of his palms upon her head drugging his senses. Through heavy lids Royal watched as his princess devoured his hardness, licking and sucking him with determined prowess that outmatched any skilled courtesan with her honesty.

Royal panted erotic encouragements in a low sailor's brogue, his hands leaving the tangled wisps of her copper hair to encircle her wrists. She cried out as he yanked her up to straddle him, his primal grunt as he turned and tossed her to her back a violent echo in the room. Then he was pulling her legs apart, his face pressing to the core of her need. His tongue circled her damp folds, his teeth grazing her as he laved her pulsing body.

A coarse finger tantalized just inside, and Josephine's hands clenched the coverlet, her body coming off the bed as she stretched to accept him more fully. Royal's pleasure at her deprivation rumbled to her ears, but he refused to give her more. He merely teased and tantalized her with nearly painful intensity.

"What would you do if I stopped right now, hmm?" he demanded to know between licks. "If I left your sweet center empty? Would you cry for another man to relieve the sultry ache between your legs?"

"Royal, please, now!" she begged. Her body was fluid, screaming for his penetration. Josephine didn't know what she would do, she only knew he could not be so cruel, even though nothing but that shone from his eyes. Panic and need cramped her stomach, uncoiling with a snap as Royal poised above her, her hot taste upon his lips as he caught her mouth with a deep, thrusting kiss.

"You know no man could resist you," he barked, plunging inside, his movements hard and fast. Their bodies seized in the heat, the stabs of pleasure Royal gave her with marked movements primal and raw. His head hung lazily, his back stooped though the grind of his hips pushed against the mound of her unceasingly. His shoulders and chest dripped with sweat as he coiled against her and drove into the sweet core that beckoned him madly. Flowing heat scalded the iron length of him.

"Royal," she screamed as he scooped his arms around her back and lifted her easily to him, upright as he now was on his knees with Josephine's legs around his own. His vindictive eyes drew her, seduced her with their dark serenade.

"Do you like that, princess?" he grunted, bucking against her even as she began to writhe against the pressure building low. "Do you like the way I take you?"

"Royal," she whined, her orgasm slowly, painfully stirring in her thighs. Royal laughed in a low demon's pitch as he bit the side of her neck, sucking the skin with starving lips. Shivers coursed up Josephine's spine, and she felt control as she knew it slip into helplessness and sensual slavery as she could never have imagined. Her body began to thunder, her limbs to shake.

"Royal, my lord, I love you," she was crying. Josephine convulsed upon him, the thick shudder and squeeze of her sheath snapping Royal's possessive control. He groaned a series of lewd phrases before he slammed into his untamed wife with a sequence of jolts and jerks. She was crying, laughing, screaming above him, her nails drawing blood in their wake as they scraped down his shoulders.

"Who do you belong to?" he asked in a pampering tone as he basked in the final waves of her, rolling her hips with his arms around her, holding her flush to him. Josephine had begun to slump, her arms outstretched alongside his neck. Her breasts were swollen and he gently licked at them, patiently awaiting her response. It came in a shaky whisper.

"You, Royal."

"My full name," he insisted, flicking a nipple with a forked tongue. He still rolled. Oh, she could feel the pressure, the wetness that undulated inside. Her legs opened wider and his still iron-hard member reached deeply. "Whom do you belong to, princess?"

"Captain Royal David Ashhurst," she whimpered, her eyes barely open as she looked at her husband. His dark appeal was incredulous, masterful, and somehow so evil at that moment. "The devil of Charleston. I am your wife, yours to hold alone."

"That is correct," he agreed, kissing the bridge of her nose, his hands petting the skin of her back. He reached a finger down to the bottom of her feminine cleft and began to stroke.

"Royal," she simpered with a squirm. "Royal—"

Josephine ached to spread her legs even wider, but she couldn't seem to and the hot twinge of her lower belly intensified. Her lotus flower craved the sword of him greedily, the rippling petals of her flesh sucking at him as she moaned in exquisite sobs. Her cries changed slowly to feminine grunts; her breasts thrust shamelessly into the air. Royal's slick finger moved back to torment the apex of her bottom, teasing at the higher cleft of her backside. Josephine felt powerful now, her fingers roughly clenched in his hair as she took from him what she wanted, the second shock wave coming quick and never ending.

Flushed and drained, Josephine slumped against him. Royal's deep laughter floated to her ears as he gently lifted her from him, her squeals of protest at their physical separation so endearing Royal nearly said it then, his eyes now soft upon the green chips of hers. Then his gaze traveled to her distended and bruised lips. The guilty pang he felt that he may have been too rough with her was comforted by male satisfaction. Her head found its home in the crook of his shoulder, and he inhaled the warm scent of her hair with pleasure.

"No more dancing with men I don't approve of," he chided one last time before stealing a goodnight kiss. "It doesn't agree with my temper."

"I hope you approve of Brad, Captain Ashhurst, for even if you don't, he is my dearest friend and shall forever remain that way," she informed him. "He doesn't step on my toes. And I can count on him to not be…slobbery. And I will have you know, by the bye, he has extended his help in any way he can. He is Carter Seymour's neighbor, after all."

They said nothing for a long time as Josephine cuddled to him, her soft hair draping across his arm. Royal's eyes grew heavy, the slender form of her beside him warm and reassuring in a way that never ceased to amaze him, how comforting and secure it was. Royal sighed deeply, enjoying the moment before he allowed himself to fall into slumber. His dark lashes fell to his cheeks.

It was then that Josephine's soft voice reached his ears, as capricious and saucy as ever.

"Now that you mentioned it, if this is always the case afterwards, Captain Ashhurst, you can be certain I shall fill my card with every manner of rakehell at any moment that proves opportune." She smiled, giggled, and rolled over.

Royal shook his head across the pillow with an easygoing chuckle. That was his princess, he surmised. And he figured that it was more than likely that he wouldn't want her any other way.

21

He sat cloaked in darkness beneath the window, staring unseeing into the misty gloom as he listened. Though they'd had the decency to keep the window shut, every scream, grunt, and moan echoed through those thin panes of glass and floated to settle upon his ears the way the wail of a hurricane at landfall overtakes the beach. He could see within his mind Josephine arching her wayward back, parting her knees to offer up that which men wanted most—that which had belonged to him. The rage, the torment, froze him; the vile sounds of their union intrigued him even as he wished for it to be erased from his memory.

Damn Blackbeard. Damn him straight to hell.

Seymour paid no attention to the ache of his soft calves as they cramped from the pressure of his weight on his haunches. Time slowly ticked by, and still Royal Ashhurst continued to avail himself of the pleasures that Seymour had bought and paid for. Seymour's own hand had brought him release twice already and still the need hadn't been exhausted. Now he knew that Josephine was all harlot beneath her bitchy airs, and he was looking forward to putting her in her place.

One thing Seymour had managed to control was his urge to shoot through the window with the hope he would be lucky. But the risk of killing Josephine before he'd had a chance to sample her wares was too great, and if he missed, Ashhurst would not give him a second chance. Seymour had underestimated Benjamin's son before; he would not make the same mistake twice. He was craftier and more resilient than any other threat he'd faced in his lifetime, and just like Benjamin, his son had that certain spell over people. Now his latest incantations had put Seymour in a bind. He could feel the walls of every room, even the humid air outdoors, closing in around him in a sudden sickening spiral.

Seymour blinked madly. Royal Ashhurst was not a social lord; people did not clamor for his presence like they did for himself. His father had been polished, like Seymour, careful of the way he did things. Royal Ashhurst was a loose cannon, with no idea of how things should be done.

Seymour had spent most of yesterday awaiting word from his couriers as to what Charleston had been mired in, and he hated what each and every one of them had had to say. Seymour sensed, too, that in their fear of him they had spoken softer words than the truth. Mumbled words about his health and his obsession with Josephine Beckham, suspicions about his reaction when he learned of her marriage to his rival. People curious as to whether or not he would show at the Montgomery's gala.

Well, he would show them. He would show them all. Seymour thought that repeatedly as he watched a big hulk of a man emerge from the shadows. The hair on his neck tingled as he recognized the face in the moonlight and the first gray streaks of dawn. Seymour edged himself a little farther away, his skin feeling cold even though the damned heat of his groin burned endlessly. But Carter Seymour wasn't stupid. He knew his eyesight wasn't as good as it used to be, and truth be told, he'd never been a very good aim to start with. No, he would go towards the docks and wait to ambush Ashhurst there.

Like father, like son, Seymour smiled, and hummed a child's tune about a pocket full of posies in his head as he disappeared into the morning mist.

* * * * *

"I will see you at teatime," Royal said, kissing her cheek as she lay snuggled in bed, the first rays of the daybreak creeping in. Josephine's sluggish eyes cleared upon her husband, who had already washed and dressed for the day.

"Leaving me again," she grumbled softly.

"Josephine, I have many things I need to do, and time is of the essence," he replied shortly, his state of preoccupation not mediated by the coming of the morning light. "I know you don't understand, and I cannot explain it, not when I don't know fully myself what to expect. Just trust me, princess—"

"Damn it all, I've grown sore with hearing that," she snipped. "And I'm telling you, I'm not staying cooped up in this house one more day." *There*, she thought contrarily. And if he didn't like it, she would be more than happy to explain the various orifices that he could stuff it.

"You are well aware why you shouldn't be out wandering," he argued, " and you were just out for an evening last night. If Kingsley lets you, not only will I know about it but I'll have his head, even though it is no small source of irritation to me that he's been spending entirely too much time with you. However, I trust him with you, and your safety is more important."

"And I shall continue to be with Kingsley until my husband sees the error of his ways and realizes living in fear every waking moment is tiresome beyond reproach," she replied smartly. "It was you who ordered him to stick to my side, captain, lest you have already forgotten. He has been a marvelously good sport, too—have you ever seen a pirate arranging flowers? 'Tis something not worth missing, I assure you."

"Do not worry, princess, the time is growing near," he hinted, leaning down to distract her in the best way he knew how. "And I wouldn't speak so loudly of flower and fluff in regards to the steadfast pirate I know. Kingsley is below stair." He had enough to worry about, and he didn't have time to explain. The bridge of his nose nuzzled her temple. He knew she couldn't resist that.

"Why? You know something you're not telling me, don't you?" she accused, feeling a wash of heat suffuse her body at his touch despite how she tried to thrust it away. "Not unusual..."

"I don't have time for this," he ground out with irritation. "Trust me or nay, I know what's best for you, even if you're being too proud to see it." He turned from her and did not look behind him.

"Royal, you tell me nothing!" she called to his back.

The door clicked shut loudly in the stillness of the bedroom. Kingsley's dark eyes seemed almost disapproving as he nodded to Royal, and Ashhurst felt his agitation grow at the love he saw for his wife mirrored in face after face.

Why was it women couldn't just accept a man's word? He shook his head, wondering why it was that the feminine segment had to analyze every little thing. He supposed it was because they had nothing else to do, but that wasn't a fault of his. Perhaps that was why he had separated himself for so long from any kind of solid relationship with one—it was so much easier to walk away and wash his hands of it than it was to solve inconsequential problems.

But he also knew he had the wisdom of age, and that even though Josephine was smart, she was not yet experienced and had led an altogether sheltered life despite her difficulties. She had held very little insight into the true world of darkness hidden behind the welcoming porticos and piazzas she'd grown up with.

Royal had to admit, however, as he peered across the street into Carter Seymour's courtyard and stately office window, his wife was a resourceful one indeed. Brad Harding had seemed unperturbed by his early morning visitation and, in fact, seemed eager for it, though the wisdom of secrecy was obvious in his mannerisms.

"Seymour has been sitting in that study since he got back," Brad reaffirmed. "Sometimes I can hear him yelling at his slaves. But he hasn't been there since I got home from the Montgomery's last night."

"Time has run out for Carter Seymour," Royal said quietly.

* * * * *

Seymour waited on the docks until the noon hour approached and still he had not seen the bloody bastard. How could he have missed him in the space of only a few lots? And where the hell was he? Ashhurst had been working on the *Courtesan* as diligently and regularly as clockwork.

Why wasn't he there today? Did he somehow know?

Seymour scurried past the towering masts of brigantines lined up in the slips. People looked at him oddly. He passed Johnny Lee Middleton, and though the man nodded politely, revulsion was scratched deeply in the merchant's countenance, his nose curling at the stench Seymour radiated. Seymour stumbled up the plank of the *Sundown Too*, cursing at the deckhand he crashed into en route. He slammed the door to his cabin and huddled in the blankets of his bunk as he thought of what they were saying about him now, and what they may say tonight. Cold sweat seeped endlessly from his body as Seymour wallowed in his fear.

Hours passed and he barely moved. Seymour watched the descent of the sun and the impending nightfall with a quivering conscience and an ache in his belly, for he could not muster the ability to eat. Noises creaked and groaned above him. The crew was obviously being careless as they went about their duties. He screamed for the seamen to cease their droning labors—but when he went above deck to berate them further, he found the upper levels of the craft deserted.

Madly he paced, hating the docks now, recognizing few. He had to find Ashhurst and kill him now. It was time—past time.

Seymour left the wharf and began to walk up the Bay, turning left to circle the governor's house. People were beginning to congregate; they didn't see him. Thank God they didn't see him, he mused. They were talking about him though. He could hear their voices.

Seymour then went south on Church Street, ignoring the bite of the mosquitoes that enflamed his skin. He went past the Beckham residence, where the silence outside disguised what still lay undiscovered inside.

Carter Seymour's butler found him in his office, a mess of papers and broken art littering the fine carpet as he paced, lost in his vengeance; Seymour was two paces from ordering the man out when he noticed the familiar seal pressed into the cold wax of the rolled parchments in the servant's dark hands. "This came a few hours ago, massah," he said.

Seymour snatched it away and tore it open, his glassy eyes scurrying across the even, slanted script, fear erupting through every pore like the legendary Vesuvius of Pompeii.

> *Mr. Seymour,*
>
>   *I have heard the petition of Captain Royal David Ashhurst in regards to the ownership of Seymour Transport, which as you well know, originally operated under the name of Lowcountry Export, and by inheritance was deeded the share of Benjamin James Ashhurst, who at the time of death held seventy-five percent of the holdings; this portion was to be held in trust for Royal*

Ashhurst until the age of twenty-one. Circumstances being what they were left the enterprise to you. However, the state of affairs surrounding the untimely deaths of Benjamin James and Anne-Marie Ashhurst, and the suspected, rather than proved, death of their only child, left the entire estate in your hands, and this may have been an oversight by the ruling judge.

The legal transcriptions on file that relate directly to this subject are incomplete or otherwise inaccurate; a motion has been filed to re-examine this case and place it in arbitration.

I understand that this will be a difficult situation for you, as well as the other parties involved. I am also well aware of the social repercussions that may ensue, so I have done my best to keep these proceedings under wraps until a decision has been reached.

Thank you for your time and consideration,
J. Rembert, Secretary to the Governor of South Carolina

Carter Seymour looked through the wide-open window to the star-speckled expanse of the velvet sky. Every flickering patch of darkness was a wraith in disguise. The chirrups of the crickets were a thousand cries born on the fluttering wings of the deathwatch. The sweet-smelling air wafted through, though it chilled him and brought him no comfort. The sounds of the butler tidying up for the evening in the other room was the magistrate come to seize him, and Seymour speculated on how this black season had come to pass. He pressed his tired body to the wall for support, his hand searching absentmindedly for the decanter on the shelf next to him, the sickness of his brain sending a tumult of visions to his eyes.

The soft light of the room still cast too many shadows. The warm ocher of the stained, paneled walls, the grain of them fine and smooth, were dancing around him, closing in upon him, splintering into the coarse wood of the gallows. Gilded plant containers held the lush green leaves of a lovely hybrid variety he couldn't even classify now nor seem to recall a time when he could; and though once he had enjoyed such pleasures, now it groaned at him, its petals a wide, searching mouth.

It was then that he made his last scramble for introspection, his hollow eyes looking above the cold fireplace to his portrait. He'd had it commissioned from Marseilles; it was a bold, knightly work of art. The artisan had been extremely kind with the aesthetics, and he used it often for contemplation.

The blade of a dagger was struck directly through his image's heart, the shimmering glint of it so bright he couldn't believe he hadn't noticed it before. And from that lethal blow hung a single tattered parchment, the writ upon it of his own hand.

* * * * *

Royal fumed over his argument with his wife, saying very little to Brad after taking his leave, other than a strict order to keep his mouth shut about his morning visitation, he only alluded to the consequences of what he had done earlier. It still cast a shadow over the rest of his day as he went to the docks, where he heard by word of mouth that Seymour had been seen flitting about the wharfs before he fumbled his way aboard the *Sundown Too*. It didn't take a whole lot of detective work to know that Seymour was looking for him. Seymour stuck out like a sore thumb.

Royal worked quietly inside the *Courtesan* with one eye turned north-easterly through the portal to where the glossy schooner under Seymour's command sat lifeless and unassuming at the other end of the line. An eerie embrace gripped his heart as he stared for long minutes. Nothing seemed to matter in the present but his revenge upon Carter Seymour, and yet it was but the series of those past events that had brought him to where he was now. There were times he'd thought he wouldn't survive or ever find a way to seize this moment.

And he thought, too, of Josephine. His marriage to her would outlast what brewed with Seymour, and far after this moment had come and gone he would still be with her. It was a daunting yet exciting vision.

He opted to let his wife stew in her own wrath and he didn't return home for tea. As the day waned and he saw Seymour leave the docks, he found himself walking towards the solid building of the government offices, the glow of the flickering lamps beside its entrance fueling his own energy anew. There would be hell to pay, and Royal grinned at the prospect.

The welcome he received from the councilmen as they gathered was about as cordial as that he had experienced at the Montgomery's. Royal kept a wicked smile upon his face as he went out of his way to greet those he knew would deride him even as he kept his eyes peeled for any sign of Seymour. Minutes from the last meeting were read, and still the proprietor did not surface.

He could feel John's gaze appraising him from the pulpit as the meeting moved forward and the details of Rhett's pursuit of the buccaneers were outlined. A list of names was read, and when his own was called, Royal cleared his throat.

"I would like more than anything to assist in this endeavor, council, but I'm afraid my duties to my wife and company shall keep me here in

Charleston," he supplied. "However, now that I have the floor, there is something I feel you all need to know about Carter Seymour—"

"Damn you, Ashhurst," came Reid's loud affront from across the room. "The man has been through enough because of you, don't you think? You shall serve to disgrace none but yourself yet again if you think this conversation has any place in this room—"

"Carter Seymour is a murderer and a saboteur, and we all have suffered. Charleston has suffered," Royal cut in, none too softly. Angry stares barbed him from all directions. "Think what you will, gentlemen, but the proof is binding and will show itself here and now." He advanced to the dais in the front of the room, his stride slow yet sure. Ears that had been stretching to overhear the commotion put their reservations to the side and gave Ashhurst their full and forthright attention, their disgust plainly showing on their fine faces. Royal made eye contact with them all, their disdain as voracious as the sea captain's own satisfaction. He slammed down the stack of parchments he held in his shaking hand, commanding respect from all in attendance. The taste of conquest was an agreeable one indeed. Royal's tenor resonated through the room, the echo of triumph a sweet sound he had torn and scratched through his dishonored life for.

"Here, in Carter Seymour's own invective, is a compilation of correspondences to Edward 'Blackbeard' Teach, in which he describes the details of this port of call and alludes to the premeditated kidnapping of Samuel Wragg and his boy."

22

Josephine frowned as she sat across from Kingsley, the closeness of the night air drifting in through the window of Royal's office doing nothing to nurse her mood into better health. The amiable black man would put his arm around her every now and again in silent comfort, and she would return his attention with a squeeze, for despite all piratical appearances, Kingsley was as cuddly as a stuffed bear. His simple reassurances that it would be all right always made her feel better, but even his tender ministrations weren't helping this time.

"Damn it all, that man frustrates me to no end," she swore. Kingsley continued to bob around the room, unbothered by her unladylike fuming even as he kept his eye on the window. It was one of the many qualities that had made Josephine so readily able to endear him as friend. "If he cared about me at all, Kings, he wouldn't disappear with nary a word like he does. I'm not asking for a full-scale recital—just a little common courtesy…"

"Yer worryin' too much, Miss Josephine," he said. "Ash just has a lot on his plate, I'm thinkin'. The *Courtesan* is out of the frame an' *Navigator* ain't got the cargo capacity to do double duty. *Stormchaser* is purty well set in her runs tae England an' wouldn't be havin' the time tae sail to the Caribbean. He turned down a good bit o' pay, though," he grinned, "tae stay in Charleston fer ye."

Josephine paused. Her eyes searched Kingsley's bearded face. "What did he turn down, and why?"

Kingsley gulped, his expression plainly telling her he wondered if he'd overstepped his bounds. Josephine blinked and widened her eyes at him, sighing as she gave him another hug. "Ah, ye doan play fair, Miss Josephine," he chastised. "I'll tell ye, but ye best not be gettin' me in any trouble."

She nodded, and he set her away from him. "Mr. Rembert asked him tae follow Cap'n Blackbeard an' his crew. Ash passed on the offer fer mixed reasons, but from what I can garner it's mainly 'cause he worries fer yer safety."

"Bah, if that were true I would see him more than the few hours between midnight and dawn," Josephine scoffed. "To be honest, sometimes I feel as if he married me out of obligation, and now he regrets his decision."

"Doan think like that, lady," he argued. "He did ask me tae stick tae yer side in his absence, so ye can rest assured knowin' his damned bellyachin' over it is his own order. An' yer a good woman, Miss

Josephine, an' smart, too. I doan think Ash's known too many of those, other 'n perhaps Madame Isabella."

Josephine cleared her throat against the lump of envy and suspicion that blossomed there, anger burning its petty core in her chest. "Yes, I'm certain Isabella Kirkpatrick holds a special place in his heart. One that I'm unlikely to ever touch," she vexed. "I'm guessing she sees more of him than I do, and I bet that makes her happier than a snake in the grass…"

"Yer jealousy is unfounded an' will only push him away, iffen ye doan mind me sayin' so, Miss Josephine," Kingsley replied gently.

"So he can act like a ninny but I can't? That's a double standard if I ever heard one," she sniffed.

Kingsley's arm draped over her shoulders, his friendly hand patting her awkwardly. "There, there, he married ye, after all, Miss Josephine. Ash wouldn't tie himself down lest it was what he wanted; an' if yer worried as tae whether or not Ash will honor his vows, I can assure ye he ain't never gone back on his word that I know of."

Josephine went to the door. Kingsley warned her not to even as she opened it. "It's so terribly stuffy in here, Kings," she complained. Her mind was afoul with frustration. God, what was wrong with her?

"Ye can't be goan out, Miss Josephine," Kingsley's rumble came behind her. "Miss Josephine—"

But she was already out the door, reveling in her own rebelliousness even though she didn't plan on going more than a turn around the block. "It's all right, Kings," she reassured, but his eyes burned with anger as he caught her arm.

"Damn it all, ye can't be wandrin'," he chastised. "Come, now—"

"Get your filthy black hands off of her," cut a voice through the darkness. The pair felt the hair at the back of their necks stand on end as Carter Seymour materialized from the shadows, madness glinting in his eyes like moonlight upon still waters of the harbor. Josephine cursed herself then, felt her fingers go numb at the realization of her folly. "Now, darkie!"

Kingsley pushed Josephine behind his back, his brown eyes simmering from the insult. "Yer gonna regret sayin' that, ye snivelin' pup," Kingsley roared, so unlike the gentle giant Josephine knew that even she felt taken aback. He did not move from his guard, but his hand was slowly moving to the pistol at his belt, an inch at a time. Wise in the ways of battle, the pirate kept Seymour's eyes with his own, his other hand making motions in the dark to divert the merchant's attention. "It was ye that I brought Blackbeard tae meet upon the point! I told Ash ye seemed familiar—"

Whether Seymour saw the burly man's action or his reaction came from unadulterated rage, no one would ever know; but a flash of fire shone in the night, the loud echo of Seymour's weapon as it discharged a bullet into Kingsley's torso and the shudder of the ground as he fell to it remained with Josephine forever.

"No!" she screamed, the world blurring around her as she ran forward, the rashness of her action blinded by the instinct for rebuttal that fed her. Her hands stretched outward, ready to claw the eyes from Seymour's face, when the click of a second pistol stopped her, his criminal laugh pirouetting a ghastly, ghostly dance with the fog.

Josephine stood as still as a deer; her heart pounded erratically in her chest as she stared, wide-eyed, down the barrel of the flintlock that Seymour was leveling on her. She attempted in vain to swallow the lump in her throat, her mouth suddenly dry. His eyes were dark and base, evil revelations emanating starkly from them. Seymour frowned as she began to inch backwards, his head cocking in a dream-like fashion to the side. "Nay, my sweetness, you will not run from me this time," he avowed, his breath a pitiful wheeze. "Such a pretty little bitch you are, Josephine. It is too bad the fact that you are a whore has made you uglier than sin in my eyes."

"Carter, put the pistol down," she advised, her tone shaky even though every fiber of her being was striving to remain calm. He only smiled abhorrently, the wilting jowls of his face barely moving with his lips. "Please, Carter; no good will come of this! You know it as well as I do."

"And why would you think that?" he queried softly, advancing until he was close enough to lift a chunky hand to her jaw, the clammy feel of his palm against her cheek making her skin crawl. His body odor was foul, his breath even more so. There was no shred of the polished social bishop remaining in his appearance. "You were meant to be mine, Josephine. You were meant to warm my bed at night, to writhe beneath me, and to feel the length of me inside you."

His grip became a bruising vice. Tears formed in the corners of her eyes, and Josephine felt the pressure of her teeth scraping against the tender flesh on the inside of her cheek, followed by the distinctive, metallic taste of blood. "Everything in me tells me that I should kill you, my dear," he warned her, brushing an oily kiss along her temple and down to her ear, leaving a sluggish trail of saliva across her skin. His tongue spiked inside the shell of her ear and his teeth bit harshly on the lobe. He chuckled deep in his chest at her soft cry of pain. "Yet I am bewitched by you, despite the fact that you've been soiled by the devil's seed. You still reek of it, Josephine."

"Carter, you've gone mad," she whispered, torn between the choice of resisting or allowing him to have his way. Every part of her urged her to fight, careless of the cost it may be to her physical person. And with that, she wasn't certain that she would be able to forgive herself if she didn't. But none of it would even matter if she did not live through it. Her eyes scanned the lane; not a soul stirred. Her gaze fell upon Kingsley's limp form, a glistening crimson rivulet spreading out across the ground from his side. "If you release me, it would prove that your heart has not been blighted. Things would be easier for you than if you continue down this road."

"Do you not realize that I have sacrificed everything for you, Josephine?" Seymour began to whine, his voice feverish and high-pitched. "I have made arrangements for you to have the finest clothes. I will have nothing served for you to eat that isn't of the freshest quality. I will make certain that there are attendants for your every whim. I will share my riches with you. And yet you still resist. I see it in your exquisite eyes." His mouth curled in a rueful fashion. "I shall break you of that, my black angel. What a pleasure it will be to see your feminine flesh reddened by the paddle, crystal tears of pain shimmering across your face even as you scream for me to punish you more."

"Carter, it has all been lost," she worded quietly yet firmly, the way a mother would to a small child who doesn't understand, doing her best to quell the sick churning of bile in her stomach caused by his overt desires. "It was never really yours."

"Lies!" he raged, his balled fist coming from nowhere to strike her alongside her face. Josephine recoiled from the force of the blow, her lip splitting open. Pearly drops of blood formed in the wake of his assault and stars shone behind her eyelids. Seymour paused, wringing his hand absentmindedly as he watched Josephine touch her fingers to her lips, her expression oddly serene. A long moment passed as he stared at her, his spirit feeling not compunction but the kernel of it.

And then he noticed she was laughing.

It started innocently enough; not much more than a quirk of her mouth, really. Josephine had despised Carter Seymour from the moment she met him, and every day thereafter she had discovered more and more reasons to support her hatred. Yet in that moment, she saw Carter Seymour for the isolated and dismal soul that he was; so consumed with the worldly things of life, he had long ago lost sight of what mattered, leaving naught but a cold, empty husk of a human being. She pitied him then, for the earth must be a bitter sort of hell for him indeed, his beliefs nothing more than exaggerated dreams.

"Avast, Josephine," he growled. His hand was shaking. The flint-lock wavered from her neck down to her waist and back again. She waited in a frightened limbo for him to squeeze the trigger, but still the bubbling laughter came, the sound shallow and void. "Avast, damn you! I'll kill you, I swear it!"

"Nay, Carter, you will not," she managed, surprised herself at how confident she sounded. "You do not have the courage to face what Royal will hand you if you do."

Seymour's face twisted in confusion and he paused, his eyes flickering darkly. "I suppose you are correct in one respect, Josephine," he groaned, his fingers slipping forward inch by inch to circle the barrel of the gun. "I will not kill you. At least, not until I am through with you, my dear—"

His arm swung through the air. Josephine caught but a glimpse as the butt of the flintlock struck her temple, and she knew nothing more.

Seymour breathed heavily through his nose as he wiped the sweat from his upper lip and chin before reaching shakily back to comb what was left of his stringy hair. All around him, the cheerily colored azaleas seemed brighter, more vivid; and then they morphed into a thousand laughing creatures, pointing at him, their horrid little bodies trembling and quaking in their vile jest. He looked down to where his Josephine lay slumped on the ground, her soft copper hair matted with blood.

Heaving from the effort to forestall panic, he hauled her over his shoulder, his field of vision hazy as he espied the empty street. The slam of a door the alley over urged his feet into motion. He could hear the faint echo of voices from the drive, and time suspended as he darted his head this way and that.

The night was hushed with but a crescent of a moon; dull pewter clouds ran out from her in threaded lengths, allowing the astral being to play hide and seek. The wind blew but the softest of breaths across the cheek of Charleston; nary a rustle sounded in the high peaks of the alder and black walnut that decorated the lane. Seymour kept to the shadows, moving slowly as he did with Josephine lying limply across the breadth of his back.

He found his tethered horse, and it took Seymour several attempts to right himself with Josephine upon its back. The horse heaved as Seymour kicked it into action, his hands squeezing Josephine against him. Seymour watched the world shift before him, the trees with their limbs outstretched, moaning with voices of the dead; the cries of the damned beckoned him as he ran to where he knew not, his haunted soul drawn with twisted need.

23

"Cap'n Ashhurst, where's Josephine?" a sailor beseeched as he stormed into the governor's offices, his hands running through his curly mop of hair. He was stopped at the door to the busy room by a tetchy guard. He leaned against the polished wood of the jamb, ignorant of the furrowed stares of those assembled in their fine wigs and cravats. Royal's attention snapped up from the maps rolled out across the table, his eyes locking on the bedraggled visitor in his simple seaman's garb.

"Nicholas, what's wrong?" Royal stood to his full height, his shoulders back. Gawking expressions volleyed through the room in fear and suspicion. "Damn it, man, find your tongue!"

"Kingsley—he's been found not a block from yer stead," Nicholas emitted, his breath hoarse in the silence that followed his intrusion, the shallow resonance of it shrinking the distance between him and Royal. "Yer wife, Cap'n...she's missing...."

Royal's body went as still as life's last gasping breath, his blood rivers of ice. A whisper of disconcertment circled the expanse, its poison cloud touching all who stood near. John's own skin chilled at the look in Royal's eyes, and he knew that any doubt of Seymour's guilt in the whole sordid affair would be all but eradicated by this horrible scene; yet the cost of it was showing plainly in the face of the sea captain for everyone to see.

"Excuse me," was all Royal said, pushing back from the table and staring straight ahead as he strode to the door, the murmur of questions and cries of shock over what was going on raising to the high ceilings behind him.

Rembert gave orders for officers to go to Seymour's house before he and Nicholas gave chase. Royal was already halfway through the next block and the pair ran towards him, sidestepping when they drew alongside to keep up with Royal's stride. "Captain, you don't have to do this alone—"

"He better not have harmed a single hair upon her head," Royal snarled, his cheek flexing, the rage inside him smoldering hotter with every step he took. "Damn it all to hell! Is Kingsley aright?"

"It'll be touch n' go," Nicholas supplied, "but he was able to confirm that 'twas Seymour."

"This is proof positive that Seymour's nefarious dealings have duped him into madness," John said before Royal's harsh, raw voice cut him to the quick.

"Do you think I give a damn about that?" he swore a low blasphemy, the pain in his words thick. "I never meant for her to…God, I've been such a bloody fool!"

"Where could he have taken her? It is doubtful he would be so imprudent as to return to his house off Meeting," Rembert puffed, "though I have sent men there. The problem is Seymour has a multitude of properties and we have very few resources to spare."

"You will spare what you have to," Royal ordered. "Check the Beckham residence. I have a few ideas of my own, sir, and I will look into them myself…"

"Royal, you cannot do this, man," Rembert petitioned him, knowing full well Ashhurst's intentions. "Let the law take him in. Don't throw away what you've worked so hard for!"

"You cannot blame me!" came the anguished response. Royal paused mid-stride, the depths of his sorrow incalculable. The secretary felt a cold shudder start at his spine and work its way to the nape of his neck, the hair there tingling at what he read in the sea captain's face. "Do not follow me, Jonathan, for, by all that's holy, I will crush anything that stands in my way."

"Royal, wait!"

The secretary was out with one well-placed punch. Nicholas jumped back, his calloused hands waving in front of his chest. Royal winced slightly at the fact that Rembert was going to have a tempest of a headache when he awoke. He only prayed that John would be able to forgive him one day.

"Take care of him, Nicholas," Royal ordered curtly. "And tell him that I'm sorry."

Royal vanished into the mist of the evening, his shadow succumbing to the arch of the oaks over the pathway. "Good luck, Cap'n," Nicholas whispered softly, though he felt a pang of presentiment at the lot that awaited Carter Seymour and what he may face before the dawn broke again. He heaved as he hoisted Rembert up by the armpits, dragging him back in the direction they had come, until, a short time later, the governor's guards found them.

The first thing Royal did was circle back towards the docks to make certain all of Seymour's ships were still in the harbor. He had counted three that afternoon, and as his eyes quickly picked out the Transport fleet moored in the rippling waters, he spied the *Sundown Too* still hitched upon *Ella*'s starboard side. He made his way up to Church Street, watching from the alley as the magistrate's men entered the Beckham home, the cries of what they found fueling Royal's passage. He raced through Charleston as if he had no loss of breath, his feet lightweight and fleet over the damp press of the earth. His vision tunneled, his vest falling forgotten behind him.

Royal visualized his limbs moving in endless unison, his back hunching over, his muscles extending; his nose was more aware of the scents around him, his rational mind focusing only on the crux of himself and his journey. Gates and walls that stood before him he imagined small and easily passable, and it was so. The ancient arts he had learned all those years ago in foreign lands graced him with their gifts as he sought to find balance in this, the final chapter of his revenge upon Carter Seymour.

Royal screamed with piercing agony as he thought of his interfering and temperamental Josephine dead in Seymour's hands, the brilliant shine in her eyes dulled to him. He could not erase the memory of her as he'd seen her last, those same eyes telling him of the love she had for him, and he knew his selfish victory was as far now as it had ever been.

He'd never told her that he loved her. Royal groaned and spit heatedly to the side as he continued on towards Seymour's livery, being careful to remain unseen beneath the spectral dance of the torches in the magistrate's hands. Curious onlookers stood agape in various stages of nightdress, their forms cast in fevered light. He had never told her that he was lost without her, that he didn't understand how he had made the last twenty-six years without her in it—for the next twenty-six would be a bleak destiny if it were to be the same.

He made it inside the carriage house with little effort, the one slave he saw recoiling with fear at the sight of him in his fell pursuit. Royal put a finger to his lips to reassure him, but there was no need; the boy fled without a sound. Ashhurst could hear the echo of voices as the magistrate advanced across the courtyard, and he paused but for only a moment.

The horses could sense the energy in the air, inside and out. They moved skittishly, kicking up particles of hay and dust. Royal narrowed his eyes, consciously slowing his breathing as he murmured a gentle dialect of tones. The sleek Arabian dug its hooves into the dirt-packed floor once, twice; and then it sputtered a soft whinny, looking impatient. Royal smiled, though it did not reach his eyes as he lifted the tack from the wall and drew the bridle over the regal animal's head.

"You will show me where he goes, won't you?" Royal cooed, stripping his sweat-soaked shirt from his body and tossing it to the side as he swung upon the gelding's bare back. He urged the strong beast forward, guiding by no direction of hand. They burst through the double doors of the carriage house, hoof beats a solid staccato across the grounds.

Several people turned and pointed towards him as he urged the Arabian on; even more recoiled at the fearsome sight he made—sweat glistened across his bare torso and dripped from a lock of his black, wayward hair. Firelight licked across the smooth skin of his arms and then revealed, for all to see in a hellish glow, the lesions across his back. He grinned wickedly, death's own light flickering in his gaze as he said not a word, riding into the darkness beneath the translucent Carolina moon. The hooves of the Arabian thudded as though they were winged, Royal himself a black rider, for the devil was what drove him now. There would be no mercy for Carter Seymour this time. Royal had learned more than one art in the dark corners of Europe, and he would use each and every one of them with unquenchable desire when he extracted his pound of flesh from his adversary.

24

Josephine mumbled dazedly, her eyelids heavy as she reached agonizingly for the light through her fogged brain. The dull, throbbing pain in her temple, mixed with the jostling movements of the horse beneath her, did its best to pull her back from waking. She could hear the fast, harsh wheezing of Seymour's breath in her ears, feel his wretched hands upon her body. Struggle as she did, her limbs would not respond, and she was trapped.

It was shortly thereafter that Josephine felt the shifting of the horse cease, and she feigned sleep as she watched Seymour from beneath the falling of her hair about her. He was everything but a display of grace, his gray hair much whiter than she could recall, his face a mess of greasy folds, his eyes sunken. He dismounted and took several shaky steps forward, his concentration not on her but upon a dark shape in the moonlight. And then his voice came, a mad drone in the blackness of nightfall; Josephine's insides twisted with fear and revulsion at the cold, demented delight within it.

"You see, Ben, I have won again!" he garbled. "Your devil child thinks he holds the cards, but nay, I have what he wants most. He can rot in hell with you, Benjamin, along with that little whore wife of yours. Charleston will never welcome any of your diseased heirs. Do you hear me, Ben?"

Seymour threw his question to the heavens, his scream of challenge weaving through the bulrush and sweetgrass reeds, dancing with the trickling waters of the Ashley River as it carried across hidden vales of the Lowcountry. His eyes shone with untamed ecstasy as he turned towards Josephine. She struggled to gain her composure, her spine a leaden rod of ice.

"Get off the horse, damn you," Seymour ordered stolidly, the temper of his eyes melting to lust, the thirst of his body rushing through every limb. Josephine was an exquisite mold of feminine flesh, and the desires that consumed him flamed higher, blinding any reason he may have left. He still could not grasp the fact that she was Ashhurst's wife, that the captain had lost himself in her virtuous arms, though he had heard their vile union with his own ears. Those same pale, lithe arms were now a dirty disgrace, her gentle fingers thorns, having been blighted by evil's touch, her hair not of golden invite but as red as the fire from below.

She looked at him with such loathing. He would revel in the feel of her, find glory in her cries of submission and suffering. He laughed and whet his appetite for her with the slip of his thick tongue as he dragged her from the steed, her weakened state little contest for him to overcome.

He sighed with relish at her moan, his slighted reason hearing her soft alto as crying for more.

His kisses were deep and gagged the back of her throat, his awful breath fanning across her cheek and up her nose. Josephine grappled for air, her hands balling into tight fists as she struck out against her molester. His teeth chewed upon her lip, the taste of her a satisfying elixir to his poison.

"You crave me inside you, little bitch in heat," Seymour growled, his hands tightening upon the shoulders of her gown. His fists tightened upon the fabric. In a rendering tear, the material ripped to her waist, the heavy spheres of her breasts glowing with an ivory sheen beneath the quiet illumination of the moon. Her nipples hardened in the cool night air. Seymour commented on the sordid perfection of them as he slapped each one. His free hand encircled her throat, the pressure of his hand forcing Josephine to suck readily for breath that came in small whistles, her eyes bulging.

And then his slimy mouth was covering one of her breasts. Josephine sobbed at the dirty feel of it, her legs clamping together even as Seymour was reaching down between them to penetrate the dry folds of her womanhood, his ramblings of his superiority and ownership of her falling by the wayside. There were no tender ministrations, no passionate, guiding hands; nothing but base, greedy profanity as Seymour's touch instigated his rape of her.

"Royal!" she cried instinctively, managing to connect her balled fist alongside of Seymour's head, his grunt at the sting of her blow intermingling with the push of his fornication. He pressed her back, fumbling at his breeches. The snap of underbrush nearby went overlooked as the pair scuffled across the ground, Josephine's defiance earning her a quick slap across her face.

Through the still of the surrounding night came the click of a pistol's mechanism. Seymour's head cocked at the sound, aware at last he was no longer alone with his beloved Josephine, the spiking of his hair at the nape of his neck telling him before he looked back, that he had come. Terror as he had never known tore into his stomach as his senses splintered. His journey ended here; the pool of his greed lapped at Royal's feet, the tip of the vessel running aground across the rough soil that ambled up to the moss-draped grave of Benjamin Ashhurst.

"Every drop of my blood burns for me to pull the trigger, Carter," Royal's voice rang across the clearing, the sweat and tears in his eyes thankfully hazing the sight of Josephine's abused and nearly naked body, for he knew if he saw her eyes he would not be able to stop the fervent rage tearing at his side. "But that is far too easy a sentence for you."

Royal's words came in a deep scratch, Josephine's cries in the darkness a terrible pall upon his heart as it echoed in his ears. "Princess, come to me," he instructed.

His tone was soft yet strained towards his wife. Josephine held her shredded gown together over her breasts as she obeyed, running to his side, her feet wet from the dew upon the earth.

Josephine flung her arms around Royal's waist, unable still to believe that it was he. And though his one arm anchored her to him, her small body circled by the curved strength of him, the fear inside did not abate. She did not recognize her husband for it was a demon beside her. Hatred carried its signature in his forehead and around his mouth, the tainted grin of his lips split wide, his teeth fanglike beneath the light of the crescent moon. His free hand held the flintlock, unwavering as it pointed at Seymour, his eyes following the aim of the barrel to his quarry. Every part of her screamed to beg for his mercy, for the sake of them all; yet Josephine knew her words would only fall upon deaf ears.

"How fitting your blood will feed the daisies upon my father's grave," Royal assured, feeling no crumb of pity as he stared at Seymour, watching the suffering in Seymour's bleak expression. His damned eyes still flitted to Josephine, and Royal swallowed the fatal taste in his mouth as he leaned down and pressed his lips to hers.

She was cold beneath his cruel affections, gentle though his kiss was. Tears slid down her cheeks, the taste of them upon their mouths as Royal twisted the blade he'd plunged into Seymour's black heart another quarter turn, his eyes watching with primal satisfaction as he proved his possession of Josephine. His lips caressed hers until she was helpless to resist her response, the flame in her heart for him roused to a low burn. With one last compelling pull of her lip by his teeth, she was mumbling her love for him.

"Don't do this, Royal," she found herself begging as he released her. "Let Rembert and the others try him. Show him who you are, who I know you to be—"

"Josephine, go to the edge of the clearing and stay out of the way, no matter what may come to pass," he ordered, his voice thick and unnatural. "Aye, princess, I wish more than anything for you not to bear witness to this, but you must understand that this time I cannot be a better man and shall be every inch the devil I have been known as…" his eyes scalded as he trailed off, his rage emanating from his entire being. The skin of his torso gleamed with cold sweat as he closed in the distance between Seymour and himself.

"Royal, don't do this—"

"Nay, princess," he interrupted, his feverish tenor akin to a heathenish howl. "That may have been possible only before he touched you, Josephine, and it was unlikely even then."

Royal Ashhurst faced his adversary, his methodical vision scanning the merchant for any sign of a weapon. He spied the glimmer of a shiny barrel in the grass, having fallen absently from Seymour's grasp as he grappled for Josephine. He circled until it was behind him and he stood between it and Seymour. Royal's blood simmered anew as he tossed his own pistol far out of reach, his arms open wide.

"Stand up, damn you," Royal ordered. "You cower like a dog, Carter. Where is your elegant, pious air now? Do not tell me that you have seen the error of your ways, that the blood on your hands should be forgiven when you brought this house upon yourself!"

Royal seized him when he did not rise, his physical superiority making a mockery of Seymour's pallid insulation. His eyes blazed inches from Seymour's own; he stared into the black abyss of them, knowing in that moment that he would never find the answer to the question that had eaten his soul and left him empty of all but revenge his entire life. "If only I had the means to watch your death come over an endless span of years, the torment of your sins forced down your gullet every waking moment," Royal smote, the power of his blows breaking bones with every strike.

Seymour felt the earth tremble and quake, the heavens spinning around him as Royal crushed his nose, his teeth, and his ribs. The elder man wept for clemency, but the gods paid no attention to his cries, the sick thud of Royal's retribution throwing him headlong into a fiery chasm of pain.

Royal stood back and shook his head, his breath whistling between clenched teeth as he kicked Seymour into the dirt. He stared down at his work, aggravated that he felt no better for it. Seymour lay in a mass of bloodied flesh, his eyes nearly hidden by swelling. He spit blood and shards of ivory from all that remained of his teeth onto the ground. "I shall not go to my grave regretting that I didn't send you to yours, Seymour," Royal bellowed. "You may as well try and save your cursed soul and tell me why you betrayed us!"

"Because no one of my respect should ever be second to a bastard or his son," Seymour laughed, his words garbled as he lay on the ground, "and try as you might, pup, you will never be more than that!"

His eyes flickered to where Josephine stood in the distance, her hands over her chest and her body shaking. "Look at her, Royal," he coughed. The captain's jaw flexed; his nostrils flared. "You have ruined her, destroyed her. Has it been worth it?" he laughed wickedly, rolling to his side. "She will hate you for this bestial side you have shown her. Go on, boy—kill me. I am susceptible to any butchery you are capable of, and it does not take a Hercules to kill me now, as I sit defenseless."

"It does not matter if you are weak or nay, Carter," Royal avowed. He circled the merchant slowly, patiently. "You were not when you kidnapped Josephine."

"Ah, that bitch tasted as sweet as honey," Seymour smiled, his tongue lagging from the corner of his mouth.

Royal growled, his eyes shading red and his dark, sinister brows pitched. "Did you rape her, Seymour?"

Seymour cast a look heavenward; the stars were shining brightly. It was a beautiful night in the Carolina Lowcountry, the scents of summer rushing in with the ocean tide. The promise of nature's cycle had bloomed anew; death seemed such an unfathomable idea in the sweetness of the season, when the celebration of life itself was all around.

Yet Seymour knew he was a ruined man. His body was broken, his crimes floating on those same winds that swept Charleston and caressed the grasses of the salt marsh. He knew that no future day would ever hold a measure of peace for him again. He smiled, welcoming Royal's wrath as he swore he would seek revenge beyond the grave.

"She cried like a mourning dove," he said.

* * * * *

Josephine sobbed as she heard Royal's guttural, primal scream, her feet propelled forward despite his direction. And then she stopped in her tracks, frozen in horror as she witnessed him twist Carter Seymour's head to the side, the snapping motion and the eerie tilt to Seymour's face too unnatural. She watched as Royal stumbled back, his body limp. He turned to look at her, age beyond his years carved in his face; but she could see a lost little boy in him, the wide, brilliant color of those eyes blending with the tears of his rage and sorrow. "Forgive me, Josephine," he mumbled, sinking to his knees. "Oh, Lord—"

She came to him and he pulled her down to her knees before him, his head tucked to her chest and her hands across the rough wounds of his back. Josephine wept as Royal squeezed her slender form to him, his groan muffled by her body. "Josephine, princess, I have failed you, as I have always done. I swore I would protect you with my dying breath—"

"Shh, Royal," she soothed, her fingers combing the slick, dark hair of his head, her heart so pained and free at once. "Seymour did not assault me, not the way you think! It was a lie—"

He was shaking his head. He sighed heavily, heartily, almost as if it were his last.

"I am no good for you, Josephine," Royal coughed, sitting back, his hands reaching up to hold her face. He stared at her, his heart still pounding with the wintry clutch of fear he'd felt when he was certain he had lost her. "But so help me, I love you, and I dread the pain my love will bring you."

She continued to stroke his hair, rubbing gently at his neck, feeling the taut muscles relaxing beneath her ministrations. Her limbs felt light and airy, her heart hammering at his admission. She blinked several times through her tears to look into his eyes, adrift as he was in his own privation.

Seymour's slain body was paces away, a surreal thing indeed. Fears of repercussion snuck their way in. She looked away, almost willing the vision to dissipate, too. "I have loved you since I met you, sir. Something about you captured my heart," Josephine smiled tenderly despite the chaos. "For I have nothing but you, though there is nothing more I can see myself wanting. You've been a staunch defender of all you see as right, my love. You have protected me at great cost to yourself without reservation. There is little that is more honorable than that. And as for tragedies…time will heal these wounds you have suffered."

Royal slowly rose, his face unreadable as he gazed at his father's glittering headstone. Weather and time had already dug its nails into the marble. He thought then of how quickly every year passed in remembrance of the one previous. And now it was over—and he felt empty, lost. He stared at Carter Seymour's body, growing cold in the mist of the night as time passed. Royal and Josephine held each other without a word. "Let's go home, princess," he murmured at length. "Though I know not what awaits."

25

The news of Michael Beckham's murder came as a jaded shock to Josephine's sentiments. The tragedy with which his life ended was a bitter pill to swallow; it seemed such a waste. She tried not to think of how his body had been left to rot for days after his murder. The atrocious stench of his decomposition billowed out the door when the magistrate's men broke in to search for her the night of her abduction, for no one had missed him before that. It was an additional source of commiseration to Josephine that no one attended his funeral besides herself and Royal except Kingsley, who managed to be present for her sake, even in bandages from his maltreatment by Seymour's hand.

The horrendous blather of Carter Seymour's crimes and his subsequent death did not slip through the cracks of Charleston society without fanfare. And while Royal was certain the colony would find a way to pin the blame upon him, even his cynical demeanor was staggered from its foundations at the heartfelt contrition he found. Who knew Seymour had been such a charlatan, they voiced, or that his social standing came as the result of an old thievery?

Royal never mentioned the fact that he had once tried to ascertain that very thing, taking the lavish condolences and sudden support in stride, as he had the displeasure voiced from the same mouths that now spouted his triumph. To most people he had nothing to say at all, unless it was to rectify any misconception they may have had in regard to his ownership of Ashhurst & Sons Shipping or any wayward comment about the scandal his wife had caused the day Blackbeard sailed into Charleston and changed their lives forever.

Summer was in full bloom; June fell into July, and July nudged into August as Charleston basked beneath the heady sun, the days slipping past unobserved with all that Royal suddenly found before him. Oftentimes he rose before dawn and did not return until well after dusk, the weight of the empire that he had at last inherited bowing his shoulders. Seymour had left the company in dire straits, more than anyone could have guessed. It was no wonder, then, that he had turned to Blackbeard in what could have only been desperation.

Where Royal had received the letters that incriminated Carter Seymour and proved his blatant involvement with Wragg's kidnapping caused Jonathan Rembert no end of mystery; and with all that transpired immediately thereafter, it took some time until he was able to extract the truth of it from the sea captain.

Even Royal did not quite fully understand how they had dropped into his lap. The only place they could have come from was from Blackbeard himself, but the idea that the pirate would have done such a gallant favor to a man he had "made an example of" was not only unlikely, but a downright far-fetched notion.

"Perhaps this was his way of trying to make up for his abuse of you, Royal," Josephine commented one evening as they bandied the issue with Jonathan Rembert over tea and tarts. Usually Kingsley joined them, yet recently he had been finding his way over to Kirkpatrick's more and more, the darkness of his skin flushing a deeper color as he mumbled something about making certain Isabella's mundane maintenance issues had been taken care of. Josephine smiled broadly at him the third time he had found an excuse to see the madame, and she wondered if there was to be another wedding before the holidays. "From what we can tell in hindsight, Blackbeard was no fonder of Seymour than any of us."

"There is honor among thieves, so it has been said," Rembert nodded. "Yet it is an odd circle of fate that Blackbeard was responsible for both contriving this odious plot and solving it as well."

"In a way, I'm very thankful for his blockade," Royal mused softly, "though I shall carry the mark of Blackbeard's whip upon my back until my last breath is drawn."

"I'm sorry that you were detained so long that eventide," John said, leaning back in the simple yet elegant silk-covered chair, the family of which now crowded the small dwelling. He said nothing for a long minute as he absently rubbed his temple. Josephine could've sworn she'd never seen her husband ever look so contrite, not before or ever after. "There were, after all, certain parties that needed placating. It is difficult to turn around years of misconception. However, I believe that most every man worthy of the description would have ultimately done the same, when placed in the position that you were." He sighed and smiled fondly at Josephine. When his eyes lingered a little longer than usual he heard Captain Ashhurst's defining cough, and at the slight narrowing of his brilliant eyes, Rembert laughed out loud. "If you think that I'm as big a fool as Seymour, you've got another think coming," he assured. "Just as Charleston can spend the next quarter century debating on whom its devil really was."

Epilogue

In November of 1718, bad weather forced Stede Bonnet to return to Sullivan's Island, where the troupe led by Colonel William Rhett, the "Scourge of the Pirates," tracked him down and recaptured him and his crew. He was returned to Charleston and tried before Judge Nicholas Trott, who scathed him for his scheming attempts before finding him guilty of piracy and sentencing him to hang. A crowd gathered upon White Point to hear what he would say as he was led to the gallows, yet the Gentleman Pirate had no last words to placate them as he followed thirty of his crew into the arms of death on December 10, 1718. For four days their rotting bodies swung from the oaks, a warning to other seditious mariners that Charleston was no longer a haven for brigands.

November was not a good month for Edward "Blackbeard" Teach, either. Lieutenant Robert Maynard, hired out of Virginia's governor Alexander Spotswood's own pocket, at last caught up with him outside of Ocracoke Inlet, North Carolina, where, with a bit of subterfuge, he gained the upper hand of the notorious pirate during a fierce hand-to-hand combat on deck. Blackbeard sustained five gunshot wounds and twenty scores with a cutlass before he succumbed to Maynard's wrath. When at last he was dead, his decapitated body was thrown overboard and his head hung as an ominous spoil of war from Maynard's bowsprit.

It did not take long for word to spread through seafaring communities that Charleston was now a danger to bootleggers of varying capacity, for if the insurmountable Blackbeard could fall because of the Carolinian's ministrations, then certainly could they; and with pressure being exerted from all sides, the pirate menace steadily vanished from the mid-Atlantic until nothing but whispered rumors of them remained on the wind.

Royal Ashhurst found, as the years passed, that superstitions died hard and old wounds healed slowly, though heal they did in time. He still saw upon occasion that same malicious glimmer in a widow's eye or in any number of councilmen's faces at the monthly assemblies. For the most part, it bothered him little. An equal number of people would smile at him on the streets, and with business booming, as it was, with the pirates eradicated, the amount of wealth he had amassed would see him and Josephine to their deathbeds even if he never made another doubloon.

There were days when Josephine irritated him beyond any sort of reasoning; at those times he would walk alone down Legare, staring at the old brick wall that was now crumbling with age, and he would remember what hard times between them had really been like. The scents in his nose had remained unchanged from that day. There were moments when he would weep to himself, for both the old pain that would never fully dissipate and the joy that he had been given as redemption.

Her pregnancy with their first child, a swarthy son whom they at last agreed to call David Benjamin after much arguing, was something he wasn't certain he would be able to endure, so violent were her mood swings. Yet, her spark of energy took all forms, and though they had their arguments, Royal was thankful for her, blessed every passing day he had been given with her. Josephine never bored him, and life was never dull. The blaze of passion between them still smoldered, a hotbed of coals one moment, a wildfire the next. She would often assist him with his records and was a priceless sounding board for his plans, her quick mind and sharp eye frequently catching things that even he had missed despite judicious attention to detail. More times than not she would be leaning over his desk, a serious expression upon her face as she analyzed whatever parchment she held in her small hands, yet business was usually the last thing on his mind at those moments, and before long his little wife would find herself being swept abovestair for the remainder of the afternoon.

Josephine always stood by him, even as Royal's head began to gray. His princess was always at home with a candle lit for him, her eyes still beckoning him with desire and the sweet sounds of his name and love upon her lips.

Author's Notes

The people who have assisted me in bringing this story to light are too numerous to detail here; and I can only hope I can be forgiven for this trespass. From those in the Northland to the fair city of Charleston, where I have found my heart and my home, I have met as many wonderful people who have inspired me to do what I needed and never failed to cheer me with their witty and poignant contributions.

Hospitality and tourism in Charleston, South Carolina, is the personification of what southern grace and charm is all about. Working in this field, first as a front desk clerk and now as a guide, has opened me up to a horde of people and experiences that I shall always keep close to my heart. This story is, more than anything else, deeply indebted to the staff and guests of the King Charles Inn on Meeting Street, who never hindered me, and oftentimes moved me when I believed all strength to be lost.

I wrote *The Devil of Charleston* long before I became a tour guide, and it was through research for the book that I found my calling and the best-of-the-best in tourism here in Charleston. Believe me when I say a tour taken with any of these fine people will leave you the better for it: Jane, Bill, and everyone else over at Charleston Tours, who gave me my first true welcome to the sunny south; Ed Grimball, the only man I know who can find a Jell-O factory in the middle of nowhere; the crew of the schooner *Sandlapper*; and the staff of Palmetto Carriage Works. Last but not least by any stretch, a very special thanks to the dashing and charming John LaVerne and his staff at Bulldog Tours, especially James Brain, Mark Jones and Eric Spabene. Without your priceless support and inspiration I don't know where I'd be. The world is a richer place with you all in it.

And of course: David, J, Mike, Eric, and all the boys down at Hyman's Seafood; the UPS guys; Captain Mike Sigler, Suzi Jackson, Eddie McBride, and Queen Anne's Revenge Restaurant on Daniel Island; my parents, for always being there; Tim Davies, of Chateaux de Bull Street fame; Johnny Curt and Christy Lyness, for their undying assistance during the penning of this novel.

Thank you all.

— Rebel Sinclair

Other Savage Press Books

OUTDOORS, SPORTS & RECREATION

Cool Fishing for Kids 8-85 by Frankie Paull and "Jackpine" Bob Cary
Curling Superiority! by John Gidley
The Duluth Tour Book by Jeff Cornelius
The Final Buzzer by Chris Russell

ESSAY

Battlenotes: Music of the Vietnam War by Lee Andresen
Color on the Land by Irene I. Luethge
Following in the Footsteps of Ernest Hemingway by Jay Thurston
Hint of Frost, Essays on the Earth by Rusty King
Hometown Wisconsin by Marshall J. Cook
Potpourri From Kettle Land by Irene I. Luethge

FICTION

Burn Baby Burn by Mike Savage
Charleston Red by Sarah Galchus
Keeper of the Town short stories by Don Cameron
Lake Effect by Mike Savage
Lord of the Rinks by Mike Savage
Mindset by Enrico Bostone
Norah's Children by Ann O'Farrell
Northern Lights Magic by Lori J. Glad
Off Season by Marshall J.Cook
Sailing Home by Lori J. Glad
Something in the Water by Mike Savage
Summer Storm by Lori J. Glad
The Year of the Buffalo by Marshall J. Cook
Voices From the North Edge by St. Croix Writers
Whitebridge Web by Kathryn van Heynengin
Walkers in the Mist by Hollis D. Normand

REGIONAL HISTORY, HUMOR, MEMOIR

Baloney on Wry by Frank Larson
Beyond the Freeway by Peter J. Benzoni
Crocodile Tears and Lipstick Smears by Fran Gabino

Other Savage Press Books

Fair Game by Fran Gabino
Memories of Iron River by Bev Thivierge
Some Things You Never Forget by Clem Miller
Stop in the Name of the Law by Alex O'Kash
Superior Catholics by Cheney and Meronek
Pathways, Early History of Brule Wisconsin by Nan Wisherd
Widow of the Waves by Bev Jamison

BUSINESS

Dare to Kiss the Frog by vanHauen, Kastberg & Soden
SoundBites Second Edition by Kathy Kerchner

POETRY

Appalachian Mettle by Paul Bennett
Eraser's Edge by Phil Sneve
Gleanings from the Hillsides by E.M. Johnson
In the Heart of the Forest by Diana Randolph
I Was Night by Bekah Bevins
Moments Beautiful Moments Bright by Brett Bartholomaus
Nameless by Charlie Buckley
Pathways by Mary B. Wadzinski
Philosophical Poems by E.M. Johnson
Poems of Faith and Inspiration by E.M. Johnson
The Morning After the Night She Fell Into the Gorge
                              by Heidi Howes
Thicker Than Water by Hazel Sangster
Treasured Thoughts by Sierra
Treasures from the Beginning of the World by Jeff Lewis

OTHER BOOKS AVAILABLE FROM SP

Blueberry Summers by Lawrence Berube
Beyond the Law by Alex O'Kash
Dakota Brave by Howard Jones
Jackpine Savages by Frank Larson
Spindrift Anthology by The Tarpon Springs Writer's Group
The Brule River, A Guide's Story by Lawrence Berube
Waterfront by Alex O'Kash

To order additional copies of

The Devil of Charleston
or
Spirit of the Shadows

call

218-391-3070

or

E-mail:

mail@savpress.com

Purchase copies on-line at:

www.savpress.com

Visa/MC/Discover/American Express/
ECheck/Accepted via PayPal

All Savage Press books are available through all
chain and independent bookstores nationwide. Just
ask them to special order if the title is not in stock.